QUEEN ME

IMMORTAL VICES AND VIRTUES, BOOK 2

AMBER LYNN NATUSCH

Cover art by Yocla Designs

PROLOGUE

VOLKER

Pain lanced through my body as the winds of my enemy pinned me to the ground, gale forces stabbing through my flesh like metal stakes. With every effort I made to rise—or to use my magic to dematerialize into the night—I failed. Her power was too great, though it shouldn't have been, and I cursed the night, whose magic had turned on me.

Without its full strength, I could not defeat her.

"News of your death will travel quickly across the lands," she said, long, dark hair blowing wildly around her as she grew closer, "and then I shall take your place. Because who would dare challenge the one who killed the unkillable—the ruthless king of the House of Air and Amethyst?"

"I'm not yet dead," I replied through gritted teeth, knowing that eventuality would soon come if I could not rally enough magic to escape. But as she hovered over me, wicked eyes already bright with victory, I knew time had run out.

She held out her hand and called a spear of wind wide enough to impale a horse, then smiled.

"Have you any last words?" she asked, a note of mocking in her voice. "Not that they matter . . . "

I let my gaze drift to the full moon above and stared at it as I silently prayed for one last surge of magic—even if it was to be my last. Dying at the hands of a traitor was a fate I couldn't stomach.

"Know that I will have my revenge."

Her cackling laughter cut through the roar of wind, and she lifted her spear to deliver my death. The sharpened tip punctured my bare abdomen as she drove it so deep it wedged in the ground below me, securing me to the pyre of my demise.

With the knowledge that she'd won making her bold, she cut off the magic tethering me to the earth—except for the deadly spear in my gut—and bent down over me to whisper in my ear. "There is no revenge in death, Volker . . . "

I struggled to speak, pain and blood loss overwhelming me as my life slipped away, much to her apparent delight. But then the moon grew brighter, and I felt a rush of magic course through me. A scream tore from my throat as I forced every cell in my body to obey—to break apart and carry me off into the dark of night, as was my gift.

My final chance.

I felt my body dematerialize as she looked on in horror, uncertain of what was happening, until I was no longer there. I let the night's breeze carry me to safety, then regained my corporeal state. Still injured, I collapsed to the ground, clutching the wound in my gut. I had survived the battle, but not yet the war.

For that, I would need something—or *someone*—rare. Someone I wasn't sure how to find. But I was an assassin of the highest order; hunting was what I did best. And as I lay back against the ground, calling my healing powers to me as best I could, I began to formulate my plan for revenge.

To get it, I would need to find the little queen . . .

CHAPTER 1
ROWE

I raced down the hall, sweat dripping down my brow as I dared a glance at my watch.

10:17 p.m. already. *Shit*, I muttered to myself as I tried to open the front door with my hands full of cleaning supplies. I was going to be late for sure.

"Rowe!" a female voice called from the kitchen. "Did you finish the half bath upstairs?"

"Yep. All done—"

"And the grout in the laundry room—were you able to get the stains out?"

"Sure was. It's good to go."

"What about the windows in the basement?"

I took a deep breath to calm myself as I practically bounced on the balls of my feet in the foyer. "Everything on your list has been checked off, so I'm going to head out now," I said as I pulled the front door open and quickly slipped through before the lady of the house could grill me about every menial task she'd made me do that day. I didn't have time for that.

Thankfully, I was only a few blocks from my studio apartment, so

I tossed the bottles of cleaner into a backpack and hopped on my longboard. The city was quieter than usual, which was oddly welcome, but I couldn't help feeling like the silence was oppressive and ominous somehow. I propelled myself faster, not wanting to stick around and find out.

I rolled up to the back of the large red-brick meeting house my apartment was attached to and hopped off my board. The bottles in my backpack jostled as I bent over to pick it up, then spilled out through the busted zipper. It was the last thing I needed. As it was, I was fifteen minutes late and counting. The buzzing phone in my pocket told me that either Adora or Danni was already trying to hunt me down, which wouldn't end well for me by the time I got to the bar. Best to rip that bandage off sooner than later.

"Hey, Adora," I said as I struggled to force the back door open. "I don't want to alarm you, but I'm running late."

"We gathered that," she said, the din of the bar making her nearly impossible to hear. "Should I leave now to come pick you up at the edge of No Man's Land?"

"I'mma need a solid twenty minutes before I'm anywhere near ready." I locked the door behind me and flipped on the light to illuminate the sad state of my room. "Maybe thirty."

"In thirty minutes, I'll show up at your door and drag you out no matter what state you're in—or the fallout—but I'd appreciate it if you were at least dressed."

I knew she was joking because there was no way she'd set foot in Fire and Fluorite territory, but she'd made her point. Hurry my ass up. "Point taken. And tell Danni I'm sorry!"

"She understands, Rowe. We both do. Your time has never really been your own."

With that sad truth hanging between us, I placed my pack down and carefully made my way over to the bathroom. "I'm jumping in the shower now. See you in thirty!"

I hung up before my emotions got the best of me and opened the door. Danni, Adora, and I had been friends long before the turmoil that had made them leave Fire and Fluorite. It had been about four weeks since I'd last seen them, and after our night out, I knew it would be forever before I saw them again.

I didn't want to waste a minute more than necessary.

Moving as quickly as I could, I turned the water on and gathered everything I'd need to scrub away the grossness of work. I managed to find a clean towel under the sink and set it on the toilet seat. Time was ticking away, so I jumped in the shower and let out a scream when the icy water pelted my skin. The water heater was old as hell and had the work ethic of a trust fund baby, so I knew it wasn't going to kick on anytime soon.

With surprising haste for someone on the verge of hypothermia, I showered and washed my hair. I nearly jumped over the tub's edge to get to the towel and its warmth. Wrapping it around my shaking body, I opened the door and darted back into the tiny living space. The twenty minutes I had remaining would disappear quickly between drying my hair, makeup, and my walk to the edge of Fire and Fluorite land, where Adora would pick me up. I didn't exactly have time to waste, so I scrambled around in search of anything clean and decent enough to wear to the club. Money was always tight, so fancy things were definitely out of reach.

I grabbed a pair of jeans, a plain white cropped tee, and the leather jacket Danni had given to me two years earlier for my birthday and threw them on. I hopped into my pants as I crossed the room in search of my boots and managed to snag my foot on the comforter dangling off the edge of the bed. The element of surprise, combined with my jeans that had only made it knee high, sent me sprawling. I crashed on my shoulder and rolled onto my back, waiting for the pain to hit. I stared up at the cracks in the plaster ceiling through my wet red curls and waited for the throbbing to begin. I wondered if this was a sign of how the night was going to go.

Spoiler alert: it was.

The copper bar top shook beneath my hand as our shot glasses slammed down in unison. Within seconds of the whiskey passing my throat, I knew that was the shot that would do me in for sure. Was it the fifth? Maybe the sixth? Seventh, possibly? It really didn't matter at that point. I'd tried to play catch-up with two shifters, a dangerous game at best.

The shots would be coming back up soon enough.

"C'mon, Rowe!" a jubilant voice shouted over the din. The wicked smile I found on Adora's face when I turned to find her standing atop the bar like she owned the place helped distract me from the churning in my stomach and my own impending doom. "To the dance floor!"

"No can do, my friend," I said, leaning heavily on the bar as the room started to spin. "I live here now . . . just leave me behind."

"Quitting isn't an option, so sayeth the bitch running this circus sideshow!" She jumped down and landed next to me with the grace of a supernatural powerhouse, which she was. I, however, was not. I was effectively a human in a world overtaken by magic and power, a truth I faced on a daily basis. Not only did I lack cool shifting abilities and magic, but I was at the bottom of the inverted pyramid as far as the power hierarchy went. I was lucky enough to have been adopted into the House of Fire and Fluorite when I was young, but it was impossible to escape the everyday reminders of just how human I was in comparison to those around me.

Especially when drinking was involved.

Girls' night was sure to be a good time—if I didn't die from alcohol poisoning as a result.

"Rowe!" Danni shouted, her face suddenly in mine, pulling me from my drunken musings. "On your feet, lady. The night is young and there's debauchery to be had."

"I've debauched enough, methinks," I said, swaying on my feet as Adora rushed by, headed for the dance floor.

Danni laughed as she grabbed my shoulders to steady me. "There's my girl: questionably conscious, but sarcastic as always."

I felt the soft brush of fur against my arm as Danni's wolf, Nova, flanked me, most likely to help keep me from keeling over. "Perhaps that's my magical ability," I said as Danni took me by the hand and ushered me through the masses to meet up with Adora. Even in my drunken haze, I could see her blue hair flaring out around her as she spun and swayed. The numbing effects of alcohol couldn't hide the tug of sadness in my chest at the sight. I'd missed them terribly since they'd left, and I knew that trend would only continue over time.

Because the Houses, as a general rule, just didn't mix—even if you leave on far better terms than they did.

I gripped her hand a little harder as she led the way, but my sadness quickly gave way to the nausea rolling in my gut. The second we joined the mob, I shouted something to Danni, then made a beeline for the bathrooms down the hall just beyond the dance floor. As luck (and the males who seemed to design every public bathroom in existence) would have it, there was a line of women as far as my blurry eyes could see. With a garbled curse, I pushed past the bodies creating a bottleneck in the narrow hallway, headed for the back exit.

The revenge of mixing alcohol waited for no man.

I slammed into the push bar on the metal door and fell into the alley beyond. My shoulder caught on the nearby dumpster and spun me around, an added effect I definitely didn't need, given my state. Disoriented and about to puke, I flailed my arms, desperate to catch hold of anything to steady me before I stopped fighting the inevitable.

My right hand grabbed something solid and held onto it like the lifeline it was. The second the world stopped spinning, Jimmy, Jack, and Johnny came back up about as smoothly as they'd gone down. Breathing hard and silently wishing for death, I wiped the sweat from my brow with the back of my hand and stood up straight—right into the man I'd grabbed onto to steady myself in the alleyway.

CHAPTER 2
ROWE

The early morning moon poured down between the closely huddled brick buildings to shine on the wall of man staring me down. Bottomless steel-grey eyes, framed with lashes as pale as his skin and hair, bored into me as I stood in shock, unable to move. Though tall and muscular, there was an elegance to him—a refined quality—that made him less intimidating somehow, which was undoubtedly by design (or courtesy of my drunken state). Because gorgeous men in midnight-blue wool coats with perfectly styled hair couldn't be killers, right?

"I'm so sorry," I said as sweat beaded on my forehead. "I didn't see you."

"As was initially intended." He stared down at me with inhuman grey eyes that slowly began to shine like the moon itself. "But now it's time . . . "

A warning blared in the back of my mind, cutting through my alcohol-driven haze with every screech of its siren until my body went rigid with realization. His aura of power was undeniable, but it was the way he analyzed me with those gleaming silver eyes that gave him away.

He was the villain of the legends and tales my mother had told me for as long as I could remember. The ghostly fae assassin made of moonlight and shadow. A killer to best all killers.

And he was standing right in front of me like a sexy beacon of death.

My mind begged my body to run, but it held fast, too paralyzed by fear to react. There would be no escaping the beautiful nightmare before me: the recently usurped fae king of the House of Air and Amethyst.

The notorious Moonlight Wraith.

I pulled my hand away from the infamous killer and staggered back a step, still too drunk for my own good, but sober enough to know I was in deep shit.

"It seems my reputation precedes me," he said in a quizzical tone.

"I . . . I . . . "

"But what I really want to know is: who are *you*?"

"Me?" I repeated, inching backward toward the door. "I'm no one. Nobody . . . "

Those perfectly shaped lips lifted at the corners. "I beg to differ." He closed the distance between us in a blink and I flinched, expecting him to hit me or stab me or do whatever it was fae assassins did, but nothing happened. Instead, I opened my eyes to find him looming above me, a curious expression on his perfectly chiseled face. "Because none can see what I really am unless I want them to. And there is only one being I'm searching for."

"Well, unless you want a useless human, I'd say your magic is funky," I said, hoping I'd just made a good point in my addled state.

His eyes narrowed at my words, and an angry rumble shook his chest. "Are you saying I'm wrong?" he asked, pressing in closer to me. My pulse raced and my chest seized as Death himself leaned against me.

"Are you going to kill me if I say yes?"

His brow quirked slightly at my response. "Maybe I'll kill you if you say no . . . "

I stared at him, my heart slamming against my ribs. "That logic doesn't give me much reason to answer at all."

"Unless I kill you because you refuse to."

I gulped back a wave of fear and nausea. "But then you wouldn't get your answer."

He canted his head and dipped his face lower to stare into my eyes. "I think you are the answer to my current predicament," he said, raking an elegant hand through his short platinum hair that shone silvery-white in the moonlight, "which means you're much more valuable to me alive than dead."

"Well, that's a plus—"

A wicked smirk tugged at his lips. "Only if I'm right."

I leaned away from him, my throat dry and my heart racing with his proximity. The weight of his presence was too much to process in my current state; I needed space—room to breathe. Instead, I found myself pressed up against the door I desperately wanted to disappear behind.

So I could get away from the violent being before me.

So I could pretend his proximity wasn't as thrilling as it was terrifying.

So I could gaslight myself into believing the whole event had only happened in my mind.

But there was no escaping him. He caged me in with his body, his coat straining over the muscles in his shoulders as he pressed his hands against the door on either side of my face. I had to crane my neck so I could look up at his face, now cast in shadow. "You don't seem like the kinda guy who's wrong very often."

Another expression that came dangerously close to a smile tugged at his mouth. "No. I'm not." The intensity of his gaze was too much, and I fumbled behind me, trying to open the door, but damn if it wasn't locked from the inside. "In a hurry to get back to something?"

"It's girls' night . . . my friends are going to wonder where I disappeared to soon. Especially Danni," I said, officially rambling now.

"She's overprotective of me and likely to come looking for me soon if I don't get back in there."

He canted his head. "And you don't want her to find us alone back here?"

I gripped the door handle harder, wishing I had Danni's strength so I could just rip it open. "I don't want any trouble—for her or me."

"I'm afraid it's too late for that," he said, "but you already know that, don't you, Miss . . . ?"

"Little. Regina Little," I said without thinking—like I hadn't grown up hearing that giving a fae your real name was a terrible idea. "But I go by Rowe."

Bonus stupidity points for throwing in the nickname.

That strange almost-smile widened at my reply as he reached forward to brush a stray red curl from my face. His proximity set off every warning alarm in my body, but I didn't move. Like a cornered rabbit, I stood and stared at the beautiful death before me and tried to ignore that things other than adrenaline coursed through me as his finger grazed my ear when he pulled away.

"*Little queen* . . . " His whispered tone was wistful and distant, and he sounded like he was lost in a memory for that fleeting moment. Then a scuff on the pavement echoed toward us, and our collective attention snapped to the opening of the alleyway and the voice calling from just beyond.

"Rowe! Girl, you can't hide from the dance floor forever . . . I'll *finnnnnd youuuu* . . . "

His hand clapped over my mouth before I could do something drunk and reckless like scream for Danni to help me—or to run for her life. Because if he really was the Moonlight Wraith, I wasn't sure if she would stand a chance against him, even with Nova at her side.

"I'll come for you soon," he said in my ear.

Then I watched with bated breath as he disappeared into the shadows as though he were one himself.

"There you are!" Danni shouted as she and Nova rounded the

corner to find me clutching the alley door. "Did you get lost on your way to the bathroom or something?" Her gaze narrowed as she took in my flustered state. "Why are you shaking? And sweating?"

"The door was locked," I said, pointing to the handle in my grasp as I avoided her questions.

Danni reached past me and tried it. The door swung open with ease. "Okay there, Midvale School for the Gifted, you have to *PULL*, not *PUSH*. Have you just been standing out here trying to open it this whole time?"

"Nope," I said, staring off in the direction the fae had disappeared.

"Does your answer have something to do with why you look like you've seen a ghost?"

My eyes went wide at her words. "Maybe . . . "

Danni folded her arms across her chest. "This oughtta be good—"

"I think I just puked on the Moonlight Wraith's shoes."

She looked at me for a moment, eyes narrowed, before her beautiful, wide smile spread and she erupted with laughter. "Oh my gods, Rowe, how hammered are you?"

"Well, less now that I puked, but—"

"I forget how easy it is to get humans drunk." She looped her arm around my shoulder to usher me back into the bar. "The Moonlight Wraith . . . " she said under her breath in admonishment. "You must have had something strong slipped into your drink if you're seeing dead guys."

"I'm serious, Danni—"

"I can sense that, which only furthers my point."

I stopped short, forcing her to half stop and half catch me as I stumbled forward with her momentum. "I mean it! He was tall and pale and gorgeous, and he practically glowed in the moonlight."

She studied me for a moment, doing the best she could to take drunk-me seriously. "There are many tall, pale, fae males, Rowe—"

"He said he needed something from me."

Her amused expression softened to one of pity. She knew my humanness was a sensitive subject at the best of times, as well as the source of almost all my misery.

"Rowe . . . think about it. Let's say it was the Moonlight Wraith—who isn't dead, for argument's sake—what could he possibly need from you?" Her words were soft and kind, but a stake through the heart all the same, because she was right. I was powerless in a world built on it. Supernaturals didn't need things from humans, other than menial tasks.

But still . . .

"It happened, Danni. I'm sure of it."

"And I believe you when you say that *something* happened back here, Rowe, but whatever it was, it wasn't an encounter with him."

"How can you be so sure?"

Fear bled through her concern for a moment before she did her best to wash it away with that amazing smile. "Because if it had been the Moonlight Wraith," she said, ushering me forward again, "you wouldn't be alive."

She led me around the corner, Nova trailing close behind us, and I stared back into the darkness, unable to shake the feeling that he was somewhere in the shadows, lurking—watching.

"I guess . . . " My words faded, along with my conviction.

"It was probably some asshole messing with you," she said, tightening her hold on my shoulders. "You know how they love to fuck with humans."

"Yeah . . . maybe."

"C'mon, drunk girl," she said in a sympathetic tone. "Let's go get you cleaned up."

She helped me back into the bar and fed me water for the rest of the night until I started to sober up a bit. As my blood alcohol level lowered, my mind started to wonder if she hadn't been right—if the whole thing hadn't been what I'd imagined at all. Even as Adora pulled up to the edge of No Man's Land on the border of Fire and

Fluorite's territory, I tried to shake the image of the ghostly fae from my mind. But something about his image just wouldn't go away—and neither would the feeling that his words had been true.

Whoever he was, he'd be back

And I definitely wasn't ready.

CHAPTER 3
ROWE

I awoke in a hazy hangover, my face smushed into the pillow so hard it was a wonder I hadn't suffocated after I'd swan dived onto the bed last night. The second I'd walked into the room, I'd passed out. Hard.

Hard enough, in fact, to have missed the alarm on my phone blaring for a solid forty-five minutes.

"Shit!" I shot up in a panic, only to drop back down when the pounding in my head crippled me. "Not good . . . so not good," I grumbled as I sat up more slowly. The second the room stopped spinning, I attempted to stand. When I didn't crash to the old wooden floor, I shuffled through the room, headed for the bathroom. "Let's do shots, they said . . . it'll be fun, they said." I took one look in the mirror and winced. My long, red waves were tangled, and my mascara had been rubbed all over my face—everywhere but my lashes, apparently, given how pale they looked in the harsh bathroom light. The only thing that appeared to be in good shape was the black stone pendant hanging around my neck that my mother had given me when I was little. It always seemed to weather the chaos in my life unfazed. "Shade is going to kill me," I muttered as I tucked it under my shirt, then cleaned myself up as best I could and got ready for the morning.

My place in the House of Fire and Fluorite came at a price; I was their maid and errand girl. Essentially, it was like the worst paid internship ever—one I'd never be promoted out of, thanks to my human status. But it kept me fed and clothed and housed, so it was still way better than being unaffiliated. That was an exercise in survival that I wanted no part of.

I glanced at my silver ring with the tiny green fluorite stone on my hand to remind myself of that fact, then stumbled out of the bathroom, nearly tripping on my purse strap lying in the middle of the floor like an ankle noose. I careened my way across the tiny apartment toward the old fridge on the far side of the room because breakfast was in order. I grabbed a couple of mouthfuls of leftover cheese pizza, then headed for the door. With no time to change, I threw on some sneakers with my jeans and tee that thankfully weren't covered in vomit, tossed on my jacket, and heaved open the heavy metal door.

My home was a makeshift apartment built into the back of the large building the House used as a gathering place for events and meetings, and occasionally rented out if the price was right. My mom and I had lived in a small outbuilding on Shade's property when we'd first come under the protection of Fire and Fluorite, but after she'd died, I'd bounced around between various members of the House, including Shade. But once I turned eighteen, I'd petitioned to have my own space. My current place had been Mathis'—the former leader of Fire and Fluorite—concession.

It wasn't much, but it was home.

I couldn't afford a car, so I grabbed my trusty longboard off the floor next to my door and hopped on. I was a solid twenty minutes late to check in with Shade for the day, and that was going to go over about as well as me chugging whiskey like I was a supernatural. He was far from the complete asshole his predecessor (and many of the alpha male types in the House) had been, but he had a lot on his plate trying to repair the damage that had followed Mathis' death. The

House was divided, and the stress of trying to reunite it had him on edge. Shade might have been a father figure of sorts, but he still had a temper, like most alpha shifters. It was partly why I'd learned early on how to defuse the shit out of a volatile situation.

I hoped I was awake enough to call on those skills in my hung-over state.

Rolling down the street as fast as I could while navigating potholes and other street snipers, I wove my way through traffic on the four-lane road outside my building. Weekend traffic was always light, but it was still busy in that part of town, which wasn't going to help my lateness. The city blurred in my periphery until I finally reached the turnoff for Shade's massive home. It was a super-modern mansion that looked like it belonged on the cliffs of California, which was somewhat surprising, given that Portland was still recovering from the portal apocalypse that had wreaked havoc on the city fifty years earlier. The one that had unleashed supernaturals on the human world.

Shade's house was at the far end of the block at the top of an incline (of course). Cars lined the street outside, all the major pack leaders within the House of Fire and Fluorite already there for a meeting.

Was I excited about this? No, but it was what it was. Another consequence of being late.

I ran up the driveway, longboard tucked up under my arm, until I reached the stairs leading to the front door and around the far side of the house to the back, where my entrance sat. With a quick punch of the keycode, I was in and hurrying through the business wing of the house, hoping to slip past the others unnoticed.

But there was no avoiding notice in a house full of shifters.

"Looks like somebody's about to get an earful," a male called out as I slinked past the dining room-turned-meeting space.

"No time to talk," I said as I ran down the hall, praying none of them would follow.

Shifters also loved to chase.

Too busy laughing at my expense, they didn't bother to follow, and I soon found myself alone outside Shade's office door. I raised my hand to knock, but a booming male voice called out from the other side before I had the chance.

"You're late."

Fucking shifter hearing.

I quickly pushed my way in and closed the door behind me for the illusion of privacy, at least.

"Sorry . . . I had a rough night—"

"I don't want your apologies or excuses, Rowe." He lifted his pale blue stare from the phone in his hand and pinned it on me. I instantly felt like cornered prey. "I want you to do your job. The one your mother agreed to when she joined this House."

And then died a year later.

I'd always wondered what she'd done to get Shade to convince Mathis to take us on. Unfortunately, I'd never gotten the chance to ask, so speculation was the name of the game. I knew it hadn't been anything sexual—Shade's mate had died years before we'd arrived, and he'd never quite recovered from that—but whatever it was, it had been enough to convince both him and Mathis to let us join.

My mother's half-witch status should have been enough, but with me—the more-human-than-not child—in tow, I wasn't sure that it had been. And since Mathis hadn't exactly had a heart of any sort, I'd eventually settled on his motives being philanthropic, at least from an optics standpoint. Fire and Fluorite didn't have a sparkling reputation among the supernatural community, which was surprisingly problematic at times. Surely, taking on a single mother with a twelve-year-old human daughter would have earned him some points to counter his being a bloodthirsty maniac.

Then again, maybe not.

"I heard you were out late last night," Shade continued, pulling me from my thoughts. His brow quirked while I silently scrambled to figure out what to say. Danni and Adora weren't exactly his favorites, so hanging out with them was a grey area at best, and also the reason why I shouldn't really have been out in public with them. It was also the reason why we'd gone to a human bar in No Man's Land, but I should have known that wouldn't matter.

All the Houses had eyes and ears everywhere.

"Yeah . . . " I said, drawing the word out longer than necessary. "I was in rare form."

"With Dannika and Adora." He eyed me across the room, and I could practically feel it shrinking with every passing second. "Do I need to remind you that you represent not only this House when you're out, but also me specifically, since I am solely responsible for your position with Fire and Fluorite—"

"No, Shade. No reminder necessary—"

"And yet I feel like one is."

I let out a breath and dared another step deeper into the room. "They were just in town for one night. It won't happen again—"

"Until it does—"

"—and I promise that the next time someone suggests doing shots, I'll run in the opposite direction." I smiled tentatively, hoping to charm him out of his simmering anger. "My stomach will thank us both for it."

He shifted in his chair as he stared back. "I heard something about puking in the alley behind the bar."

"Yep . . . that might have happened. Not one of my finer moments, I realize, but it seemed like a better plan than doing it *in* the bar, so . . . "

He let out a breath as he uncoiled himself from his black office chair and stood behind his desk like the wall of intimidating shifter he was. Then he smiled at me like he used to when I was younger, and the tension in my shoulders melted away. "Your ability to find a silver lining in life's low points would be far more admirable if it weren't so inconvenient."

"I know," I said with a sigh. "I'm sorry, Shade. I'll do better next time. I promise."

"I'm not sure there can be a next time, Rowe, not with Adora and

Dannika. Not for a long time, anyway. Things here are strained enough—you know that. Galivanting around town with perceived enemies isn't a good look at the moment, and it adds to the complexities of your position in the House."

"I'm sorry . . . I didn't think about that."

His mouth pressed to a sympathetic line. "I know you are, and I can see that you didn't, but I need you to be smarter about things from here on out, okay?"

"I'll try."

"I'd expect nothing less," he said as he pulled a sheet of paper off his desk. "Now, this is your list for the day. You're getting a late start, but I need it all done regardless."

"I understand," I replied in a soft tone. "If that's all, I'll get to work right now."

"That's all," he said as he sat back down, "unless there's anything else I need to know about last night."

I stopped short, panic coursing through my veins. Telling Shade about the Moonlight Wraith could only end in one of two ways: with him laughing at me like I'd finally lost my mind, or with an interrogation I was in no shape for if he thought I hadn't. Neither sounded like a great option, and given Danni's reaction the previous night—followed by her logic—it didn't seem necessary to fill him in. Besides, it wasn't like I could even tell him anything, really. The bits I could still remember were a bit fuzzy and random, essentially comprising a very sexy-but-scary fae telling me something about a problem he thought I could solve. And something about finding me again.

After that encounter, if it ever came, I could decide whether or not Shade needed to be filled in. Why deal with a problem today you can put off until tomorrow?

I looked back to find Shade looking up at me expectantly. "Nope. Nothing else to report."

"Then I guess we're all done." I opened the door and stepped out into the hall. "Make sure you find Andreas before you leave. He said you didn't answer any of his messages last night. I think he was worried about you."

I pulled my phone out, and sure enough, there were four unanswered texts from the man in question on the screen. "Ugh . . . I'm never drinking again."

"I'll believe that when I see it," Shade replied. I looked back again to find mischief in his eyes as he smiled at me. "Now get out of here."

"Aye aye, Captain."

I nodded and hurried out of the room, closing the door behind me. I hovered in the hallway long enough to fire off an apology text, complete with a random assortment of emojis, to Andreas, Shade's son, who'd always been around while I was growing up. He'd been seventeen when Mom and I had joined Fire and Fluorite, and he'd most definitely been my teenage crush. He'd always looked out for me—still did, for that matter—but there was no love lost between him and the girls, which had made things difficult for us all at times.

He wasn't going to be thrilled to hear who I'd been with last night.

Before I could even put my phone away, the man in question rounded the corner in all his shirtless glory and smiled at me. "The party girl lives," he said as he pulled a threadbare tee over his head.

"Barely."

"No thanks to your partners in crime." The change in his mood when he alluded to the girls was notable, and I started to rethink my plan to keep the details our outing a secret from him. As if it were possible to keep secrets at all in Fire and Fluorite.

Bad news traveled fast.

"Andreas—"

He raised his hand to cut off my explanation. "I already overheard Dad reading you the riot act about them, so I'm not going to add anything. You know how I feel about those two." He took a cautious step closer, and the tension in his shoulders eased a bit. "You also know how I feel about you, so I'm going to drop it for the sake of our relationship."

I let out my breath in a whoosh and wiped my damp brow. "Good, because I'm really in no shape to argue right now."

His mischievous smile returned. "Adora made you do shots, didn't she?"

"She did indeed."

"And you tried to keep up with them, didn't you?"

"Guilty as charged."

His eyes narrowed. "Is that why you puked in the alley?"

"Does everyone know about that?" I asked as a wave of panic crashed over me. Because if someone really had witnessed my alley vomiting spree, then maybe they'd seen me with . . . whoever the hell had been with me.

He laughed at my response, which made the dimple in his right cheek pop. Andreas was absolutely, and quite frankly, offensively good-looking. His body was perfection, and his face was straight off a romance novel cover. And that smile he was flashing used to make me feel some kind of way when I was younger, but with age, I'd realized we were never destined for romance.

Aside from the girls, he was my best friend and ally.

"One of the guys mentioned something about it this morning," he said. "And thanks for leaving me hanging last night. It's not like I was worried about your drunk ass getting home or anything."

"Yeah . . . I'm not sure I was even capable of operating my phone at points in the evening."

He propped his shoulder against the wall and folded his arms across his chest. "And yet you got home okay."

"You can thank the girls for that."

His smile fell away. "Not a chance."

"It's a figure of speech, Andreas. I don't actually want you to thank them."

"Hell would have to get pretty frosty before I'd even consider it."

I quirked a brow at him and leaned against the wall to mimic his posture. "What if I asked you to? Would you do it then? For me?"

A low growl rumbled through the hallway. "That's a big ask, Rowe—"

"Hypothetically speaking, of course."

He pushed off the wall to loom over me. "If they'd truly protected you? Kept you safe? Then yes, I would. But I'd probably die the second the words left my mouth, so keep that in mind if your hypothetical ever becomes a real thing."

"Death by apology," I mused. "Not exactly the Achilles heel I'd have expected, but—"

"Andreas," Shade called from inside his office, interrupting me.

"Looks like Dad needs his favorite second," Andreas said with a wink.

I stepped aside to let him pass with a grand sweep of my arm. "Then don't let poor little old me keep the important male types from getting their work done."

He laughed and shook his head as he passed by, and I cringed internally at my nerdiness. "You're cut off from historical fiction for a while."

"That's fair," I replied as I hurried down the hall to the back door. "I'll see you later."

"Maybe try texting me back if I message you."

I spun around and saluted him, nearly tripping over my feet in the process, then all but ran around the corner. I could hear Andreas' laughter following me, letting me know that my awkwardness hadn't been missed. I wondered if that was partly why he enjoyed having me around, if I was like a funny stray dog you take in that does weird stuff like chew on its own leg or bark at the wall for no reason, but it's cute and lovable so you keep it. It felt like a valid explanation for our relationship, given his position in the house and my complete lack of one.

Or maybe I just appealed to the humanity in him that didn't often have the chance to show itself.

Trying to force the blood reddening my cheeks to disperse, I rushed out of the house and down the street, headed for my first stop of the day. I was in for a long afternoon of scrubbing floors and washing windows for the heads of every pack within the House—and the mocking I knew I'd receive once word of the night's shenanigans spread like wildfire. Nobody could rival the gossiping ability of bored suburban housewives like supernaturals. I swore they subsisted on power, fear, and the misery of others.

As I skateboarded my way out of Shade's neighborhood, I wondered if maybe that was why my mother and I had been brought into the House.

Maybe we were perfect sources of at least two of those things.

CHAPTER 4
ROWE

Hours later, I found myself in the vast meeting hall, ready to finish up the last of my tasks for the day. The upside was that my commute home couldn't have been shorter. The downside was that I had about three thousand square feet of wide-plank wood floors to scrub before I could crash for the night.

With a deep sigh, I hauled my bucket out of the sink in the bathroom and headed for the front entrance. The wall sconces cast a dim light around the room without the grand chandelier turned on, and I wondered how I'd missed the switch when I came in.

"Guess I'm more tired than I thought," I muttered to myself as I headed for the main panel near the doors.

"How unfortunate," a voice called from somewhere in the darkness.

I shrieked as I wheeled around. The bucket I was holding crashed to the floor, spilling soapy water everywhere, and I clutched my chest as I tried to remember how to breathe.

From out of the shadows stepped the Moonlight Wraith, something close to amusement sparkling in those deep grey eyes.

"You're like a damn ghost," I said, then realized the irony. "Is that your assassin skill of choice? You just scare people to death with your stealth? Because that makes some of the stories about you a bit disappointing, if I'm being honest."

His cool gaze assessed the room, then fell on me. "One of them . . . but I'd love to hear your stories some time so I can attest to their accuracy."

I stared at him in the scant light of the room as he slowly approached and realized I really hadn't been hallucinating in the alley the night before. Hadn't imagined the whole thing. Because there he was, standing right in front of me, looking every bit the powerful being his reputation promised; and the set of his square-but-sculpted jaw told me he'd come to finish whatever he'd started before Danni had interrupted him.

Nothing about this situation was good. I needed a way out, and fast.

"You can't be here," I said, looking past him to the doors as though one of the packs might come barreling through at any moment. "You're not in No Man's Land anymore. This is Fire and Fluorite territory. If somebody shows up—"

"I'll be long gone before they cross the threshold. Your precious shifters aren't known for their stealth, outside of a fight." He took a step closer, stopping in a beam of moonlight shining through the floor-to-ceiling windows. "Your concern, though amusing, is unnecessary."

"I'm not *concerned*," I lied, knowing that I was one hundred percent concerned about not only the reappearance of the terrifying fae assassin, but also being caught between him and whoever might stroll in at any moment. "And they're not *my* shifters . . . "

"Of course." His patronizing tone seeped into my pores and irritated every cell in my body. His arrogance made me want to scream, but I knew better than that, so I kept my mouth shut. "But you are a member of Fire and Fluorite, are you not? Wouldn't that make them your shifters by default?"

Fair point.

"Is that what you came to talk to me about?" I asked, annoyance sneaking into my tone. "My somewhat unconventional House membership?" I folded my arms across my stomach, and his eyebrow cocked in response. Whether it was in surprise or challenge, I wasn't sure, but my sudden urge to bolt from the room so I didn't have to find out grew by the second. I swore the intensity of his stare could have melted glass, and I wasn't sure my mortal skin could hold up against it for long.

Whatever he'd come for, I wanted to get it over with. Fast.

I swallowed. "So . . . you wanna tell me why you're here?"

His hands spread wide in 'ta-da' fashion. "I told you I would find you soon."

"Yep, I remembered that part from last night—"

"That's surprising—"

"—but what I don't remember is why," I continued, ignoring his jab. "Why do you want to see me at all?"

He took a step closer, and I took one in retreat. Stopping short, he canted his head at me and assessed me with a narrowed gaze. "Are you afraid of me, Regina Little?"

"Absolutely," I said without hesitation.

He smirked in response. "Good." The thick wool of his deep navy coat pulled against his broad shoulders as he clasped his hands behind his back and leaned toward me as if he were about to share a secret. "A certain individual didn't fear me enough," he whispered in a gruff voice. "She thought she could take my power—my position—and kill me, but she was wrong. And she will pay dearly for that error." Ice slid down my spine at his words, and he pulled away just enough to stare me down. "That is where you come in, little queen—"

"It's Rowe," I reminded him, wishing my tongue knew when to play dead. "Why do you keep calling me that?"

He quirked a brow at my question. "Your name means 'queen little'. I merely altered it to flow better," he said matter of factly before continuing with his train of thought. "Now you, *little queen . . . you* are my ticket to vengeance and the restoration of my title."

I gawked at him like he'd taken leave of every single one of his senses, but the conviction in his expression never faltered. He believed what he'd said with every fiber of his being, that much was clear, which made me wonder if I not only had the most notorious fae I knew of standing before me, but the most mentally questionable one to boot.

One who, by all accounts, was supposed to be dead.

The ridiculousness of the entire situation eroded my composure, and I soon found myself struggling not to laugh. But the harder I tried not to, the more my shoulders shook and my stomach contracted, and I knew it was game over. The church giggles were about to hit me like a semi-truck, and there was nothing that could stop it.

Even the rational knowledge that it was highly likely to piss off the clearly unstable fae in front of me.

"I'm sorry," I said, covering my mouth as though that could withhold the nervous laughter bubbling over.

"You think this is *amusing*?" At his words, I swore the temperature in the room dropped thirty degrees.

"Nonono . . . I just . . . it's just that . . . " Words failed me, which was so not helpful at the moment. Volker's eyes seemed to gleam from deep within in anger, and I begged my nervous system to kick in that fight-or-flight response any second now, but it didn't; the laughter kept going, even when I grew desperate for it to stop. "*I'm* your ticket to vengeance?" I barely got the words out without doubling over. "*Me*? But why . . . and *how*? You know I'm human, right? There is literally no way I can help you." It was that final line that seemed to register in my mind and pull me from my outburst. If I made him believe that I couldn't help him, then what would his next course of action be? The cold reality of death suddenly rushed over me.

My laughter ceased.

Volker, stoic and silent, closed the distance between us with one quick step. I craned my neck to meet his gaze, then instantly wished I hadn't. Those dark pewter eyes were now pale and glowing, an escalation from the subtle gleam moments earlier, and the tension in his chest and shoulders only made him more intimidating. I stood there, breath caught in my throat, awaiting whatever wrath he was about to throw down.

From what I'd heard about him, the former king of Air and Amethyst had a reputation for efficiency. At least it would be quick, right?

"What we believe and what is true are not always one and the same, little queen." His words were cold and restrained and altogether terrifying, but there was a note of truth in them that I couldn't ignore. "I know your mother was a witch, powerful enough to gain acceptance into the House of Fire and Fluorite. I know that you were allowed to remain, even after her death. And I know you must have power, even if you do not."

"If that's true, how come I never noticed? Or anyone else, for that matter?"

The brightness in his eyes dimmed slightly, making them easier to face. "I don't know."

Convenient.

"Suppose you're right. Suppose I have some great power that my mother never thought to mention and nobody in the House is able to detect, even though they're shifters with heightened senses of all kinds. What is it I'm supposed to do with it?"

He took a step back and eyed me tightly, as though he were weighing out his response. "I want to use your power to restore mine—to return it to what it was before an unknown source disrupted the magic of the night a few weeks ago." Judging by the tension in his face and body, admitting this was just about the last thing he wanted to do, and I understood why. Weakness of any kind was something supernaturals hated. I, however, was really used to it. "This disturbance has left my magic . . . *unreliable* at times," he continued, "which allowed the current queen to make her move. I need it stabilized in order to regain my seat as king of Air and Amethyst."

I choked on a laugh, then quickly coughed to cover it up. "So you want to juice up your powers with ones I'm pretty sure I don't have?"

"Yes."

"So you can get your revenge?"

He exhaled hard, frustration creeping into his demeanor. "Yes. I would not be here otherwise, risking potential exposure."

It was very apparent that Volker, former king of the House of Air and Amethyst, wasn't used to needing others. A smarter person would have known not to push that button, but I was not that individual, so push it I did.

"So you need me . . . "

In a flash, his face was in mine, eyes again glowing a silvery white that nearly blinded me. "*Want*," he growled in my ear, "not *need*. An important and necessary distinction, little queen. One you'd be wise to remember." I tried hard to breathe with him so close and terrifying. "Do not believe for one second that your life is so valuable to me that I won't bring you to your knees and make you beg for death," he seethed. "My power may wax and wane, but it is sufficient to end your life without effort—after I get what I want. Your House is in turmoil, and by the time they even realize you're dead, I will have found another way to reclaim mine and amassed an army." His hands gripped my arms so tightly that I thought they were going to explode, and that eerie glow returned to his eyes, bathing me in the pale grey light of death. "Your life is of no consequence to me, Regina Little. Don't allow a false sense of security to cloud your judgment moving forward." I tried to respond, but no words would come out. All I could do was stare into the cold face of the Moonlight Wraith and silently pray. "And if you tell anyone about my existence or my plans, I will make you wish you'd never stumbled into that alley."

Knowing that there was no way out, I stretched my neck until my lips were at his ear and whispered back. "You can't make me help you."

His grip tightened as he pressed his body against mine. "Oh, I think I can."

I swallowed hard at his threat. "I'm fragile," I reminded him. "You wouldn't want to break me before you got what you wanted."

"I won't . . . I have impeccable restraint."

"Because you're so good at what you do?"

He pulled away enough to show me a wolfish smile. "Exactly."

He let me go and stepped away. I folded my arms across my chest to hug myself and rubbed the soon-to-be bruised skin near my shoulders. Sad, scared, and angry, I stared at him as he loomed a few paces away. It was clear that he wasn't bluffing, so I had no intention of testing him further. I'd either do whatever it was he wanted me to do voluntarily, or I'd pay the consequences. And if what he'd just done was even the slightest taste of what he'd do, I'd take a hard pass on that.

I couldn't help but wonder how unhinged he'd become when he realized I didn't have a lick of power to my name—that I was as human as the daughter of a half-witch could be. No way was that going to end well. I needed to buy myself time to figure out a way out of this mess, if there was one to be found at all.

Suddenly, the Wraith went rigid, his attention turning to the front door of the meeting house. With lightning speed, he receded into the shadows. An eerie disembodied voice called to me from the darkness. "Remember, little queen, I'll be keeping my eye on you."

He disappeared without another word, leaving me standing against the wall, breathing hard and sweating like I'd just run a mile in the desert. His words were a thinly veiled threat, and I had no doubt that they were true. I couldn't breathe a word of this to anyone; I was on my own in this mess.

With that sobering reality in mind, I made my way over to my cleaning supplies and got back to work.

No sense in letting all that adrenaline go to waste.

CHAPTER 5
ROWE

I woke up around noon the next day and stretched out starfish-style on the bed, luxuriating in the fact that it was Sunday and I didn't have to do a damn thing all day long. My one day off a week was my prized possession—a sacred thing—and I had big plans to lay around all day and watch old movies. Laziness was a trait I excelled at when given the opportunity.

After I got cleaned up and tidied my room so it didn't look like a tornado had hit it, I searched for my phone so I could order a pizza. It started buzzing as though it knew I was hunting around for it, and I dove under the bed to grab it after the fourth ring.

"Hello?"

"You need to come in today," a grumpy female said, not bothering to greet me, not that she ever did. Myra was standoffishness personified—I'd learned that the hard way early on.

"Myra, it's my day off—"

"I don't need a lesson in what day of the week it is, Rowe. What I *do* need is an extra set of hands to help me serve, since Sasha decided to fuck right off through one of the portals yesterday and hasn't been back since."

"Ugh . . . *whyyyy*? Why am I the one you had to call?"

"If it makes you feel better, I called everyone else first, but they all knew you'd be the one to cave and do the right thing, so they said no."

"Am I that obvious?"

"Your need for cash is, yes," she replied without skipping a beat.

"That's harsh—"

"But true, so why don't we cut the shit and you just agree to come in so I can hang up and get back to what I was doing—which heavily involves plotting Sasha's demise?"

I groaned again for good measure, then hauled myself up from the floor. "I'll come in if you let me in on that revenge."

"Deal. Now move your ass. I need you in here by one—it's a double shift."

"MYRA!"

"Bye, now."

She hung up before my impressive combination of swears escaped.

"Don't freak out, don't freak out," I muttered to myself as I ransacked my closet for the only clean black jeans I had and a shirt to match. The best I could do was a graphic tee turned inside out. If Ravi, the owner, wanted to get pissed at me for my attire, he could run his establishment shorthanded.

The bar/restaurant combo resided deep in the heart of No Man's Land, which meant I needed to haul ass if I planned to make it there on time. I grabbed my leather jacket and a granola bar before scooping up my board and darting out the door. Was my hair a situation? Yes. Did I have time for makeup? No. Was I happy about either of those details? Absolutely not, but there was no way around it, and really, nobody at that place gave a shit about what I looked like. Even at my best, I couldn't rival Myra's beauty. If she was there, I was invisible.

I stumbled through the back entrance that dumped you right into the thick of the kitchen at ten past one.

"You're late!" Ravi shouted at me as I made my way behind the line to his office to leave my things, his flawless brown skin shimmering with sweat in the bright lights. He dabbed his brow with the back of his sleeve as he rushed between the stove and the prep area.

"Pretty sure Sasha is the one who's late and I'm the one saving your ass, so maybe bring your attitude down a notch or five?"

He shot me a sideward glance, then fully turned when I slipped off my coat and he saw my shirt. "You are not wearing that!"

"Then I'm going home, because it's all I have."

"Here," Myra called out as she cut through the kitchen like a fish through water, black hair gleaming with an oil-slick, iridescent sheen. "I have an extra."

She grabbed her purse off the hanger on the wall and pulled out a shirt. I prayed it wasn't identical to the skin-tight v-neck she had on. It may have shown off her boobs amazingly, but I lacked what she had and the shirt would have only showed that point off more.

I let out a sigh of relief when I saw it was a crewneck.

"Thanks—"

"Don't thank me yet. It's a shitshow out there, and it's not even prime time."

"What's going on?" I asked as I turned my back to the kitchen and pulled my tee over my head.

"Who knows? It's good for tips, and that's all I really care about."

"Still saving up to buy your tail back?" Yael yelled over the din. I yanked Myra's shirt on in time to look over my shoulder and see him staring at her, a wicked smile tugging at his mouth. "I don't think that's how it works, Myra dear."

"I didn't pawn it, you uppity shit."

"Oh, that's right. You crossed the wrong members of Sea and Serpentine, and now you're in timeout," he replied, feigning a pout that accentuated his full lips. "How long is that going to last, again? Was it fifty years? Seventy?"

"Long enough for me to find a way to kill you and dispose of your body without anyone ever learning what happened to you," she replied, slipping behind him in an almost seductive manner. She grabbed the ten-inch chef's knife off the counter and began twirling it against her fingertip. "I still have many allies in the sea," she said, her pleasant tone—that I'd never heard before—belying the simmering rage brewing behind those sapphire eyes. "They're extremely discreet."

"If you kill my cook, I'll call in some favors to deal with you," Ravi threatened. "So how about all of you just do the jobs I pay you to do, in the one place that would hire you in the first place, and be grateful for it."

Yael said nothing. Myra grumbled under her breath as she walked away. And I kept my head down on my way to the front of the house so I wouldn't get pulled into any more petty bullshit. Because as much as none of them would admit it, Ravi was right. The place was called *The Riff-Raff* for a reason. Any outcast from any House was welcome there, which made it unique. It was rare to have so many Houses dubiously represented at the same establishment, let alone be staffed by them. It made it tense as hell at times, but Ravi was the king of cutting through everyone's shit to keep the ship righted. And damn, did the staff test that ability on the regular.

"I'm going to gut him and feed his entrails to the fish," Myra said as she loaded a tray with beers from the bar. "Fucking fae bastard. It's like he's forgotten why he's here."

"Why *is* he here?" I asked, following her lead and loading my tray with drinks.

She turned to me, eyes sparkling with delight. "You don't know?"

Aw shit. Mischief Mermaid Mode unlocked.

"Nope, but I can see that you do and are dying to tell me, so . . . " I swept my hands wide to invite her telling of the tale.

"The queen kicked him out."

"Huh . . . "

"That's not the good part, you twit," she said, her amusement waning as she scolded me. "She threw him out because he dared to ask a question about their former king—stupid shit. His arrogance knows no bounds."

"You mean the Moonlight Wraith?"

She shot me another disappointed look, then jerked her head for me to follow. "Was there another king of Air and Amethyst recently dethroned and killed? Or do they not tell you humans things at Fire and Fluorite?"

"I know things!" I argued.

"If you say so." She walked up to a massive table filled with equally massive males and started slapping beers down in front of them with little care. The amber liquid sloshed over the rims, splashing the table and the arms of those that had ordered them. I rushed behind her, serving drinks along with napkins and apologies.

"She must have slipped," I said, wiping off the arm of some guy I didn't recognize.

"She's a fucking mermaid," he snapped back. "She can control tides, so I think keeping beer in a glass shouldn't be a big stretch."

"It isn't," she said as she continued around the table. "I just don't fucking care." She punctuated her response with a saccharin smile, and I immediately knew it was going to be a long day.

"Okay," I said, scooping the final beer off her tray, "I think I can handle this, Myra. Why don't you check on your other tables?"

"Fine. We can talk more about Yael later, then." She walked away, and I let out a breath.

"That one has a real fucking attitude problem," one of the guys grumbled as he watched her walk away.

"Everyone that works here does," I explained, setting his beer down in front of him. "That's why Ravi hired me—to help clean up the mess."

"I guess you're pretty good at that, given the shit you do for Fire and Fluorite," he said with a laugh. The others at the table started to chuckle along with him like they were all in on some joke I'd missed.

"Someone has to do it."

"And I bet you do it *really* well, don't you, red?" He grabbed a strand of my hair and tugged it a little too hard to be comfortable.

"Myra will be back when she fucking feels like it to take your order," I snapped as I tried to pull away. But the hold he had on that strand was too tight, so I stood there helpless while he held it hostage, much to the amusement of the others at the table.

"I'd rather you take my order."

I'm going to kill Sasha when she gets back.

"Too bad she's not your waitress," a male voice said from behind me, "and she isn't on the menu, either, so let her go." I looked back to find Andreas standing there, anger simmering in his glare. "She's a member of Fire and Fluorite. Fuck with her and you fuck with me."

"You and who else, Andreas?" the hair-tugger replied as he relinquished his hold on me. "Your House is in shambles right now. They have bigger issues to deal with than this human servant of theirs."

Andreas leaned forward, gently pulling me behind him. "I don't need anyone else."

"Okay," I said, grabbing his arm to pull him back a step or twenty, "I think we're all set here." I turned back to the asshole who'd started it all. "Like I said, Myra will be back out to get your order in a minute."

"And like I said," Andreas added, "Rowe is one of us. Remember that next time you consider fucking with her."

I hauled Andreas away amid a barrage of colorful takes on his final statement, each one making my cheeks flare crimson. By the time we'd put enough distance between the table and us, I thought my face would combust. "Are you okay?" he asked as I tried to calm down.

"I'm fine," I replied in a weird hushed shout of sorts. I took a deep breath to try to settle my nerves—unsuccessfully. "It's not my first time dealing with assholes."

He glared over me at the table I'd all but dragged him from. "Mine either."

"I'll bet. Now . . . you wanna tell me what you're doing here?"

Right on cue, a bag of takeout appeared on the bar beside him. "Oh . . . that makes sense."

"The better question is, why are *you* here?"

"Sasha bailed into a portal, and I'm apparently the only one who works here with a sense of loyalty."

He pulled his hard stare from the grabby assholes and smiled at me. "One of the qualities we all love about you."

"Oh, I think that ogre over there thinks you have a whole different set of reasons for why you all love me."

Andreas shot him a murderous look. "I'll just bet he does."

"I had that under control, by the way. I would have been fine."

"I'm sure you would have," he replied as he paid for his food with a tiny vial of shifter blood, "but if it's all the same to you, I'm not going to stand by and let anyone treat you that way."

"One of the qualities I love about you," I said, using his words against him. Only I didn't have a 'we' to diffuse the loaded meaning, and blood heated my cheeks once again.

"As much fun as this is to watch," Myra said, sidling up beside us, "and it *is* fun—because it's painful—I need you to actually work." She handed me a tray full of orders and pointed to the table they belonged to. "Feed them before I have to stab someone."

"I guess I should go," Andreas said, shooting Myra a sideward glare.

"Sexy *and* perceptive," she clapped back. "Throw in some daddy issues and a dark side, and I might be interested." He opened his mouth to reply, but she cut him off with an outstretched hand. "It's a joke, biceps. Now take your food and bugger off so your girl here can do what she's getting paid to do." She turned on her heels and hurried off to the kitchen—and someone else to terrorize.

"Any chance she's getting her tail back soon?" Andreas asked, and I couldn't help but laugh, even if it wasn't really funny. The truth was that nobody knew, even Myra, and buried deep down underneath that frigid bitch persona was a homesick mermaid, desperate to return to the sea.

"No clue."

"Well, I'll gladly chuck her back into the Pacific whenever she does." Andreas grabbed his bag and tucked it under his arm. "You gonna be around later?"

"Much, much later."

"Then I'll see you tomorrow when you check in with Dad."

"I'll be there with bells on," I replied as I adjusted the tray on my arm. "But I should go before Myra and her sharp tongue return."

He smiled at me, then turned toward the door. "I'll throw her back into the Pacific without the tail, too," he offered, "if she needs to cool off."

"Try it and you'll lose a hand," Myra barked as she entered the dining area again. Andreas' laughter followed him out. "A word of advice: he may be hot and funny and whatever, but he has trouble written all over him."

"Say what, now?"

"The nice ones always do."

I gaped at her in confusion. "That literally makes no sense at all."

"That's your amateur status talking," she said, taking back the tray I was idly holding. "Once you're a big girl with some experience under her belt, you'll understand."

"Excuse me?"

"Take him, for example," she said, jerking her head toward a shady-looking guy in the shadowy corner I hadn't even noticed. "He's been staring at you since he arrived. *That* one has promise."

"So, just to be clear, being a creeper is a *good* thing, and being a solid friend is *bad*?"

She smiled with genuine pride. "Exactly! Now you're catching on."

I stared at her in silence for a second. "Mermaids are weird."

"Says the human trying to fit into our world."

Customers shouted at us from across the room to deliver their food, and I quickly dispatched the full tray in my hand. On my way back to the kitchen, I caught Myra's arm, a thought occurring to me.

Creatures of the sea were long known for harboring secrets—knowledge that didn't always make its way onto land. Maybe she could help me figure out if I actually did have power.

And if so, how to use it.

I leaned in close to her, and her eyes narrowed with suspicion. "What if I wasn't human?"

"What?"

"I said mermaids are weird, and you said so are humans—"

"Yeah—"

"—but what if I'm not?" I repeated. "What if I have power?"

"I mean, you're technically not human because you're like one quarter witch or whatever, but you clearly don't have any magic or power." She swept her arm wide, gesturing to our surroundings. "Hence the reason Ravi lets you work here. You're an outcast, too."

"That's not what I mean—"

"Then what *do* you mean, Rowe? Because I have a tray full of food getting cold and a finger-snapping bitch at table four who's about to be wearing it if she doesn't knock that shit off," she said, raising her voice loud enough for said finger-snapping bitch to hear.

Maybe she was right.

Maybe this wasn't the right time to have this talk, for many reasons.

So instead of fueling tensions further, I shut them down entirely. "Ravi!" I yelled at the kitchen. "Myra needs a snack break, *STAT*."

"Is she hangry again?" the boss yelled back.

"Very, and about to make bad life choices because of it."

"Myra! Get your ass back here."

She smiled like a snake about to strike and handed back the tray for the eightieth time. "Enjoy."

With nothing else to say, she turned on her heels and disappeared into the kitchen, leaving me with the bitch, the meatheads, and the creeper in the corner—not to mention the rest of the building.

I raced around like a rat in a maze, taking orders and delivering food, internally kicking myself for dismissing Myra, like that wouldn't bite me in the ass. When I finally stopped to take a breath, I found myself standing in front of the creeper, ready to take his order.

My gaze lifted from the ticket pad in my hand to find the unfamiliar man staring at me. "Can I take your—" My words stopped short when the steel grey eyes assessing me registered.

The Moonlight Wraith smiled at my realization. "I told you I'd be watching."

CHAPTER 6
VOLKER

She stared at me wide-eyed, and I couldn't help but think that was her default expression.

She'd worn it earlier that morning when she'd raced out of her apartment to go to yet another place of employment. She'd worn it when she'd argued with the Sea and Serpentine girl, and again when the brute at the table had grabbed her arm. The only time it had been absent was when the shifter had rushed in to aid her. His chivalry hadn't seemed to faze her, which meant she was used to such acts from him—an ominous sign, indeed, indicating that he was never far away.

And that would be a problem.

When I'd followed her to this bizarre haven within the neutral territory, I hadn't intended to make my presence known to her. My mission had been simply to observe her behind the safety of glamour, to see if she disobeyed the rules. But something about the way she had looked at the shifter changed things.

She needed a reminder of whom she was dealing with.

Of what was at stake.

"What . . . " she said, the word barely wheezing past her lips, "what are you doing here? And *how*?"

"The how appears obvious, does it not? As for the why—I wanted to make sure you were obeying the rules I set forth last night before we were interrupted."

"This was a test?" she asked, disbelief tainting her tone.

"Of sorts." She swore under her breath. It was particularly amusing. "Do you always make scenes wherever you go?" I asked, earning further ire from the fiery being unwittingly masquerading as a human; this source of great power parading around the city underneath their noses. Not even those close to her knew what she was, and their ignorance would be my gain.

"Are you always a cryptic dick?" she countered, earning a glance from the table behind her. The fear I'd seen from her the previous night was all but gone, replaced by an irritation that those who knew me would never dare show. Was it a false sense of security she felt, being surrounded by others? Or the thought that her wolf might appear from nowhere yet again to save her? Or was it the hint of exhaustion tugging at the corners of her eyes and rounding her shoulders that made her bold, too tired to think through the potential ramifications of her choices?

Whatever the answer, I found her unexpected behavior darkly intriguing. I leaned back in my seat and stared at her for a moment longer before answering. "Perhaps."

Her annoyance grew in an instant. "Are you going to order something?" she asked, her frustration plain in her expression. "I don't need snappy-fingers lady crawling up my ass."

"She won't."

"Oh? Are you gonna bully her too, then? Is that your MO?"

"Are you always this brave when surrounded by others?"

"Do you always answer a question with a question?"

"Would it bother you if I did?"

"Is that really a question?"

"Is that?"

More creative swearing under her breath.

This time, I allowed my amusement to show. My reaction only seemed to anger her further. "I have to go," she said as she turned to leave.

"I wasn't banking on the shifter," I said, pulling her to a halt.

"Andreas?" she replied with care. "What about him?"

"He's a potential complication, to say the least."

"Why?"

"He seems rather invested in your well-being."

Her brow creased as she contemplated how best to reply, but her hesitation was response enough. "He's my friend."

"Your *friend*?"

Her eyebrows drew together in anger. "Yeah, my friend. Does that surprise you?" she asked. I nodded slowly, and she scoffed. "Because I couldn't possibly have friends?"

"No."

She stared at me expectantly, waiting for me to explain further. When I didn't, her cheeks reddened and she took a deep breath. Something about seeing her so flustered was fascinating to me—the way she didn't bother to mask her emotions was both foreign and refreshing. It was in direct contrast to life in Air and Amethyst, with all the games and plots. A House filled with deceivers of the highest caliber.

She, however, was anything but.

"Then what?"

"I did not expect you to be so . . . *close* with a high-ranking member of Fire and Fluorite. Or what remains of it."

"*Close*?" she replied, emphasizing the word as I had. "Close how? Like 'in a relationship' close?" I nodded. "Yeah, no," she said, nearly choking on her reply. "Your radar is way off on that one."

"Is it?" I asked, needling the little queen further. "He doesn't have a reputation for having friends."

"Well, he's the one that friend-zoned me a lifetime ago, so yeah, I'd say you're way off."

"Perhaps he's changed his mind."

"Definitely not."

"For his sake, I hope you're right. I wouldn't want him getting in the way."

She glared at me with fire in the depths of those emerald eyes. "He won't."

Our silent standoff continued until the raven-haired mermaid called for her. "Are you working or flirting?" she shouted over the din as she approached. "Because I didn't take that break only to have to do double the work once I came back out." She sidled up next to the little queen and stared at me, heat in her eyes. "If you're too dumbstruck to take his order, I can manage it for you," she said as she lifted the ticket pad from her hands.

"I've decided not to stay," I informed her as I slid out from the booth to tower over the two of them. "Maybe another time, Regina Little."

Without looking back at her dumbfounded expression, I headed for the door, the mermaid's words trailing behind me. "Told you the creeper was more promising."

I smiled to myself as I disappeared through the exit. They were both rather amusing.

It would be such a shame to have to end them.

CHAPTER 7
ROWE

"Hey, Yael?" I shouted over the clanking of dishes and running water.

"Yes, little human?" He spoke that word with the inherent disdain of a fae—like he couldn't actually help it. Like that was just his default setting or something.

"What's the fae queen like?"

He glanced across the line through his dark lashes, green eyes gleaming. "There is no good way for me to answer that question. At least not if I ever wish to return to her good graces."

"As if you could," Myra argued from the far side of the room. "At least I know my punishment has an expiration date, however far in the future that might be."

"Wait," I said, trying to keep up and failing miserably, "are you saying he might *never* get to return to Air and Amethyst's lands . . . be a part of their circus again?" I dared a glance at Yael, but he merely stood there, jaw muscles straining as he glared at Myra, who appeared to give zero fucks at all. "What did you do to deserve that?"

His pale gaze turned to me and pinned me in place. "I allied myself with the wrong leader, apparently."

"So you were loyal to the Moonlight Wraith?"

"In life, yes."

Interesting . . .

"And once he was out?"

"Nyssa—I mean *the queen*—never even gave me the chance to sever that allegiance and swear fealty to her. I was not the only one, but I was the one of least importance, so instead of killing me, she used me as an example of what happens to those who dare to question her rule—even though I technically didn't even do that. I merely asked where Volker had gone."

"That's awful, Yael," I said softly. "I'm so sorry."

"Yes, well, at least I didn't flee like some of his closest advisors and ambassadors did, or die at her feet like so many others, so that's something."

Myra came up beside me and grabbed a stack of plates from the stainless steel counter. "Don't pity him too much, Rowe. His asshole personality more than outweighs his sob story."

"Don't pity me at all," the fae replied, eyes sharpening like daggers aimed at her back.

"How about you all actually do some work while you have this impromptu care-and-share moment?" Ravi's voice preceded him as he walked in from the front of the house. "There's no point in that anyway—none of us are returning to our former glory, and you're only kidding yourself if you think otherwise."

Silence settled on the room like a thick fog, choking out everything else.

"But—"

"You wouldn't understand, Rowe," he said, cutting me off, "so just let it go, unless you want someone in here to start poking around in your wounds."

"I just don't understand how the queen can do that. How she can be such a fascist without anyone standing against her."

The clatter in the room slowly grew again as the others went about their closing tasks. Yael, however, stood stock-still across from me, staring. "Because she was powerful enough to overthrow the Moonlight Wraith. And he's the only one who could challenge her—if he weren't inconveniently dead." I stiffened at his words, and I was damn sure he noticed. But there was no way for him to know what part of his sentiment had elicited my response. Right? "Volker was an arrogant asshole, but he was fair and just, as far as fae rulers go."

"The queen is a raging cunt," Myra added, and Ravi choked on a mouthful of water, coughing it across the countertop I'd just sanitized. "In case you haven't had the pleasure."

Myra's outburst earned her a smile from her fae adversary. "I will neither confirm nor deny that—though I wish I could."

The conversation fell off after that, each member of our motley crew seemingly reflecting silently on all they'd lost and on what I assumed must have been the truth of Ravi's words. It was one thing for me to feel like an outsider within my House, but to have really been a part of something so grand only to have that ripped away was a different kind of punishment altogether.

How painful it must have been for them to even talk about it.

With guilt niggling, I hurried about my closing tasks, doing all I could to steer clear of the solemn environment in the kitchen—the one that I'd all but caused. I stopped in around midnight to grab my to-go container with the dinner I'd never gotten to eat, my jacket, and my board, then left without even saying goodbye.

I'd already made a spectacle of myself that evening. I didn't wish to cause any more undue harm.

The light breeze caressed my face when I stepped out into the early morning moonlight. Everything was quiet and still and peaceful—which rarely described the city of Portland—and I loved every second of it.

I dropped my longboard and started down the road, my cold pizza in hand. I knew it wasn't going to taste good, but I was exhausted and starving, so I didn't really care. Beggars couldn't be choosers.

My turn was approaching, so I leaned into my heel edge and took a wide right to avoid the massive crater in the center of the intersection. It had nearly swallowed me whole once before; I had the scars on my elbows to prove it.

The streetlights on the road beyond were nearly all broken, so I focused hard, squinting against the darkness. A cloud drifted in front of the moon, cutting off the only real light source available, and I cursed under my breath as I did all I could to avoid any bumps or potholes ahead. And as I rolled through the shadows, headed for the safety of home, something appeared in front of me out of nowhere, giving me no time to stop.

I veered right and buried the nose of my board in a pothole, which sent me—and my to-go box—flying. I landed hard on my shoulder and rolled a few feet before stopping. With a groan, I pushed myself up to stand, only to find the carnage that was my dinner lying in the road before me, cheese-down on the pavement.

My longboard righted itself and rolled until it ran into whatever had sent us off course in the first place. I looked over to see someone kick the tail end up and take the board in hand with ease. Someone I recognized—barely.

Someone I really wasn't in the mood to see.

Volker's glamoured appearance stood off to my left, my board in his hand, staring. He was undoubtedly pleased with the chaos he'd caused; that seemed like a fae thing. His gaze drifted from me to the pizza lying only feet in front of me, and amusement twinkled in his eyes as he took a step closer.

"I wouldn't eat that if I were you."

My temper boiled over, but even that couldn't blind me to the fact that there was nothing I could do to him, so instead, I grabbed a piece that had landed atop another, checked it for any nastiness, then lifted it to my mouth and took a big ole bite. He watched as I chewed it dramatically, a flicker of something in his steady expression. Probably disgust, given that I doubted he'd ever had to eat road pizza before, but I couldn't be sure.

"I'm starting to get stalker vibes from you, Volker," I said around my mouthful. "It's not a cute look."

"I'm merely keeping an eye on my investment," he replied as he approached, his gait casual but his vibe anything but.

"Is that what I am? That implies that we actually have an agreement, and some kind of payment, which I sure haven't seen." I waggled my pizza in the air. "I wouldn't be eating this if I had."

"You think you're in a position to negotiate?" he asked, eyes narrowed and sharp.

"I think I'm hungry and tired and not in the mood for your shit, especially after you ruined my dinner."

His eyes drifted to the sad-looking slice in my hands. "*That* is not dinner."

"It is for some of us." I took a step closer, prepared to take another dramatic bite in front of him, when I felt something squish underfoot. I looked down to see the contents of the other slice sticking out from under my shoe. I lifted my leg, but the pizza was firmly affixed, thanks to the congealed cheese. No amount of flinging or shaking seemed capable of knocking it loose. Finally, with a massive front-kick motion, I managed to free myself of my fallen dinner. It flew across the street and stuck to the window of a car repair shop, and I watched it slide slowly down the dirty window like it was clinging on for dear life before it hit the sidewalk with a splat.

Volker cast a wary look at the pizza, then at me, which made the whole situation that much more ridiculous, and I couldn't help but laugh. At him. At myself. At the poor piece of pizza whose destiny would never be fulfilled.

"What are you doing?" he asked, voice thick with disdain.

"Laughing . . . you should try it sometime. You might like it."

"Doubtful."

I shrugged. "If you can't find shit like that amusing, I'm pretty sure you're the definition of uptight."

He turned slowly to face me, cutting my outburst short. "Why would anyone want to laugh at themselves?"

His haughty arrogance seeped into my pores, sobering me in a heartbeat. "Because it's funny? Because some of us are used to being the butt of the joke, so it's easier to beat everyone else to the punch? But I guess you wouldn't know much about that, would you?"

"No, I wouldn't. Only one has ever dared to laugh at me before."

"One?" I repeated, surprise overtaking me. I mean, I knew he wasn't exactly the sort to be fodder for others, but only one? Really? "Lucky bastard," I muttered to myself.

Something that dangerously resembled a smile tugged at the corners of his mouth. "He might be inclined to disagree with you . . . if I hadn't slit his throat for his affront." His mesmerizing grey eyes bored into mine, and I cracked under the pressure. Nervous laughter erupted from me again. He leaned in closer. "Do you find retribution entertaining as well, little queen?"

"No—"

"Because I can assure you, I take that subject deadly seriously."

I bit my lip, trying hard to retain my giggles, but failed miserably. "Pun totally intended?"

"Keep laughing and perhaps you'll find out." A crackle of energy washed over me, and I shivered. "Now, if you're finished with whatever that was, we should be on our way."

"Where?"

"To your place."

"Why?"

He looked at me as though the answer were obvious. "So we can find your power."

"You mean that power I know nothing about and don't think exists?"

Silence.

"Yes. That power."

I sighed heavily, and my stomach growled. "I'm way too hungry and tired for that right now—"

He leaned his face closer to mine. "And yet you'll do it, because I want you to."

My surge of fear was quickly eclipsed by anger. "You think looming over me with that mean, fake face of yours is enough to make me do whatever you say? Better think again. I've grown up around alphahole shifters trying to browbeat me into doing things. Bullying is their default language. So all your dick-swinging is doing is making me want to dig my heels in and do the complete opposite of what you want, because it's about the only power I can wield against you." He stared at me with an eerie calm that had me rethinking my outburst, but instead, I doubled down and kept it going in the hopes that maybe I could make a point that would save my hide. "Did it ever cross your mind that maybe I would help you if you just asked nicely?" He looked at me like I was speaking Greek; like nothing I'd said made any sense. "Maybe not everyone needs to be threatened into compliance. Maybe you could have just pled your case and waited for my response before all your 'help me or else' bullshit. You might be surprised by my response—especially after tonight."

His eyes narrowed. "What happened tonight?"

I took a deep breath and tried to focus—to choose my words carefully. I didn't want Yael to suffer for what he'd shared. "I learned what the queen did to those left behind after she usurped you—how ruthless she was to anyone brave enough to show loyalty to you."

"And how did you learn this?"

Careful, Rowe . . .

"I work with someone who was cast out of the House because of that loyalty, and it sounds as though he was one of the lucky ones. Others were killed without question. He lost his place with Air and Amethyst, and is now forced to live in the neutral zone and work in a kitchen because of it, with no idea if he can ever return. So yes, I would have agreed to help you if you'd simply asked, because someone like the queen doesn't deserve to rule."

"And you think I'm better suited, do you? That I would not have done the same had our roles been reversed and I had overthrown her?"

I shook my head. "My friend said, unprompted, that you were

fair, as far as fae rulers go, and that you were the only one that could stand against her. He has no reason to lie, so I believe him."

I wasn't sure what I expected him to do at that moment. Turn on me for overstepping, maybe? Ignore my logic and return to his threatening tactics? Maybe worse? But what I most certainly did *not* expect was for him to assess me in silence until his mouth twitched with amusement.

"You *believe* him?"

"Yes."

"You think I deserve to rule Air and Amethyst?"

"I think she doesn't . . . "

That hint of a smile widened. "Close enough."

"So . . . " I replied, folding my arms across my chest, "are you going to ask nicely or not?"

The smile quickly turned to a smirk. "Little queen, will you help me usurp my usurper?"

"Yes, I will. Now that wasn't so hard, was it?"

"Surprisingly not."

I stared at him, head canted to the side. "Not everyone has a hidden agenda, Volker. Sometimes people are willing to help because it's the right thing to do."

He mimicked my posture. "Not in my world."

"Then I feel sorry for supernaturals."

"But you are one, remember? My world is your world."

"It sure doesn't feel that way," I said, reaching over to take my board from his hands.

"That's why I've come to you—to see if we can't find these powers of yours."

"You couldn't wait until I got home to do that creepy appearing thing? You had to do it in the middle of the fucking road and ruin my food?"

He shrugged with a grace I sure as hell didn't possess. "Just a reminder that I can find you anywhere, at any time."

"Hmm . . . that sounds like a threat. And here I thought we'd just gotten past that."

"Old habits," was his only response before he turned and started walking down the road toward my home.

I stared at his back, doing all I could to try and make sense of the fae assassin I'd never be rid of until I discovered this power I was sure I didn't have and he got his revenge. He was so certain—so calculating—that I was starting to believe that maybe he was right. Men like him didn't come to conclusions like that lightly. But still, I couldn't wrap my head around having power that I couldn't feel. Couldn't access. Something about it all was off, but I couldn't begin to understand how or why.

While I stood there trying to figure it all out, he glanced over his shoulder at me, his smug expression as maddening as it was alluring. I took a deep breath, scooped my to-go box off the ground (because littering), and rolled my board down the road behind him, ready for him to stop at any moment and knock me off course again just for shits and giggles. Did I understand him? No, but I did understand his desire for revenge.

The circumstances surrounding the death of my mother when I was young were suspicious at best. She had been murdered, that much we knew, but the fact that no killer had ever been found had always bothered me. And in the few moments I allowed myself to slow down enough to sit with my thoughts, I'd wonder about it. If she'd ever have justice. If her killer would ever pay for what they'd done.

And it was in those quiet moments that a small, dark part of me emerged, demanding vengeance for her, even though I knew I'd never get it.

But I could help Volker get his. And with Yael's endorsement of the former ruler, I felt even better about that possibility.

The Moonlight Wraith was more than the myth perpetuated, or at least it was starting to look that way. If not, I was potentially about to aid and abet one of the most notorious killers the world had ever seen.

Not that I really had a choice.

CHAPTER 8
ROWE

We walked into my apartment, and it was impossible not to see the expression on Volker's true face immediately devolve. "So this is how Fire and Fluorite treats its minions?" he asked, taking in the tiny space. "How charming."

I popped the final bite of my road pizza into my mouth and chewed thoughtfully before answering with my mouth full. "Could be worse."

His steely gaze fell back on me. "Could it?"

"At least I have a House," I replied with a shrug.

"Is that what you call this?"

"I meant 'House' in the grander sense . . . as in Fire and Fluorite."

"I see . . . "

"Says the homeless fae with no House at all," I muttered under my breath.

"Are you sure you want to play this game with me?" he asked, that cool tone belying the fire burning inside him.

"It's not a game to me. Nothing about any of this is a game—it's my life. Literally."

"Mine as well," he reminded me. "I'm glad we're on the same page about that."

His stare made me squirmy, and I quickly found something else to focus on—like the state of my room. Never had there been a better time to finish cleaning it than that moment. I rushed around like a wild woman, scooping up dirty clothes and tossing them into my already full laundry basket like a tidying hurricane.

Volker watched in silence, and I could only imagine what deprecating things he was thinking.

"Was there some sort of illegal substance or spell in that poor excuse for food you ate on the way home?" he finally asked. I paused to look over my shoulder on the way into the bathroom and found exactly what I was expecting looking back—the physical embodiment of incredulity.

"Nope. Neither."

"Then where did this sudden rush of energy come from?"

"I only have two modes, Volker: busy or deceased." I snatched the towel I'd used earlier off the curtain rod where it hung and stuffed it under my arm. When I turned to exit the bathroom, Volker was right there, lingering in the doorway.

"I'm quite certain 'deceased' isn't a mode, little queen."

"Fine. Try 'crazy or coma'. Better?"

His expression soured further, as if that were even possible. "No—"

"You're the worst, you know that?"

"Then help me get my revenge and be rid of me forever."

"Let's unpack this power thing a bit, shall we?" I asked, dropping my armful of laundry onto the heaving basket. "You're really committed to that being true, so can you at least tell me about this alleged power of mine that's going to solve all your problems?" My request was met with silence, and it dragged on for longer than I was comfortable with, forcing me to speak before I exploded out of my skin with anxiety. "My mom was—at best—half witch, as far as she knew, which is likely why she was able to secure a position in Fire and Fluorite, with me as part of the package."

"So you admit you're not human."

"Not fully, but who is anymore? Bloodlines are so muddy now."

"Which then begs the question: what was your father?"

At that, I shrugged. "Mom never talked about him, but if he'd been anything other than human, I'm pretty sure she would have used that to her advantage when joining a House. And per your own observation," I continued, earning a quirk of his brow, "I'm not exactly a big deal in Fire and Fluorite, so—"

"You assume he was human."

I shrugged. "I asked her about him once when I was maybe ten or so, because I was getting old enough to realize that her generic answers about him were meant to discourage the conversation. She told me he was, and I quote, 'a useless sack of shit who never cared about either of us'." I hesitated for a moment, blindsided by a wave of emotion. "She was murdered a couple of years later—before I was old enough to demand real answers. But I remember the look in her eyes when she answered me that day, and it still haunts me. My guess is that he was a bad person—which I guess is kinda evident in the fact that he abandoned my pregnant mother and his unborn child."

Volker stared at me for a long moment. "Being an asshole is hardly a trait exclusive to humans."

His words pulled me from the weight of sadness dragging me down. "You think my dad was supernatural?"

"I think it isn't your mother's blood that makes you what you are."

His intense eyes held my gaze, and I did all I could not to shrink away. "And what is that, exactly?" I dared to ask.

Volker unfastened his coat, and my eyes quickly skimmed over the chest muscles visible through his tight white shirt beneath.

"The answer to my problem."

His response yanked my mind back to the topic at hand, which was unfortunate, given that it was far less fun than ogling the gorgeous fae. "Ugggh," I groaned before pushing past him to toss another handful of laundry into the basket. "The. Worst."

Volker snuck up behind me, and my heart lurched into my throat. He smelled like danger mixed with crisp night air—or what I imagined that would smell like—and I inhaled reflexively before I realized what I was doing. I turned quickly to find him staring down at me and my reddened cheeks.

I knew he was death incarnate—had heard the stories of his kills —but with him standing there in front of me in the dim light of the room, it was impossible to ignore how hot he was. He emanated power and danger from a dapper, seductive exterior, the perfect façade to bely the killer beneath.

"You want to know?" he asked, his voice low and gravelly and everything a girl could want to hear from him under different circumstances. Very different circumstances. "You're a wellspring," he said, as though that meant anything to me.

"Okay . . . "

"This power does little to benefit you directly. It doesn't make you faster or stronger; doesn't give you spellcasting or shifting abilities, either."

"Sounds lame."

"But what it *does* do is strengthen and amplify the abilities of others, and it can restore magic lost. As I told you, something has been amiss with mine, even before the queen usurped me. I assume that's why she was able to do it at all. With my power unstable, I need your help to take her out."

Realization hit me like a sledgehammer. "You need me to restore your magic so you can kill the queen?"

"In a sense, yes."

"Okay," I said, trying to filter through all he'd said, "then why can't you just plug into me or whatever and take what you need, if it's a passive power?"

"It's not that simple. If it were, I'd have done so without your knowledge."

"How do you even know this?" I asked, my mind reeling with questions and unknowns. "I mean, I've never even heard of a wellspring before, and I hear about a lot because I'm basically invisible to most supernaturals. They say all kinds of shit in front of me without thinking twice."

"I know this because I met the previous wellspring," he replied with something that sounded dangerously like a note of sympathy—but for whom or what, I had no idea.

"Previous . . . as in there's only *one* of us?"

"At a time, yes."

"Well, what did you learn from the last one?"

"Many things—though he'd already gone mad by then."

Something about the way he said those words raised my hackles. "What happened to him?"

Volker's expression darkened. "He killed himself. Wellsprings are extremely powerful in their own way, but that power also creates instability if it does not have an outlet. Without one, they slowly deteriorate and implode—or so it seems."

Holy. Shit.

"Like . . . what kind of outlet are we talking about here? Because I am all about them if it keeps me from going off the deep end."

"It's complicated, but think of it like burning off energy, in a fashion. You must vent it off or into something else to keep the balance."

"But why don't I feel this? Shouldn't I feel it?"

"I don't know."

"Says the guy who brags that he basically knows everything."

"I cannot know how someone else's power feels. No one can."

"Well, that doesn't really help me, now does it?"

"What I *do* know," he continued, mouth flattened in irritation, "is that, without a being to channel your ability long-term, your life will end as your predecessor's did."

"And let me guess, you're willing to volunteer for that position?"

A wolfish smile graced his face. "Yes. I am."

I paused for a moment, mulling over the unknowns and

potential ramifications of giving the Moonlight Wraith my unfound power. There was no way that, if he did somehow get his hands on this wellspring power and regain his position, that would be the end of it. Even with diminished power, he was still a force to be reckoned with. I could only imagine how he would be with a constant stream of additional power feeding him.

"How do you know that would even work?" I asked, trying to buy myself time. "I mean, you said yourself that the last wellspring was already crazy by the time you met him."

"It will work."

"And you couldn't possibly be wrong about that?"

That fucking smirk returned. "No."

Irritation prickled my skin. "Where was this all-knowingness when the queen was plotting to overthrow you?"

The smirk died in an instant. "Would you like me to show you some of my escalated intimidation techniques now? Because if you continue to speak to me that way, I'll take that as a yes." He leaned forward, and a chill rippled through the room like the warmth of the sun had just fallen away and night had rolled in. "You'll find out just how ruthless the House of Air and Amethyst can be."

I held his gaze as best I could with my legs shaking beneath me. "I thought we talked about this already," I replied, a note of warning all my own lacing my tone. The tension in the room amped up with every passing moment, and I wondered if our agreement only minutes earlier had already been thrown out the window; if under that cool, placid façade of his was a roaring temper just waiting to be unleashed.

I folded my arms across my chest and did my best to emit a sense of confidence I sure as hell didn't feel in that moment. "What if you're lying about the madness to trick me into allying with you, or whatever you call this long-term connection?"

"I'm not lying because I can't—"

"*Can't lie*?" I scoffed, cutting him off. "That's literally all the fae do. They scheme and connive to get what they want. It's practically your trademark."

Volker looked at me for a moment before doing the unexpected. Instead of lunging at me and slamming me against the wall, he threw his head back and laughed—like really laughed. I wasn't sure which was scarier.

"Who told you that?" he asked as he lowered his gaze to me. "Your mother? Or maybe it was the pup at the bar." My silence sobered him from his morbid amusement and he pressed closer, leaving little space between us. "The fae are not all as cunning as you've been led to believe, little queen."

"At least one was cunning enough to unseat you and take your power," I argued without thinking. My regret was instant.

His grey eyes narrowed to slits, and I wondered if I'd pushed him too far. If our tentative alliance would go up in flames. "Careful, little queen . . . my patience is not endless. Nor is my fuse."

"I'm sorry. I didn't say it to be a dick. I'm just pointing out the obvious," I said, talking so fast it came out like one big run-on sentence. "Not everything is a personal attack, Volker. Not everyone wants to cut you down."

"I feel like your life speaks to the contrary."

"What's that supposed to mean?"

"It means look around you. Does your House treat you as they do the others? Do you live as they live? Eat as they eat?" He cast a dubious glance at my roadkill pizza box.

"Do you think I'm a joke?"

"I think you are to this House—"

"Woooow—"

"—I think they mock you while you toil away at the menial tasks they deem beneath their great power. I think you scratch out an existence while they thrive. I think you will live this way until death takes you, and they will not mourn you for a single moment."

I shook my head, though I couldn't deny the numbness I felt at his words. "No . . . that's not true . . . "

"Isn't it?" he asked, shifting forward until his body pressed against mine and we moved backward together until I bumped into the wall. "Isn't that exactly what's happening here?"

"No . . . "

"*No?*"

I slipped my hand between us to relieve the pressure in my chest, only to find it still there once the weight of him was gone.

"They're my family."

"No they're not. That's just the pretty lie they've fed you for years. They don't treat you like family."

"Yes they do," I argued, though it sounded weak even to my own ears.

"Do they? Tell me something, then, are you invited to rituals and parties? Are you in attendance for House matters of importance?"

"Yes! I go to those sometimes!"

Something close to pity flashed in the depths of those pewter-colored eyes. "By your own invitation, or with others who take it upon themselves to include you?"

Ouch. The truth impaled me as I thought back to those events—and the fact that, for every one of them I could recall, Andreas had brought me along.

"I . . . you're twisting the facts."

"Am I?" he asked as he stepped back a pace. "Or am I elucidating a painful truth?"

Anger prickled in my veins, which conveniently eclipsed the sadness threatening to pull me down. "So maybe things aren't perfect here, Volker, but that doesn't mean you're right," I said as I lunged at him, finger jabbing his chest. "Shade took my mother and me in—gave us protection through the House and himself as second. Without his kindness, we'd have been scraping by out there in No Man's Land with the humans and magical rejects."

"He did indeed," he replied calmly. "I can't help but wonder why that is . . . "

"What's that supposed to mean? Shade has always been good to me."

Volker scanned the room with his eyes in slow, dramatic fashion. "Yes, I can see that."

I instantly saw red. "Not everyone cares about material things and beauty like the fae do—"

"Another thing you've been taught about us, I see—"

"Well, you sure don't do much to contradict it with your fancy clothes and your perfect, smug face—" I cut myself short and willed my cheeks not to flush redder than they already were.

Judging by the look on that aforementioned perfect, smug face, I failed miserably.

"No, please, do go on," he said, dark eyes twinkling with delight.

"I'm just saying that I like my apartment—"

"Good—"

"—and I like my life just fine—"

"Great . . . "

I folded my arms across my chest and took a step back to keep from doing something I'd definitely regret—what that would be, however, was highly in question. Despite my desire to punch him in the face, there was a conflicting desire to stroke the perfect contour of his jaw right after I did.

I shook my head to knock those thoughts loose, then continued my argument. "Shade said he'd move me if I wanted, and I turned him down."

"Little queen, you can keep your life and your apartment and do whatever you want with both, for all I care. Just give me what I want, and we'll all be happy."

"Doubtful," I mumbled under my breath.

"Worried the truth will ruin your sunny view of your life?"

At that, I smiled, doing my best to mimic the air of arrogance he constantly exuded. "Oh no, I didn't mean *me*—I meant *you*. It's doubtful *you'll* be happy. Because, let's be honest, you're just as delusional as you seem to think I am if you believe you can take your former House back and move on like nothing ever happened. Have you seen the state of Fire and Fluorite after everything that went down? Shade and Andreas are still trying to stabilize it, and that shit pales in comparison to a full-scale usurping." I stood there for a second to let my words really sink in. "You can't just kill the queen of Air and Amethyst and then carry on."

His brow furrowed. "And why not?"

I scoffed at his hubris. "Because she's probably just the tip of the iceberg. It's hard to stage a coup by yourself—in fact, I'm pretty sure 'coup' implies that more than one individual was involved—"

In a blink, he spun me around, hips pinning me against the wall, caging me in. "My revenge will deal with them all," he whispered in my ear, his knuckles turning white as his fingers dug into the plaster near my face. "*Anyone* who dared to cross me."

I couldn't breathe, fear and something wildly more dangerous holding my chest captive. The pressure of his weight against my body was too much and not enough, and my addled brain was thinking things that were just as dangerous as the fae I'd pissed off.

And yet, I couldn't banish the image of him slowly unfastening my pants and sliding them down my legs from my mind.

"With the help of this mystery power of mine?" I asked, my words low and husky.

His mouth grazed my ear, and fire shot through me. "You are either with me or against me, little queen. I would hate to have to torture you for breaking our agreement . . . "

He released his hold on the wall long enough for his hands to fall to my hips. His fingertips bit in hard, and every ounce of blood in my body surged between my legs. I sucked in a breath and reflexively pressed back against him. "Then I guess it's a good thing I'm not."

"I suppose it is . . . " He took a deep breath to assuage his anger, his exhale ruffling my hair, then relaxed his hands. I spun around to face him and found him staring at me with that impassive expression I was growing to hate. "Your power is not a mystery, little queen—its absence is. A problem I plan to solve tomorrow—"

"*Tomorrow*? But I thought—"

"You need some rest," he said, cutting me off as he quickly made his way to the door.

"But—"

"Sleep well, little queen." He pulled the door open and smiled wickedly back at me. "And sweet dreams." Without another word, he disappeared from sight. The door closed, leaving me standing there, breathless, wondering what the fuck had just happened.

That unanswered question kept me up all night.

CHAPTER 9
ROWE

Morning hit me like a kick to the nuts.

I was exhausted from lack of sleep, stress, and a million other things, but that didn't change the fact that I had to get up and get shit done. Slacking, sadly, wasn't an option.

A quick shower and coffee woke me up a bit, but not nearly enough to answer the call from Myra flashing on my phone. There was no way I was going into the restaurant. That place had already sucked up way more time that I didn't have.

With a defiant smile on my face, I rushed over to Shade's house to see what he needed from me that day. When I walked in the back door, I could hear the chaos echoing down the hall long before I got near his office, but the second I stepped into the hallway, it went quiet. Damn supernatural hearing.

Andreas stormed out of the room, raking his hand through his dark hair, and turned in the opposite direction. Shade stepped out after him like he wanted to stop him, but he didn't. Instead, he looked over his shoulder at me as I stood stock-still in the hallway, staring like a deer in headlights.

"Good morning, Rowe," he said, letting out a sigh. "I need you to do something for me today."

"That's why I'm here," I replied with a smile.

He forced one in return, but it never reached his eyes. The tension in his expression and his body remained, and I couldn't help but wonder what in the hell they'd been arguing about. In all my time around them, I'd only seen them fight a handful of times, and that had been mainly during Andreas' teen years—until the recent turmoil at the House set tensions high. He'd been his father's right-hand man, third to our former House leader behind his father until recently. I hated knowing that the stress of Fire and Fluorite's situation was causing waves between them.

House politics were a real fucking bastard.

"I need you to run some errands in town. When you're done, I need you to check in here, then head over to Townsend and Marsh to see if they need anything."

I groaned inwardly. Marsh was all right, but Townsend was a knuckle-dragging idiot who thought dad jokes were the pinnacle of humor. Cleaning for him was like being trapped—while sober—in the worst comedy show that you couldn't escape for hours. "Okay."

He gestured for me to follow him into his office, then handed me a stack of envelopes addressed to various people, some I knew and others I didn't. I tucked them in my shoulder bag and turned to leave. "Rowe," he called after me. "Is everything all right with you? You seem off."

"I just have a lot on my mind, that's all."

He quirked a brow, his fatherly concern palpable. There was no way I could involve him in my debacle for myriad reasons, but there was also no way I could keep up the pretense that all was well and expect him to believe it. He might have been insanely busy, but he wasn't blind. And I was a shitty liar. Not exactly a recipe for success.

I weighed my options while he looked on patiently, then landed on something I could ask him that would be both believable and potentially helpful. "Shade?"

"Yes?"

"Do you know anything about my father?"

His brows rose with surprise; I guessed he hadn't expected that particular line of questioning. He took a deep breath as he rounded his desk to stand before me. "The only time I discussed him with your mother was when she first came to me about joining Fire and Fluorite. I needed to know if there could be a claim on you from someone within another House, because agreeing to take you both on under those circumstances would have meant potentially feuding with them, and Mathis would have needed to know, for all our sakes."

"And?" I asked, impatience weighing down on me.

"All she said was no . . . no other House would care. I took that to mean that either your father didn't know he had a daughter to claim, he was dead, or he wasn't a member of another House because he was a rogue or human. Any way you sliced it, it didn't matter, and given your mother's body language and change in mood when I asked, she had no intention of elaborating further, so I let it go. I knew what I needed to know to protect the House."

"Okay . . . "

Shade sensed my disappointment and rested his hand on my shoulder. "Why is this suddenly of interest to you? You've never once asked about him before."

"I don't know . . . I guess I've just been thinking about where I came from lately. With Mom gone, I thought maybe it would be nice to know if he was alive . . . maybe meet him." I dared a glance up at him and found sympathetic eyes looking back. "I bet that sounds kinda childish, doesn't it?"

"There's nothing wrong with wanting to know the truth about who you are, Rowe. Who you come from."

"Too bad I don't get to know." I forced a smile and turned to leave before my emotions could get the best of me.

"Rowe, I need you to do one more thing for me, okay?"

"Sure, what's that?"

His lips pressed to a thin line. "Be careful in No Man's Land today."

"Why? Is something happening?"

He shook his head, but the worry creasing his brow remained. "No, nothing specific, but . . . just be careful all the same?"

"Always," I replied, fear tightening around my throat. "I'll see you in a bit."

He mumbled something under his breath as I walked out the door, and I couldn't shake the feeling that something deeper was going on. Whatever he and Andreas had been arguing about had really knocked him off balance, which was unnerving at best. His low-key warning didn't help, either. Shade had never shown concern when sending me on errands before.

That fact haunted me as I rolled through Fire and Fluorite territory, headed for No Man's Land—and potential danger.

I spent the better part of the morning delivering documents to various embassies and businesses without incident. After I dropped the final one off, I breathed a sigh of relief. Despite my best efforts, Shade's surprising warning had gotten to me. As I walked down the steps of the investment company where I'd had something signed for our House, I looked forward to stopping by Shade's place and then heading home.

Then I remembered I had to go to Townsend's. Any happiness that had dared to seep in disappeared in a second.

I rolled down embassy row, the tall, historic buildings towering over the rest of the city like watchful guardians. For whatever reason, I'd always loved them when I was younger. Mom and I would wander downtown for hours together, and I'd beg her to stroll past them until she relented. As I slowly rode down the street, I felt her presence, a sense of familiarity washing over me. It grew with every passing moment, until I questioned whether it was a memory or something in the present I didn't understand.

I hopped off my board and kicked it up into my hand as I looked around, focusing on that feeling. It was coming from behind me, and I turned around to see a petite brunette in the distance, hurrying off in the opposite direction. The tight bun atop her head had me doing a double take. My mother's hair had always been like that; and she had been the same size and build.

And there was that growing sense of familiarity that I couldn't ignore.

Before I knew it, I was running toward her, calling to her like I'd completely forgotten she was dead. "Mom!" I shouted over the din of the city.

She didn't slow.

I tossed my board down and jumped on in one smooth motion, then pumped my leg as hard as I could to close the distance between us. She was all I could see amid the chaos of the city—all I cared about in that moment. And with every inch closer I came, that feeling grew stronger.

"Mom!" I yelled again as I neared. "Mom, it's me!"

When I was within feet of her, I jumped off my board and lunged to grab her shoulder. But before I could reach her, a hand clamped down on my wrist and yanked me back. A tall, beautiful male glared down at me like I'd just run over his dog, and another quickly joined him, putting himself between me and the woman.

"Mom?" I called again, craning my neck to see around the two blocking my view. Through a tiny gap between them, I could see the brunette beyond. She turned slowly to face me, and my heart sank to my shoes. I shouldn't have been surprised that it wasn't my mother, but whatever that feeling was that had driven my actions, it had been too strong to ignore. I hadn't stopped to think about what I was doing, and now I was in the death grip of some goon in the middle of downtown, wondering what the fuck was wrong with me.

And judging by the looks on all their faces, they were, too.

"I'm sorry," I said sheepishly. "I thought you were someone else."

She cut a look to the guy that had me by the arm, and he let me go. Then she turned without a word and continued down the street with the bouncer-types behind her.

Not wanting to cause any more chaos, I grabbed my board off the street where it had rolled into the curb, then took off down the road, headed for my home turf. Once I was out of embassy row, that feeling I swore I'd felt was nowhere to be found, and I questioned whether I had ever really felt it at all, or if the memory of my mother had just blindsided me so hard that I'd confused past with present.

By the time I got back to Shade's, I was wondering if I was starting to lose it; if my refusal to accept and properly process my mother's death had finally reared its ugly head, manifesting in full-on delusions. Because that was what I needed, on top of the fae assassin and the magical powers I supposedly had (according to said fae assassin) but couldn't manifest.

I was glad that Shade was out when I returned. After knocking on his office door three times, I tried the knob and found it open. I quickly ran in and dropped the document on his desk before rushing out, closing the door behind me.

And turning right into Andreas.

I clapped a hand over my mouth before a screech escaped me. He stared down at me, clearly amused by how startled I was. "Dad's out."

"I see that, Sherlock. Thanks for the tip."

He threw his hands up in surrender. "Damn, girl, what's got you all worked up?"

I let out an exhale, letting my lips flap inelegantly in the process. "I think I'm losing it, that's all."

"Care to expand on that?" he asked, still towering over me in the long hallway.

I quickly relayed my bizarre encounter, and he listened intently until I was finished, then stood there in silence like he wasn't quite sure how to respond. But really, what was there to say? "Are you feeling okay?" he finally asked, concern etching his brow.

"I'm good. Probably just tired."

And crazy.

"You know you can talk to me about anything, right? Regardless of what's going on with the packs and the House and everything," he said, placing his hand gently on my shoulder. "Whether I like your relationship with them or not, I know Adora and Dannika leaving has been really hard on you, and you've been weathering backlash for their actions—"

"It hasn't been that bad," I lied, trying to dodge the subject.

"Doesn't seem that way. And you're working like a madwoman, Rowe. Maybe you need a break."

"I'm fine, Andreas," I said, trying to convince us both of that. "Not having Danni and Adora here has been difficult, and I *have* been working a lot lately, but I do have friends at work—and you. It's not all bad."

"I'm not sure Myra and the others at that restaurant fall under the 'friend' umbrella, since I'm pretty sure any one of them would douse you with lighter fluid and strike a match if they thought your death would earn their positions back in their respective Houses."

I scrunched my face. "That's an oddly specific example."

"True," he said with a smile, "but you get my point."

"Kinda hard not to after the bonfire analogy, but yes, I see it, and I'm under no delusions that Myra wants to sleep over so we can braid each other's hair and swap secrets."

"Good."

"I'm also aware that Yael wouldn't deign to step inside my apartment for fear that my standard of living might be contagious. And Ravi is just . . . Ravi," I said, trying to find a way to sum up my enigmatic boss. "I'm not sure he's friends with anyone . . . including himself."

"That sounds about right."

I ribbed Andreas with my elbow, and he had the good form to pretend to be hurt. "But they're not as bad as you think they are."

"I doubt that."

"Andreas!" I shouted as I slapped his arm away from me. "Don't be such a snob—that's Yael's specialty."

Any amusement slowly bled from his expression, and he stood there in silence for a moment, just staring. "And what's mine?" he finally asked, breaking the oppressive quiet.

I struggled to find an answer when the full weight of his stare pressed down upon me like that.

But I managed. Eventually.

"Distracting me when I should be working."

He smiled with approval. "So I'm distracting, huh?"

"Oh, boy . . . here we go."

"In that case," he continued, ignoring my jab, "I'm going to double down on my distractiveness—"

"Not a word—"

"—and ask what you're doing on Friday."

"What I'm always doing on Friday. Working."

His wicked smile widened. "What if I could get you out of it?"

" . . . Then I guess I wouldn't be working?"

"Which would make you available to come to a party at my house."

"What party?"

"The one I'm going to throw that you're coming to."

"But—"

"I'll deal with Dad. I'll tell him you're delirious and seeing ghosts and need a break. Just say you'll come."

Nervousness swirled in my guts. "What about the others . . . aren't some of them still salty about my connection to Danni and Adora?"

"My party. My guest list. They can fuck off if they don't like it."

"Or they can start shit and be total pains in my ass."

"Not if I'm there."

"Which you can't be every minute of the night."

"Is that a challenge?" he asked with a quirk of his brow.

"Nope. Just an observation."

"Well, how about I leave it like this: the party is here on Friday. I'll be there. All your favorite whiskeys will be there. And I'll even play that Bowie song you love so much no less than four times if you show."

"No work *and* 'Rebel, Rebel'?" I asked, pretending to mull over the offer in grand style. "I could be persuaded."

"Good. Now get over to Townsend's house," he said with a wink. "I hear he has some killer new jokes for you. He was bragging about them the other day . . ."

"Shoot me," I said with a sigh. "It's the humane thing to do."

"I'm afraid I can't do that, Rowe. You're the featured guest at my party." He smiled wide as he turned to leave. "Now get your ass moving—and stop being so easily distracted."

CHAPTER 10
ROWE

Townsend's comedy set was even worse than promised.

I rolled up behind my building, exhausted, starving, and dumber for having narrowly survived the pun-fest of the century. All I wanted was alcohol, a lobotomy, and a coma deep enough to block out the world for a week.

What I got instead was a visit from the Moonlight Wraith.

"Late night with your little wolf?" he said in my ear, causing me to scream and throw my keys in the air as I started.

I turned around to face him, clutching my chest, and found amusement sparkling in those charcoal eyes. "What. The. Fuck?" I said, breathing hard as I scoured the ground for my keys. "Are you just going to keep lurking in the shadows so you can scare the shit out of me? Don't you have anything else to do, like stalk the queen and learn her schedule and weaknesses, or whatever it is assassins do?"

"I'm working on that," he replied, looking not at all ruffled by my outburst. "Once I have what I came for, she'll be no match for me."

"Did you happen to figure out how to elicit my supposed power since last night? Because it didn't magically avail itself to me today while I was running errands and working my ass off."

"How disappointing," he deadpanned.

My blood pressure skyrocketed. "I am so not in the mood for this right now."

"In the mood for what?" he asked, stepping in front of me.

"You," I replied, flapping my hand around at my back step, "skulking around, uninvited."

"I think 'skulking' implies a lack of invitation—"

"I mean all the spying and random appearances."

"I prefer 'observation and unexpected visits'."

I stared at him incredulously as I tried to calm my breathing. "I'm starting to understand why the queen wanted you dead."

Volker leaned in close, his nose only inches from mine, and assessed me for a moment. "Hmm . . . is that a hint of madness in your eyes I see, or is it just me?" He pulled away with a smug smirk on his face and all I could think about was smacking it away. Not that it would have worked, but my imagination made it look good, so it seemed a viable option.

"Oh," I said, folding my arms across my chest, "it's definitely you."

"Then perhaps you should dig down deep into that well of power you possess and figure out how to access it so you can rid yourself of me."

I stared at him for a moment, silently trying to do what he'd asked just to shut him up, but of course, nothing happened. So instead, I shoved my hand into my jeans pocket and made a show of looking for something. Volker watched, that annoying, impassive expression intact, as I slowly withdrew my hand and held it up in front of him.

With my middle finger extended.

"I found this . . . does this help?"

"Not you, no."

"Maybe my power is with my final fuck," I continued, my tongue fueled by hanger and exhaustion, "which would be super convenient, because then I could give them both to you at once." His eyes flared white, and the flash sobered me in an instant. "Listen," I said, throwing my palms up between us in surrender, "I'm starving and grumpy and too tired to think clearly right now, which is only going to make me say something I'll regret—"

"You haven't already?" he asked, irritation in his tone.

"Are you going to hurt me because of something I said?"

"Not yet . . . "

"Then no."

He looked to the moon above, then back to me. "The night is still young. You have time."

Choosing to ignore him, I unlocked the door to my apartment and pushed it open. Without invitation, he followed me inside.

"So, back to my powers," I said as I flipped on the lights and headed straight for the kitchen. "What's the plan? Surely you and all your ancient fae knowledge should have an idea of how to wake them up or whatever." I yanked the fridge open and buried my head inside.

"They do not need to be woken," he said as the back door clicked shut. The sound of heavy footfalls on hardwood echoed through the room, eclipsing the hum of the fridge fan.

"Well, they need something!" I snagged a piece of pizza out of the half-open box on the top shelf and stuck it in my mouth as I grabbed two beers and a container of cookie dough. With the grace of a drunken elephant, I shuffled backward so the door could fall closed on its own and ran right into Volker, butt first. I yelped and shot forward, dropping the beers and cookie dough. Somehow I managed to snag the pizza out of thin air, but smeared sauce all over my questionably clean sleeve, so it was a goner.

Pouting an appropriate amount, I dropped it into the trash, then picked up my mess.

"You seem jumpy," he said, and I could practically hear the smirk he was wearing when he spoke.

"Maybe you shouldn't creep up on people."

"Your home is the size of a shoebox. Where else would you like me to stand?"

I popped up to find that fucking smirk staring back at me.

Bastard. "Outside would be great."

"I cannot figure out what's wrong with your power if I'm outside."

"Fine," I said as I opened the fridge again and grabbed the last, lonely slice of pizza, leaving the empty box to deal with later. "But you owe me a pizza—two, actually."

"If that will improve your mood, I'm sure it can be arranged."

Frustrated and hungry, I brushed past him to the two-person dining table in the center of the kitchen and sat down for the first time all day. I placed the pizza and beers down, then took a breath and leaned back in my seat, stretching my arms high above my head. I dared a glance at Volker and found his eyes raking over me. Especially the swath of skin sticking out from the hem of my shirt.

I quickly sat up and took a bite of my food. "You'll have to talk while I eat because I'm starving and dangerously close to dying of low blood sugar."

Volker took a seat across from me while I stuffed my face, his distaste plain in his expression.

I took another bite and chewed it slowly before speaking. "So what's the deal? How are you gonna evoke these reticent powers of mine?"

He leaned back in my kitchen chair like it was his throne and looked down his elegant nose at me. "You're going to give them to me."

I looked at him like he'd taken leave of his senses, but he seemed unfazed. "Say what, now?"

"You're going to give them to me."

"Um . . . pretty sure that's not a thing, Volker. And, side note, if it was that simple, then why the fuck haven't we done that already?"

"It *is* a thing—just not one you're going to like, so I didn't lead with it."

"And why wouldn't I like it?" I asked, knowing that he was probably right; I wasn't going to like the answer.

"Because if you were in control of your abilities, you could simply use them to recharge me, so to speak," he explained. "No permanent solution would be necessary."

"But I'm not."

"Exactly. Which is why more drastic measures must be taken."

"Drastic . . . " I said around a bite of pizza. "I don't like the sound of that."

His smirk returned. "Do you remember that madness I told you about? What happens when you don't have a target into which to channel your magic?"

"Yeah . . . "

He leaned forward on his elbows, dark eyes twinkling in the light of the room. "What I'm suggesting would be the answer to that problem, as well as the solution to mine."

"And how would we accomplish this?" I dared to ask, dreading the answer.

"Through a blood bond."

"Nope," I said, shaking my head like a wet dog. "No way that's happening—"

"It may be your only option—"

"You mean *your* only option," I countered, "because *I'm* not the one who needs my power in the first place. I'm not the one trying to kill the queen."

"A fair point but a moot one, I'm afraid, little queen. You've already agreed to help me, and the fae are very particular about agreements."

Dammit.

"Can I get out of whatever the hell this blood bond is once you get your revenge? Because it sounds pretty fucking permanent."

He nodded. "As I understand it, yes. The wellspring has control over who they connect to, so they should have control over whether or not the connection is severed."

"*Should*? Why do I not like the sound of that?"

"Because it implies that this probability isn't guaranteed."

I took a deep breath and tried to weigh my options. I was already in too deep to back out, not that Volker would let me, and I would be kidding myself if I didn't admit that somewhere deep down inside me, I wanted to feel that power—to claim my magic, if for no other reason than to feel like I truly belonged in the supernatural world. The niggling at the back of my mind about how the last wellspring had offed himself was motivation as well, to say the least. Would being bound to Volker for a lifetime be the worst thing ever, if the alternative was slowly going crazy? Maybe yes; maybe no.

Regardless, I still didn't really have a choice. Telling him no didn't seem like an option, even if I wanted to. I guessed I'd find out soon enough whether his "I can't lie" statement had itself been a lie.

"Fine," I said, shooting up out of my seat. "Let's get this over with."

Shock filled his eyes for a split second before he was on his feet beside me. "Give me your hand." He reached his toward me, and I placed mine on top. A flash of silver-blue light illuminated my apartment, and I shielded my eyes until the glow dimmed to a bearable level. When I looked again, I saw a massive sword that looked like it was made of moonlight itself nestled in Volker's hand like it was an extension of him.

Suddenly, his nickname started to make a whole lot more sense.

"Uhh . . . whatcha gonna do with that?" I asked, nerves fluttering in my gut.

"As the name implies, there must be an exchange of blood for this to work."

"Of course."

His eyes dipped to my upturned hand, then jumped back up to meet my gaze. I tried to ignore the hint of amusement I found in them. "I promise I'll be gentle."

"Why don't I find that reassuring?"

A smile slowly spread across his stunning, ghostly pale face. "Because you're smarter than you look."

"You son of a—"

The sharp sting of his blade piercing my skin cut off my retort.

Blood puddled in my hand, and I tried to pull away so I could apply pressure to it, but Volker held it hostage as he carved a line through his own palm around the outline my hand created. His blade disappeared into thin air, and he used his free hand to clamp our palms together and hold them so I couldn't run away.

At first, I felt nothing but Volker's heavy gaze on me, undoubtedly waiting for my power to course through him and deliver on the promise. Anxiety tightened my chest as I thought about what would happen if that power didn't come; if he'd been wrong about me after all. I knew way too much for him to go on his merry way and leave me in peace.

Panic bloomed the longer we stood there, inches apart, with no sparks of magic to be found, until I couldn't even breathe. My knees gave out, and I collapsed to the floor as pain lanced through my chest like a dagger trying to carve out my heart. I let out an anguished cry, and Volker dropped down beside me and released my hand. Breathing hard, he hovered over me, his hands looming nearby but never making contact, as though he was scared to touch me and make things worse.

"Did it work?" I ground out through gritted teeth.

In response, he backed away slowly, and the stabbing in my chest abated. I took a few deep breaths and pushed up onto my knees to face him. "Do you feel any different?" he asked.

"I feel pain—but it's getting better." I wiped the sweat from my brow and tried to stand. I teetered on my feet, and Volker was suddenly at my side to steady me. I looked up into those endless grey eyes, and for a moment, I could have sworn I saw a hint of concern.

Whether it was for me or the vengeance he saw slipping through his fingers, I wasn't sure.

"Is that what my magic is supposed to feel like?" I asked between deep breaths. "Because if it is, I don't want it. I'll go mad in a day."

He straightened slowly and stared down at me. "That was *not* your magic," he said in a dark and ominous tone. Not a great sign coming from the fae killer.

"You felt it too?" I asked. He merely nodded in response.

I pushed off my knees to stand before him, uncertainty tainting the air between us. "So what do we do now?"

His jaw clenched so hard I wondered if his teeth might shatter. "I don't know."

CHAPTER 11
ROWE

It took a solid five minutes to recover. By then, the pain was fully gone, and all that was left in its wake was hunger and the low-key sense of dread I'd felt from the moment I'd met Volker. So, status quo.

He didn't say a word to me as he sat across the table, staring at me like I was a puzzle he couldn't quite solve. The weight of that stare was a lot to weather, so by the time he spoke, I'd polished off the better part of my beer.

"As I see it, only one of three things could explain why that didn't work," he said as he laced his fingers behind his head, his wool coat spreading to expose the tight shirt beneath it—and the even tighter muscles straining the thin white fabric. "The first option is that I'm wrong and you're not the wellspring. The second is that your powers have been somehow taken." He paused for a moment and watched as I took a huge bite of pizza. "You eat like a wild animal."

I shrugged. "Extreme pain makes me hungrier. Sue me."

"Perhaps you should eat more during the day."

"Is this really what you want to talk about right now?"

"Your physical well-being could be a factor in why your magic is . . . off."

"My 'physical well-being' is just fine," I argued. "I eat as much as I can, when I can, but I work a lot, so it isn't always ideal."

His eyes narrowed ever so slightly, and I could have sworn the temperature in the room dipped a degree or two in an instant. "They treat you like a slave."

"Except I'm taken care of—and I get paid," I noted.

"Not very well."

I shrugged. "It is what it is. Now . . . what was that third option?"

A frown tugged at his full lips before he spoke. "Option three is that your abilities have somehow been suppressed by magic. And since it cannot be option one, and option two seems highly unlikely because it would be virtually impossible to do without you realizing it, I'm working off the theory that it must be the third."

I choked on a laugh (then nearly a bite of pizza). "Glad your hubris hasn't been shaken by this evening's misadventures."

"It's not hubris if I'm right, which I am."

"Really? Because that didn't seem to go to plan, and you were pretty confident beforehand, so . . . why are you still so convinced I'm the wellspring?"

"Because I am," he replied, his expression tighter than it had been a moment before.

"That's not an answer."

He leaned forward on his elbows. "Yes. It is. And I'm right about the second option as well because, per my estimate, you would have been around eleven or twelve when the previous wellspring died, which means that if your power had been taken, you'd have been old enough to remember."

Realizing that I wasn't going to get anywhere arguing, I let it go and moved on to something he might actually be willing to expand on in a helpful manner. "Okay, so if it's door number three, how in the hell do you even begin to figure out the logistics of that, let alone how to undo it?"

"That's what I need to determine." He balanced his chin on his fists, leaning in even closer to me, and suddenly the room seemed a lot smaller. His skin seemed to glow from within, giving him an ethereal appearance, but his harsh, angular features offset it in a perfect blend of ruggedness and beauty. It was impossible not to stare in wonder—even given the circumstances. "Tell me more about your mother. She was a witch, was she not?"

"Half-witch," I corrected. "Her father was human."

"Was she powerful?"

"Powerful enough to bind my wellspring magic on her own? No . . . I don't think so," I said as I cracked open the second beer. Volker's inhuman eyes watched as I put it to my lips and took a long drink. Realizing I'd never asked if he wanted one, I reached it toward him. His gaze drifted to the offering, then back up with eerie slowness. Then, to my surprise, he took it.

"Why do you say that?" he asked.

I opened my mouth to answer as he raised the bottle to his mouth. His lips parted slowly and he licked them just a little before taking a sip, his eyes pinned on me the whole time. I stared as he drank, his Adam's apple bobbing elegantly with every swallow, and I wondered if I'd ever seen such a basic activity look sexier in my entire life. The corner of his mouth turned up, as if he knew exactly what I was thinking; then he slowly licked the rim of the bottle before placing it down on the table.

I'd never been more jealous of an inanimate object.

"Umm . . . " I hedged, trying to clear my head, "I mean, I never saw her really use any power. Like ever. She would imbue things on occasion for the former leader of the House and for Shade—make potions and tinctures—but nothing of the magnitude I think it would take to do what you're talking about."

"But she would know other witches," he pressed. "Witches who were more powerful than she."

I shook my head. "She didn't really have a lot of friends. We joined this House when I was young, and from then on, it was just the two of us. I would go with her to clean for the others. We lived in a small outbuilding-turned-apartment on Shade's property until she died. After that, I bounced around a bit, then landed here." I gestured to the room for effect, and his brows pressed to a deep V in response. "I don't remember other witches—aside from some of the others in the House—but I don't think they're especially powerful either."

He mulled over my words for a moment, then leaned closer. "How did she die?"

Sorrow washed over me at his words, and I worked hard to keep the pain I felt from my face. "She was murdered. The killer was never caught. Beyond that, I don't know any details. I'd just turned thirteen when she died. I think Shade and Mathis wanted to keep a lot of what happened from me at the time, which doesn't bode well for the circumstances."

"No, it does not."

I swallowed back my emotions and quickly stuffed the final bite of pizza into my mouth to buy myself time before speaking; if not, the tightness in my throat would surely give me away. Volker watched in silence, foregoing the opportunity to dig further.

"So," I said, taking the beer back from him so I could chase down the pizza—and my emotions—"I'm not sure Mom is the golden ticket you're looking for. If it was another witch, I don't know who."

I grabbed the tube of cookie dough and squeezed it. In my emotional distress, I apparently squished it a wee bit harder than necessary, and the dough shot out onto my shirt. Par for the course. "Fuck," I said, jumping out of my seat. I raced over to the bathroom to try and do damage control, but the more I tried to clean it, the more I just smushed it into the fabric. Anger shot through me, and I let out a frustrated growl as I ripped the shirt over my head and snatched the one I'd slept in off the bathroom floor, momentarily forgetting that a fae assassin was sitting at the table nearby, watching my every move.

I tried to tug the shirt down quickly, but it caught on my bun, leaving me exposed. "For fuck's sake," I muttered as I waged war with the cotton adversary blinding me to the killer in my kitchen. The second the fabric relented and fell into place, I found Volker standing inches away from me, staring at my chest.

"What is this?" he asked as his deft fingers reached beneath my collar. My skin flushed where he'd touched it, and my breath hitched in my throat as he pulled out the necklace I'd worn since before I could even remember. The necklace my mother had given me.

The one with the exact same stone she'd always worn.

I watched with rapt attention as his thumb rubbed gently over the iridescent black rock. It glittered in the scant light as he examined it with a reverence I didn't fully understand.

"It was a present from my mom," I said, my voice a bit breathless. The short chain of the necklace had him so close to me that all I could think about was his overwhelming presence, the intensity of his gaze, and the feeling that coursed through me every time his finger accidentally brushed against my throat.

"This is gabbro," he said as though I hadn't just spoken. "It's the most powerful stone for imbuing."

His iron gaze met mine just as his words took hold in my mind. "Wait . . . what are you saying?"

"I'm saying that this stone is what's interfering with your magic." He let the shiny brown-black stone fall to my chest, but his stare held fast. "I'm saying that your mother was a far more powerful witch than you think."

CHAPTER 12
ROWE

It took a second for my brain to catch up to his words.

My mother had magically hidden my powers? My mother had kept them secret from me my whole life? I didn't want to believe it—couldn't believe it. But then I remembered the way she'd constantly tuck the necklace beneath my shirt if it popped out while I was playing. The way she'd check it at bedtime, securing it under my pajamas as if she were saying goodnight to it as well as to me. It had never struck me as odd; my mother had loved order and routine. It had just seemed like a part of her. But now, with this new knowledge, it cast a very different light on those memories.

Maybe she'd done it to protect me, but I'd never know. The truth had died along with her.

To his credit, Volker stood patiently and watched as I tried to filter through this new information while a barrage of emotions undoubtedly played out on my face.

"I . . . I don't understand," I said softly. "Why wouldn't she tell me? Even if she wanted to suppress my power, why not at least tell me I had it?"

"Perhaps she planned to tell you when you were older—but until then, I imagine it had to do with plausible deniability," he replied, his body still trapping me in the bathroom.

I caught myself leaning closer to him, my mind so heavy with sorrow that I wasn't thinking clearly. A part of me was so desperate for comfort—for consolation—that I wanted to forget that he was the Moonlight Wraith and lean into his strength; to bury my head in his chest and cry and scream and unleash every emotion threatening to escape me because of my mother's duplicity. I wanted him to hold me close and tell me it would all be okay—to lie to me, as she had. But the second my forehead grazed the lapel of his heavy wool coat, the reality of who he was and what I was doing kicked in.

I suddenly needed space in the worst way. I had to get out.

Nudging my way past him, I stumbled into the main room and propped my hands on my knees as I fought for breath. "What the fuck is going on?" I asked myself, knowing I didn't have a good answer.

"Take it off," Volker said as he walked up behind me. "I need to see if it works when you're not wearing it—when it's not connected to you."

Something niggled at the back of my mind at his directive. Something cold and scratchy and altogether uncomfortable. I stood up and turned to look at him. "I've never taken it off before."

His eyebrow cocked with surprise. "*Never?*"

"Never. Like, I literally can't remember a time it wasn't hanging around my neck."

"Take it off," he repeated with a sense of urgency I didn't understand.

I raised my arms slowly, as if they were suddenly made of stone, and reached behind my neck to unclasp the silver chain the gabbro hung from. My fingers fumbled with the delicate mechanism, slipping off every time I tried to pinch it open. "I can't get it," I said, frustration in my voice.

In a blink, Volker was behind me, nimble fingers taking charge. I waited for the necklace to lift off my chest as he unfastened it, but seconds passed with nothing but the hammering of my heart in my chest and his frustrated mutterings to fill the room. "It's magically sealed," he finally said, dropping it against my neck. "Your mother was a clever one, indeed."

"I guess that answers your question about it needing to be connected to me to work."

"So it would seem." He stepped in front of me, his proximity such that the sweet smell of night assaulted me again. His eyes locked on mine as his hand raised and wrapped around the gabbro stone. "This might hurt," he whispered as he leaned in closer still. Then he yanked the pendant forward, trying to break the chain against my neck. Unfortunately, all that did was give me a wicked case of rope burn and slam my body against his as I lurched forward right into his ridiculously firm chest.

"Motherfucker!" I shouted, clasping the back of my neck where the chain had dug in. "You could warn somebody before you do shit like that."

"I literally did—"

"That was a generic heads-up. I mean actually tell me what you're about to do." *Asshole.*

"This is going to require magic to remove," he said as he pulled back a step and extended his hand out to the side. Seconds later, the glowing sword was back in his palm. "Now, I need you to listen *very* carefully, little queen. I'm going to cut the chain with this, but you need to be perfectly still, understand?"

I eyed the wicked-looking weapon growing nearer with every passing second. "Like, 'don't breathe' still?"

His face lingered only inches from mine as he whispered, "still like a marble statue."

I stared at him, my body trembling with fear and adrenaline, knowing we were totally fucked if that was what the task required. "You realize I'm never still, right? I'm constantly moving. Hell, I'm shaking right now."

The back of his hand gently pushed the wispy tendrils of hair that had escaped my messy bun over my shoulder, and the shaking diminished ever so slightly. "Perhaps I should knock you out first." His sultry tone directly contrasted the words he spoke, as if he were trying to lull me into agreeing.

I looked up into his piercing eyes and frowned. "I'll take a hard pass on that, thanks."

His fingertips trailed along the sensitive skin of my neck until he took the chain in his hand. "Then don't move, and all will be fine."

"Says the guy who isn't going to lose his head if he's wrong." With no other options, I took a deep breath and let it out slowly, hoping that would help accomplish the impossible.

Volker gently lifted my chin with his index finger and leveled his gaze on me. "You have to trust me."

There was something so soft in his tone—so genuine and comforting—that I felt my shoulders relax and still; felt the knot in my stomach release. I stood there in silence for a moment that felt like a lifetime and stared into the eyes of a being who'd terrified me only days earlier. But that fear was gone, replaced by a sense of calm I couldn't fathom, especially while my face was being held captive by a killer.

"I do," I murmured, nodding lightly.

"Keep your eyes on me," he said softly, "no matter what." I swallowed hard as I did as he asked, focusing solely on the ethereal glow of his face as his terrifying moonlight blade grew nearer. "The blade will burn if it touches your skin, and it will cut through your flesh with ease. So I really do need you to hold still."

"Okay . . . I'm ready," I replied before I caught my breath and held it.

I could feel the strange chill of his weapon as it hovered near my skin. He pulled the chain taut to create as much distance between it and me as possible, but even though it was standard length, the sword felt awfully close to my face as it tugged against my neck when he pressed his blade to it. The pressure grew as he leaned into the task, and a strange sulfur smell filled the room as the metal crackled and sizzled.

I closed my eyes and prayed it wouldn't cut through it with a sudden jerk, leaving the blade to continue on through my face.

"Eyes on me," he growled, his voice strained with concentration.

They snapped open to find him staring at my neck, his face still inches from mine. His exhales ruffled the stray hairs around my face, and I tried to focus on the tickle they created instead of the pain blooming in the back of my neck as he applied more and more force against the spelled necklace. And it worked for a while, until a searing pain lanced through my cheek as his blade met my skin. "Volker . . . " I said, my voice shaking with pain.

"I've almost got it."

The blade bit in further, and I tried to suppress the scream bubbling up at the back of my throat. "Volker . . . "

"Just a bit longer . . . "

Tears streamed from my eyes as the freezing burn ripped through my jaw. The scream I was terrified to let out finally won, and an ungodly, strangled cry escaped me as I tried in vain not to pull away.

Volker's blade disappeared in an instant, and his hand cupped my cheek where his sword had just cut through my flesh. The pain abated immediately; the stench of sulfur and burning skin did as well. All that was left was me with a tear-stained face, breathing hard while his glowing eyes raked over me, assessing me for other wounds.

Once he was satisfied I was all right, he let me go. "I cannot remove or destroy it without harming you in the process," he said, pulling away quickly. He retreated backward until my entire apartment spanned between us. "We will have to find another way to break the spell."

His eyes finally met mine, and something close to worry tugged at their corners. Worry that his plan was about to fall apart or worry for something else, I didn't know, and didn't get a chance to ask. Without another word, he rushed toward the door, his hand hovering over the knob. He stood there for a moment, his back to me as he hesitated, then spoke. "Are you all right?"

"Yeah," I said, rubbing my face where the wound should have been, as though I could still feel it. "Don't worry . . . your wellspring is intact."

His hand gripped the doorknob and squeezed it hard enough for the metal to groan in his grasp. "I wasn't asking about the wellspring."

Surprise washed over me at his words. "The human's fine, too," I replied, my voice barely a whisper.

He turned just enough for me to see that perfect, haunting profile, then gave a tight nod. Unlike his normal dramatic exit, he walked through the door in silence, with no parting warning or threat. The door clicked shut behind him, and I collapsed onto the edge of my bed, adrenaline still surging through my veins at an uncomfortable level. My knees bounced as I chewed on my nails, thinking about everything that had just gone down.

Volker had been right; my necklace was suppressing my power somehow. But it was the questions raised by that knowledge that plagued me as I sat in my silent room wondering how in the hell we were going to figure this out.

And what had spooked Volker enough to send him running from my apartment.

CHAPTER 13
VOLKER
THIRTEEN YEARS EARLIER

I scoured the woods outside the city, hunting the one who'd dared to invade my territory—the uninvited threat looming in the shadows. But I was the monster to be feared, not him, and so I continued on, following the faint pulse of magic that filled the cool night air. It was erratic and heady and impossible to ignore. And as I neared its epicenter, I heard a low voice murmuring, the note of desperation plain even from far away.

It grew louder and more urgent as I approached.

His back was to me as he stooped near a tree, his head clamped between his hands as he pulled at his hair. He didn't seem to notice me at all as I stepped into a break in the trees. I quickly glanced at the full moon before I called my blade. The silver-blue light filled the forest, drawing the man's attention.

He was on his feet in a second. "Why won't she help me?" he asked the night air as he turned to face me. His dark auburn curls shot wildly from his head, and his green eyes were wide and rimmed with madness. "She refused to take it," he rambled as he took a step toward me. "She said she didn't want it—turned me away so long ago. And now everything's falling apart—for us both."

"What is?" Despite his apparent madness, I couldn't help but ask.

"The plan!" he snapped, wielding that crazed stare like a weapon. My moonlight blade glowed at my side in preparation. "It wasn't supposed to end like this . . . " He growled in frustration and tugged at his hair. "If only she'd done what I asked!"

"If who had done what you asked?"

"It doesn't matter now," he muttered to himself as he frantically paced a tiny patch of grass as though the trees had caged him in. "It's too late."

"Too late for whom?"

His feet went still and he looked at me as though seeing me for the first time. "Me." He took an aggressive step forward, and I lifted my blade, pointing it at him. "You don't understand," he continued, unfazed by the threat. "It's too much, and no matter what I do, I can't escape it!"

"You cannot escape death," I said, raising my blade.

He sneered at the threat. "That too."

"What else is there to escape?"

"You know," he said, lips curled in a snarl. "You all do. It is the curse of this gift—the price of so much power. Power you can never have." He pointed an accusatory finger at me as he stepped closer. "It's not safe with you." He shook his head furiously, then resumed his pacing. "Too much power . . . "

His fragmented messages culminated into a resounding truth I could scarcely believe. "You're the wellspring—"

"Don't say it!" he screamed, clutching his head. "Naming it makes it worse—gives the power power, and I can't have that, no no no . . . it doesn't need that." He yanked at his hair that burned red and gold in my blade's light. "I have to find a way." He stopped short and lifted those eyes filled with insanity to me. "Are you the way?"

"I am the way to death," I replied.

My threat didn't faze him at all. "No . . . the way to stop it."

His conflicting words confused me. "To stop the madness?" I asked. "I could bind your gift to me to stop it, yes—"

"NO!" he shouted, his behavior devolving once again. "No, no, no . . . you're not listening. *Nobody ever listens. And if you won't listen to me, then you won't listen to* her, *either."*

"Who?" I asked, irritation bleeding into my tone. "Who is she?*"*

"She wants nothing to do with it—but at least she let me help with the spell."

"What spell?" I asked, trying to redirect his incoherent ramblings as pity tugged at my chest. He was so far gone that I knew killing him would be a mercy. But something about his words niggled at the back of my mind, and I couldn't shake the feeling that there was something more to what was happening—that he had not found his way to me by chance.

Then, in a moment of clarity, he looked at me with the fierceness and conviction of a man determined to accomplish one final, sane task before succumbing to insanity forever. "The one that will hide her from the world," he said, voice steady and stern.

"Who?" I asked, inching closer, the mystery his madness was slowly unveiling sucking me in with every passing second. "Who must you hide?"

Silence fell upon him as his eyes lost their focus, his lucidity disappearing as quickly as it had come. "I love her," he said softly. "I love them both . . ." His wandering gaze found mine yet again, and deep in the green depths was a resignation I'd seen before. The kind that dwelled in men with nothing left to lose. "Would you tell her something for me?"

My brows furrowed. "Tell her what?"

He let out a slow breath. "Tell her I'm sorry."

Before I could ask who the message was for, he lunged forward and impaled himself on my gleaming blade. His eyes shone white as it sucked away his lifeforce, as it did all its victims, but this time was different. I tasted the power of the wellspring as his heart slowed and his skin grew pale, and he raised his face to look at me one last time.

"My little queen."

With a final breath, his body went limp.

And somewhere in the world, a new wellspring was born.

CHAPTER 14
ROWE

I woke up the next day, blissfully clueless for about five seconds as I sat up and stretched. But by the time my arms fell back to my sides, the memories of everything that had happened the night before bodychecked me back into reality.

My mother had magically suppressed my powers with my necklace somehow—and now she was dead. My mind reeled so hard from the implications that I felt dizzy. I staggered over to the sink and poured a glass of water. Clinging to the counter, I chugged back as much of the cool liquid as I could on an empty stomach. It growled in protest.

After a couple of deep breaths, I felt a bit better. I made my way to the bathroom and got cleaned up. Staring into the mirror, I realized just how exhausted I looked. My sleep had been fitful, riddled with strange dreams that had seemed too real to be dreams at all, and the dark circles under my eyes were testament to that. I needed a vacation in the worst way.

Too bad that wasn't in the cards.

As if my financial instability had summoned her, my phone

started ringing. I checked the screen to find Myra calling, which clearly didn't bode well for my day. "Hello?"

"Rowe?" Myra yelled into the phone, the din of *The Riff-Raff* nearly overpowering her voice. Confused by how busy the place sounded, I glanced at the time on my phone. It was already noon.

"What's up?" I asked, already well aware of the answer.

"Sasha still isn't back, and shit's gotten crazy over here. I let you off the hook for ignoring my call yesterday, but I really need you to come in."

"Uggggh," I groaned, shuffling out of the bathroom. "Why can't Ravi drag someone else in there?"

"Because he's Ravi and he knows you'll come. Now, I'm gonna need you to haul ass over here ASAP."

"No."

Silence. "*No?*" The note of surprise in her voice was quickly eclipsed by simmering rage that would surely propel her into Fire and Fluorite territory just to drag me into work. Probably by my hair, if she was really in a mood.

But I had bigger problems to worry about than an understaffed restaurant I only worked at part-time (normally). "I'm sorry, Myra, but I'm not coming in. I've got some crazy personal shit going on."

She remained silent for a moment, but I could still somehow hear her anger through the phone. "Rowe," she said, her voice eerily calm, "if I promise to help you with your problem, would you come in? Now. *Please.*"

"You can't help—" I cut myself off as Volker's words shot to the front of my mind. *Gabbro . . .* Gabbro was a *sea* stone. Myra was a *mermaid.* If anyone could tell me about it, she could—or at least she was the only sea creature I knew who might be willing to help me, which basically made her an expert in my mind. "Okay, I'll come in if you'll help me with my problem," I said, choosing my words carefully. "We'll call it a favor owed."

Her hesitation was plain. Sea creatures, much like the fae, took bargains and deals and favors very seriously. To be in someone else's debt was no small thing by their standards. "Fine. I'll owe you a favor."

"One you can't discuss with anyone. For any reason."

"Obviously . . . wait, why? Are we burying a body? Because I'd have helped with that just for fun—"

"No, we're not burying a body," I replied as I rushed to the closet for the black clothes I'd worn the other night. I really needed to do laundry, STAT. "I'll be there in twenty."

"Make it ten," she said, then hung up in true Myra fashion.

Bitch loved to get the final word.

For once, Myra hadn't been exaggerating.

I walked into the restaurant and found myself in a crowd so deep it was nearly impossible to shoulder my way through. I didn't recognize who they were or what House they were from, but they were loud and drunk and definitely not leaving any time soon.

My necklace questions were going to have to wait awhile.

"There you are," Myra said, grabbing my arm to haul me through the room as though she were twice my size—or a bulldozer. "Ravi is in a mood, so steer clear of the kitchen as much as you can and just run drinks for now. Poor Stella is bartending; I've seen her break down in tears no less than four times in the past hour."

"Great . . . "

"Just remember: head down, tits up. Follow that advice and we'll get through this without committing a homicide." She disappeared into the fray, and I shoved my way to the bar, where Stella was most definitely crying while pouring drinks. I quickly hopped over the counter and started taking orders.

No point in trying to deliver drinks that hadn't even been made yet, right?

Ten minutes later, Stella's breakdown had ended, and I was ready to actually help serve again. Myra grabbed trays from the kitchen and practically threw them at me to deliver for her. It was like being tossed into a tornado. I had no control over which path I took to the tables, the room too thick with bodies. By the time an hour or two had passed, I was sweating, dehydrated, and starving.

"When are they gonna leave?" I asked Myra during a slight lull.

"Looks like never, but it's slow enough for you to take a break now. Ravi will just have to deal with it."

"Then he'll have to deal with you taking yours at the same time, because I need to talk to you about that favor."

Myra glanced over her shoulder at the kitchen, then jerked her head in that direction. "All right. Let's go out back." She turned on her heels and backtracked through the ruckus in the kitchen to the back door. She shoved it open and headed out into the crisp evening air. The light was fading, but the remnants of sun reflected off of Myra's hair, cutting the black with a warm glow. "What's going on?"

Without explanation, I pulled out my necklace and showed it to her.

Her eyes widened at the sight. "That's gabbro."

"It is."

She turned her suspicious gaze to me. "How did you get this?"

"My mother gave it to me when I was very young—I don't remember a time without it."

"Gabbro is used for *very* powerful spells, Rowe," she said as she lifted the stone with a reverence that surprised me coming from her.

"So I hear—"

"What do you think it's for?" she asked.

I leaned toward her in conspiratorial fashion, careful to keep my voice as low as possible. "I think it's to suppress something."

"Like what?" she asked, her tone incredulous. "You're basically human. There's nothing to suppress."

"Or maybe I'm not. And maybe there is."

She pulled away enough for me to see her scrunched features. They displayed her utter confusion in the most comical way. "But that makes no sense. Why would anyone want to suppress your powers if you aren't human? You're nothing in this world without them. This isn't some cheesy movie where being supernatural is to be kept secret."

"But what if it was safer for my power to be kept secret?" I countered. "What if whatever is being suppressed inherently endangers me?"

She stared at me thoughtfully for a moment. "You said your mother gave you this stone? And she was a witch, correct?"

"Half-witch, yes."

Silence. "Did she have any friends that were sea witches? Someone she could have gotten this stone from?"

"I guess. I have no clue, though. I was way too young to know when she gave it to me, and we were pretty much on our own for years until she went to Fire and Fluorite." Her brow furrowed as she contemplated my answer. "I never thought anything about it until last night. She used to tell me it was a charm to protect me. We both had one—"

"Wait," she said, cutting me off, "your mother had a gabbro stone too?"

"Yeah . . . why?"

"*Why*? Because that potentially changes everything," she said as though I were a complete and total moron. "They wouldn't have been spelled separately, Rowe. I'd bet my shot at getting my tail back that they're linked, which wouldn't make sense if they were protection charms." She looked at me for a moment, sympathy in her eyes.

"Why not?"

"Because your mother is dead and you're not."

Ice impaled my heart at her words. "But . . . "

"Did she die of natural causes?" she asked, though I could hear the guilt in her voice at the question.

"No," I whispered in response. "She went missing one night and never came back. I was thirteen, so I was spared the details, but I overheard Shade and Mathis talking one night about her murder."

Her lips pinched together. "I'm sorry, Rowe. I really am."

"Thanks."

She stared at me, her hesitation plain. "We know that stone wasn't for protection, which leaves me questioning a whole lot of shit right now."

"You and me both—"

"You said that you think you might have power that it's suppressing . . . where did you get that idea?"

Ummm . . . "Someone suggested it."

"Who?"

"I can't say."

She folded her arms across her chest. "Can't or won't?"

"Both, actually, but not because I don't want to. It's just not an option."

She assessed me for a moment in a way that would have surely made Volker proud. "You're just full of surprises tonight, aren't you?"

"Apparently. Now, can you help me figure out what this stone is for—and how to remove it?"

Shock washed over her as she reached for the stone again. "You can't take it off?"

"Nope."

She tugged and yanked and tried the clasp, to no avail. "It's been spelled in place," she said with true disbelief in her tone. "That is no small magic, Rowe. Whoever did that had to have immense power."

I shrugged, unsure of what to say. "My mother didn't have it, I know that much."

"Unless the stone suppressed hers, too." Myra looked thoughtful for a moment, mulling something over in her mind. "Your mother's stone . . . do you have it?"

"No."

"Do you know where it is?"

"I . . . I have no idea. I imagine she was buried with it, but I never saw the body, so I don't know."

"Well," she said, pushing up her sleeves, "we'll likely need it to break the spell and unleash whatever it is this stone does. Who knows . . . maybe you're the most powerful witch who's ever lived."

"Or maybe I'm a weapon to wield, and my mother knew it," I countered, the weight of what we were playing with pressing down upon me.

"There's only one way to find out," she said, her expression sober as she stared at me with those sea blue eyes, begging me to put the pieces of the puzzle together. When it was clear I hadn't, she stepped closer and lowered her voice. "You need to dig up her grave and find it, Rowe—"

"*What*?" I shrieked. "No, Myra! That's disgusting. I can't do that—"

"You don't have a choice," she said, her fingertips biting into my arm, "not if you want to break this spell. Gabbro stones absorb magic like no other. If two have been used to seal a spell, then there's no chance you can undo it without them both. You have to get your mother's."

Cold sweat slid down my spine as the truth of her words settled on my mind. It wanted to reject them—and tried several times—but regardless of how macabre the suggestion was, she was right. I had to get Mom's necklace.

The screech of the metal door pulled me from my downward spiral as Yael walked out, a cigarette pinched between his lips. "What are you two vixens discussing out here when you should be inside slaving away like the rest of us?" he asked as he struck a match to light his cigarette. "Something unseemly and nefarious, no doubt—"

"Rowe needs to dig up her mother's grave," Myra said so bluntly that Yael actually choked on his first inhale.

I shot her a death stare. "What about the whole 'can't tell anyone' agreement we had?"

Myra shrugged. "I didn't tell him why, which is the real secret. Besides, what's Yael going to do? Tattle on you?" she asked, totally unfazed. "Like he has any pull with anyone anymore . . . "

Yael, totally ignoring our sidebar argument, finally pulled himself together. "I'm sorry, I think I just hallucinated. Did you say *dig up a grave?*"

"Yes," Myra said. "Her mother's."

Yael turned his green eyes to me and looked at me like he was truly seeing me for the first time. "Well now, this night just got astronomically more interesting."

"I don't think I can do it," I said to Myra, whose attention was all on the gorgeous fae she loathed. "I know I have to, but . . . I don't think I can actually bring myself to physically do it."

Her gaze slowly slid over to me. "You can and you will because, as you said, you have to." Her harsh expression softened slightly, as though she had just remembered the subject at hand. "But I'll help, if you need me."

"Count me in, too," Yael said, raising his hand for effect. "I highly doubt this endeavor will disappoint."

"You're the literal worst, Yael," I said as I pushed past him toward the door. "And Myra, forget I ever said anything to you about this."

Before either could say another word, I threw the heavy metal door open and stormed inside. Everyone in the kitchen parted like the Red Sea to let me pass, even Ravi, who just stared at me in silence as I grabbed my things and punched the door to the front of the house open. I didn't stop until I hit the street out front, my feet pounding the pavement as I ran through No Man's Land, tears welling in my eyes.

Because, as much as I hated to admit it, Myra was right.

If I wanted to get to the bottom of my magic, I'd have to dig up my mother.

CHAPTER 15
ROWE

It took me three days to find the nerve to do the unthinkable. Three days to convince myself that I was strong enough to face what I'd find in that grave. Three days to realize that there was no way around my fate.

And three days without any sign of Volker.

I tried not to let my mind run wild with the potential reasons for his absence and failed.

Then I tried to ignore the potential reasons for why it worried me so much and failed yet again.

Without him at my side, I stood at the edge of the cemetery, shovel in hand, praying the cloudy sky above would keep me shrouded in darkness while I worked. If I was caught in the act, I was basically fucked, because I was way too emotional not to crack under interrogation. The whole truth about Volker was certain to come out, and even though Shade might have understood why I'd done what I'd done—and that was a big 'might'—my actions couldn't be kept secret. The whole House would learn about the Moonlight Wraith, and Volker's vengeance would be turned against those I cared about when his plan was ruined.

My mother's grave was under the shade of a massive oak tree, which thankfully provided further cover for my morbid task. Dressed in black with my hair tucked up into a beanie, I spiked the shovel into the ground and took a deep breath in preparation.

"I can do this," I said to myself, wishing I didn't have to. Volker's absence gnawed at me as I gripped the wooden handle tighter.

I hadn't seen him since he'd left my apartment following the necklace debacle. Hadn't felt him lurking in the shadows. At first, I'd welcomed the break; then worry had set in. I wondered if he'd been found. If he'd been taken to the queen and executed—again. With no way to contact him and nobody to ask, the uncertainties ran in my mind on a loop. By day three, I was just irritated with it all.

With him.

With my conflicting feelings about him.

The scary assassin who'd accosted me in the alley behind the bar had been all but gone since the night he'd tried to cut my necklace off, and try though I did, I couldn't help but wonder why. Why he'd been so gentle with me. Why he'd looked so afraid when I'd cried out. Why he'd rushed out of there after making sure I was okay. I knew he needed me alive to get his revenge, but it had seemed like more than that—like he actually cared. And I wondered if maybe I cared more than I wanted to admit too.

But then he'd disappeared for days without a fucking word.

My ruminations soured at the thought.

"You don't need his help," I muttered under my breath as I eyed the spade buried in the ground, begging me to dig up that first mound of earth. But I couldn't move. Instead, I strangled the handle and stared at that pierced ground, thinking about what lay six feet below.

Then a cool sensation prickled my skin right before a pale hand wrapped around mine and a low voice murmured in my ear. "Perhaps you should let me do this, little queen."

I glanced over my shoulder to find him staring down at me intently, his body so close to mine that the crisp scent of night enveloped me, and I let out a breath of relief. "Where the hell have you been?"

"That's a long story," he said, pulling my hand away from the shovel.

"Why are you here?"

"That's a much shorter one," he said, a smirk gracing his ethereal, moonlit face. "Because you're here." He looked to the ground at my feet, and the smirk fell away. "And for such interesting reasons . . . "

"My mother had a necklace just like mine. Myra says we'll likely need it to break whatever the spell is that's keeping my power withheld."

"The mermaid would likely know of such things, given her connection to the sea."

"So here I am. Grave-robbing."

His lips pressed to a grim line. "I see."

Silence fell upon us, and I couldn't help but notice how close he still stood. How his open coat brushed against my back. How his outstretched arm encased me. And where I would have once felt fear in his presence, all I felt was a bizarre sense of relief—of comfort.

I shook my head to try to knock some sense into myself, then took a step away. "It would have been nice if you could have at least dropped a note or done one of your creepy stalker bits so I knew you were still alive these past couple days. Disappearing was a dick move."

Those dark eyes looked me over and amusement tugged at his lips. "I thought you'd welcome the reprieve."

"I did, until I started worrying about all the things that could have happened to you, so don't do it again."

"I don't plan to."

"Good."

"Good."

More silence. My eyes turned to the ground at my feet and my throat tightened. "I really don't think I can do this, Volker," I said, my voice threatening to crack. "She was my world . . . "

He closed the short distance between us again, and the pain in my chest abated ever so slightly. "Then I guess it's serendipitous that you have me to do it for you." Something dangerously close to sympathy penetrated his stare. "You were a child when she was taken from you; those memories should remain pure."

Tears pricked the backs of my eyes, and I bit down on my lip to hold them back. But my efforts failed, and I felt the first teardrop slide down my cheek. Volker watched it as it fell to my jawline. Then, with liquid grace, he lifted his hand and wiped it away before it fell to the ground.

He rolled it between his fingers until it disappeared, then yanked the shovel from the ground, only to drive it back in again and again with unimaginable force. Dirt and grass flew around us, and I stepped back until my back hit the tree. Morbid though the scene was, I couldn't help but marvel at his strength while he worked. How his biceps strained against his fitted coat. How his jaw flexed as he heaved the earth into a pile next to the grave.

What would have taken me hours, he did in mere minutes.

The clank of metal against wood pulled me from my lustful thoughts. Head back in the game, I inched forward as he maneuvered in the hole to open my mother's casket. The hinges creaked as he lifted the top, and I watched his expression like a hawk, looking for any small sign of what he saw inside.

"Volker?" I called, but he didn't reply.

The longer he stared, the more my anxiety drove me forward, until I was peering down over him into the casket that I'd secretly hoped would be empty. But it wasn't, and I gasped at the sight of my mother's remains; just bones, with scraps of fabric covering them. And no necklace to be seen.

"It's gone," I said, my words escaping on an exhale like I'd been punched in the gut—which was exactly how I felt.

Volker still said nothing. Instead, he looked up at me, something strangely akin to resignation in his pewter eyes. "My mother's necklace is gone. Do you get that? It's gone, which means all of this was for nothing—and you're not getting what you want, because we don't have a fucking clue where it is." Still, he didn't react. "Why aren't you freaking out right now?" I asked, tears again rolling down my cheeks as my barely withheld emotions erupted. "Why aren't you totally losing your shit? You should be raging like a madman, and here you are, all calm and cool while I have a meltdown. Like you knew it wouldn't be there or something . . . "

His silence nearly undid me.

I watched as he climbed out of the grave with a grace no human could ever possess, silently pleading with him to say something—anything. Instead, he towered over me from the top of the dirt mound he'd created. He looked like a god on high, and the clouds above parted to allow the moon to shine down upon him, framing him in eerie blue light.

Then he opened his mouth and shattered the illusion with three words.

"Because I did."

CHAPTER 16
VOLKER
THREE DAYS EARLIER

I stormed out of her apartment, knowing how close I'd come to sacrificing her. My singular focus on removing her necklace had eclipsed the bigger picture. If she hadn't cried out—hadn't broken through to me—I might have killed her to break the magic tethering that necklace to her, and with that, killed my chance at revenge.

Yet somehow, as I'd looked into her terrified eyes, my vengeance no longer mattered. I was consumed by her fear and by the sudden vision of her lifeless body in my arms. I needed to find another way.

I had to get away from her as quickly as possible.

The night welcomed me with open arms as I disappeared into the darkness, needing an outlet for my unsettled emotions. And so I hunted Nyssa down.

I knew she'd recently left her territory in the forests of Northern Canada, a hiccup in my plan, but it was only a matter of time before I found her. The fact that she was on the move at all was surprising, but even more so when I found her two days later on Portland's embassy row. Why she was there was a mystery. One I neither liked nor trusted.

Regardless, it was an advantage I hadn't expected. The embassy, though large, could only house so many guards. She had no army. No reinforcements. Once I learned her movements—and took stock of those closest to her—I would know how best to exact my revenge, provided the matter of Rowe's necklace could be remedied.

A problem I wasn't quite ready to face again just yet.

Atop an adjacent building, I crouched in the shadows and watched. She was staying in the penthouse, which was little more than a room of windows—one I knew well, since it used to be mine. The lights flicked on as she entered, a guard on her arm. He removed her thick fur cloak, exposing the strapless crimson gown that trailed behind her. But that wasn't what caught my eye. A dark stone hung from her neck; one that looked painfully familiar.

Without thought, I disappeared into the night air to rematerialize on the Juliet balcony off the penthouse. Pressed sideways against the narrow space between the windows, I dared a closer look. The queen's guard was on his knees before her, lifting her voluminous skirt over his head. Seconds later, her head lolled back as she cried out. With her distracted, I pressed against the window to better see the stone hanging at her throat; to see if my suspicion was correct. To see if it was indeed a gabbro dangling from a silver chain—just like Rowe's.

One look told me my eyes had not deceived me.

Anger rose from deep within, and I felt the glass beneath my palm creak as I leaned harder against it. Nyssa's head snapped to attention at the sound, but I'd already disappeared into the darkness yet again.

I didn't stop until I was outside Rowe's apartment, where I could process this bizarre twist of events. But the more I thought it through, the less bizarre it became. From the moment I'd narrowly escaped my own assassination, I'd wondered why Nyssa had chosen that moment to make her move—if she'd somehow known that my power had been disrupted. But now I wondered if there hadn't been some other reason. Something she had done to ensure her success.

Her necklace was identical to Rowe's, though the stone appeared smaller. And given how rare gabbro was to procure, let alone imbue with magic, my mind began to swirl with theories. What if Rowe's mother had had a necklace just like hers? I hadn't been able to compre-

hend how the wellspring power could be suppressed, but it had seemed the most likely reason why Rowe felt none of it. But what if it wasn't that at all? What if the gabbro did something else entirely?

What if Rowe's mother had sought to siphon her power—draw it down to keep her precious daughter from going mad one day? Most mothers would do anything to keep their daughters safe, and after what I'd seen of the wellspring madness, she would have been wise to want that. Her murder made sense if someone had found out about this potential connection to Rowe and guessed its meaning. Someone like an ambitious fae who sought to rule Air and Amethyst . . .

Though this theory had holes, it also had merit. And if it proved true, it would mean that I wouldn't have to remove Rowe's necklace—I'd just need to take her mother's from the queen. With it, I could tap into the power I needed to stabilize my own, as well as to take my revenge. And afterward, that power would still be mine to call, as long as I had the gabbro. I'd have a connection to the wellspring that she could never take away, an advantage I hadn't bargained for.

The plan was as simple as it was flawless.

And yet not.

Even if my theory was correct, there was one rather large complication: Rowe.

She had initially been a means to an end, but had quickly turned into a curiosity of sorts: a strange, amusing being unlike any I'd ever met. Walking away had been the plan in the beginning, because all I'd cared about was seeking revenge and retaking my throne. But now . . . now I wondered if that would be so easy. Stealing Rowe's power through the necklace would mean deceiving her, not to mention leaving her alone and weak in an unstable House, surrounded by supernaturals that—though she thought otherwise—did not care about her.

Why did a strange pain gnaw at my chest at the thought of abandoning her to that fate?

The click of the door unlocking sounded through the alley and Rowe appeared, dressed in black, with a hat hiding her flowing red hair and a shovel in her hand. I held to the shadows as I followed her through Fire and Fluorite territory until she finally arrived at a cemetery. I hid behind an oak tree as she stared at what could only be her mother's grave, prepared to do something that would surely break her.

And while a temporary rush of adrenaline coursed through me at the confirmation of my suspicion, it was quickly shut down by the look of anguish on her face.

That foreign pain in my chest returned and drove me from the shadows.

Her emerald eyes went wide before they narrowed to angry slits. Before she could launch into a rant, I began to explain. "To clarify, I was not certain. It was a hunch of sorts."

"A *hunch*?" she replied incredulously.

"I wondered if perhaps she'd had a necklace to match yours."

"Didn't I tell you she did?"

"No, you must have left out that detail between the shocking realization that your mother had suppressed your power and me trying to carve your necklace from you." The note of guilt I felt crept into my tone, and her expression softened at the sound.

"And you bailing the second that failed," she added. "You didn't exactly give me a chance to fill you in as you bolted from my apartment."

"I thought it best at the time," I said, not wishing to explain further. Admission of the fear I'd felt at what I'd done would only have led to more questions; questions I did not want to answer.

"Were you mad? Is that why you haven't been back since?" Though she tried to hide it, the hint of disappointment in her eyes was as plain as the moon above.

"I wasn't mad," I replied. "I needed to find the queen." I let my gaze fall to the grave next to me, then back to her. "It appears you were quite busy in my absence . . . "

"Yeah. I've known for a couple of days that I needed to come, but I just couldn't make myself do it. And you were nowhere to be found to force the issue." The sting in her voice as she spoke those words was raw, and I wondered if her bleary eyes allowed her to see me flinch as her blow landed. "But I guess we're both all caught up now. My mom had a matching necklace, and now it's gone, so I'm willing to bet someone stole it from her."

"Either in life or death—which one remains unclear. As does whether or not it was the motive for her murder."

She took a step toward me, steel forming in the depths of her sad eyes. "You think someone might have killed her just to get the necklace?"

"I think the state of her body illustrates the lengths someone went to in order to obtain the stone."

She stared at me for a moment before her gaze drifted to the now-closed casket. "Why do you say that?" she asked, her voice hollow and empty and so full of pain, it filled the air around us.

My jaw clenched as I inhaled, not wanting to share the answer, but knowing I must. "Because her head was severed from her body to remove it." Those emerald eyes went wide, and more tears spilled. I fisted my hands at my sides to keep them still. "Which means her necklace, like yours, was probably charmed to stay in place."

"Oh my gods—"

"There is no way to know if the wound was incurred before or after her death," I continued, hoping that speaking would distract me from the pain in her eyes. "It appears that no one has been here recently to dig up the grave, unless someone with the magic to restore the earth afterward did so."

She looked at me for a moment, pondering something. "Is there a way to find out? Could someone tell if anyone disturbed the ground before us?"

"There are fae that can. I believe the one from your restaurant, Yael, possesses such a skill. He might not be powerful enough, but it's possible."

She bit her lip, her hesitation plain. "What if I asked him to come?"

"Here?" I asked, disbelief in my tone. "Now?"

"He was there when Myra and I were discussing this," she explained. "He kinda barged in just as we figured out that grave-robbing was in my future. He was all about it—maybe *too* all about it, now that I think back—but he doesn't know anything else. About you or the wellspring or anything. He just knows I had to dig up my mother's grave, and he offered to help."

"And you trust him?"

"I mean, trust or not, we may have to take that chance." When I said nothing in response, she rambled on. "He's the one I already told you about; the one who was cast out for his loyalty to you, if that helps reassure you."

"It does—minutely. Regardless, we cannot leave the grave looking as though it's been disturbed, so there is little choice in the matter. Beings I can heal to varying degrees, but the earth, I cannot. Tell him to come."

She pulled out her phone and quickly typed in a message. Once she finished, she tucked it into her back pocket, then stared up at me. Gone were the tears she'd shed for her mother's fate. Gone were the shock and disbelief. All that was left was the burning fire of vengeance that I knew all too well.

"Volker?"

"Yes, little queen?"

"Promise me something. Promise me you'll help me find out who killed my mother."

I took a step closer to stare into her determined eyes. "I may already know."

Her nostrils flared with anger. "Tell me."

I hesitated for a moment, quickly weighing just how much I should tell her. "During my recent absence, I was tracking the queen. It seems she's come to the embassy here in Portland, though I don't know why—yet. When I saw her, I noticed she was wearing a gabbro necklace; one that looked identical to yours. That's why I was not surprised that your mother's was missing."

She stumbled back a step, and I caught her arm to keep her from falling into the grave. "You think she has it?"

"Yes. I do."

"Do you think she killed my mother?"

"Of that, I can't be certain. Not yet."

Her lips pressed to a thin line. "We need to get that necklace."

"Agreed."

"And Volker," she said, squaring her shoulders to face me like a warrior, "if I find out that it was that bitch who killed her, I'm afraid you might not get your revenge."

I felt the corner of my mouth upturn. "And why is that?"

Her expression mimicked mine, and I felt a surge of excitement rush through me. "Because I'm going to rip her fucking head off with my bare hands."

I smiled with delight at the thought. "You would have to fight me for the privilege."

She didn't even flinch. "Then I guess you'd better hope it wasn't her."

"I'm starting to think I should."

The buzzing of her phone cut the tension between us, and she pulled it out to find a response from Yael. "He says his break is in five, so he'll meet me here," she said, her features scrunched with confusion, "even though he doesn't know where 'here' is."

"He'll find you with ease," I replied as I tossed the shovel into the grave. "Some of us are rather gifted at that." I turned to leave, afraid of what might happen if I lingered much longer. Of what the heady promise of her bloodlust might make me do. *She's a means to an end*, I reminded myself. *Nothing more.* "I'll see you soon, little queen."

Before my dark desire made me do something I'd surely regret, I dipped into the nearby shadows and disappeared from sight.

CHAPTER 17
ROWE

It felt like the cemetery was a revolving door of randomly appearing fae; only minutes after Volker was swallowed by darkness, Yael appeared out of nowhere. I'd barely had time to dirty my clothes to sell the lie that I'd been the one to dig the hole before he showed up, somehow looking elegant in his black pants and shirt with a white apron. One that never seemed to get dirty, despite the chaos in the kitchen.

He strode toward me, a tiny smirk tugging at his lips. Then he stopped only feet shy of the hole and stared down at it with morbid fascination. "Are you sure you're human?" he asked, disbelief in his tone.

"Yeah," I lied, "of course I am. Why?"

He continued to eye the gaping hole in the earth. "I just wouldn't have expected you to be able to dig all that up. You must be exhausted." His gaze lifted to find me standing stiff as a board, shovel in hand.

My shoulders rounded on cue, and I drooped against the wooden handle as much as it would allow. "Totally, which is why I really need your help."

"To clean up this mess?" he asked, stepping closer. "Or for something else—like collecting your mother's body?"

"I didn't come for her body; I came for something on it. Something that isn't there."

"What?" he asked, something close to genuine curiosity in his tone.

"A family heirloom. A necklace, to be exact. I need it, but it's gone," I said, unable to keep the sadness from my voice at the thought. Silence fell between us as I mustered the nerve to ask him for the real favor I needed. The fae, in my limited experience, didn't love to talk about their specific powers, and I was about to ask him the limits of his. I winced a bit as his name left my mouth. "Yael . . . your power . . . it's related to the earth somehow, right?"

His eyes narrowed immediately. "Yes. Why?"

"Because while I could use some help filling in this hole, what I really need to know is if anyone disturbed my mother's grave before me, and I'm hoping you can determine that."

His elegant features tightened. "You want to know if I can determine who took the necklace."

"Yes . . . or at least if it was taken from her after she was laid to rest."

"That's a bold request—"

"I know, and I wouldn't ask if I didn't—"

"—but you've piqued my curiosity with your grave-robbing mystery, so I will do as you ask. Without expectation of a favor in return."

I let out a breath of relief. "Thank you."

"Do not thank me yet," he said as he slowly crouched down and pressed his hand to the earth. "I don't know if her grave has any tales to tell . . . "

He closed his eyes and hummed a melody, soft and sweet, as his hand caressed the inside edge of my mother's burial plot. The earth began to vibrate in tune with his song, shaking the ground I stood upon while I looked on in awe. Then, as quickly as it had started, it stopped, and Yael stood. "No one has moved this earth since the body was interred. That doesn't really help you, does it?"

"It does, just not in the way I'd hoped. I'd suspected it was spelled so it couldn't be removed."

His eyes narrowed yet again as he stared at me. "Then how is it gone?"

I considered my options carefully, knowing that Yael was smart and shrewd, just like Volker. Lying wouldn't work, but divulging too much wasn't a stellar plan either. Then again, maybe it just didn't matter anymore. "My mother was killed when I was thirteen, and I'm starting to wonder if the necklace was the motive behind her murder."

He studied me carefully. "It must be very powerful for someone to risk a war over it."

"War is only a risk if you know who did it, and her killer was never found."

"Then I'm left to wonder how hard Fire and Fluorite tried to find the one responsible," he said, edging closer. "The Moonlight Wraith may have been many things, but disloyal is not one of them. He did right by those in his House, and if any member of Air and Amethyst had met an untimely death, he would have hunted the killer to the edge of the earth and beyond until they felt his wrath. I'm surprised your leaders did not do the same. Besides, how hard could it be to find someone with a necklace that harbors some powerful spell or magic? One you would easily recognize, I assume?"

Good fucking question. "I guess I'll find out when I track the killer down—and kill them."

Yael's suspicious expression gave way to one of concern, something I'd never seen from him before. Not where I was concerned, at least. "Be careful, Rowe," he said as his brows pinched together. "You're playing with fire, and I think we both know how that ends."

I forced a smile. "I've watched you and Ravi in the kitchen. I get the gist."

Yael smiled back—one filled with actual, genuine amusement.

"You're entertaining, for a human," he said, retreating a step. "Try not to die on this mission of yours, would you? Myra will be insufferable if you do—"

"Why? Some days, I'm not sure if she even likes me."

"Oh no, not because of that," he replied, smiling wider still. "We just won't have you as a buffer anymore."

His delivery was perfection, and I couldn't help but laugh. "And with Sasha still MIA . . . "

"Exactly. I'm glad you better understand the stakes now."

I smiled at him, a tiny warmth brewing in my chest. "I do. I wouldn't want you all to suffer in my absence," I said before my smile faded and awkwardness settled in. I looked up at Yael as I fought to keep my emotions at bay. "Thanks for this, Yael. Really."

"I would be lying if I said it wasn't nice to be needed again. For something other than menial labor."

The weight of his words impaled me, and I reached out and took his hand in mine without thinking. He looked down at where they were joined before his eyes snapped up to mine, wide with surprise.

"You'll get back to where you belong, Yael—I know it." I squeezed his hand, then let it drop as I turned and walked away before my tears could fall. It had never dawned on me that Volker's quest for vengeance might not be solely for his own benefit; that he might be doing it to help those like Yael, who had been displaced for their loyalty. And to avenge those that had died because of theirs.

"I guess I'll just stay behind and clean up your mess," he called after me. "Literally."

"I'll make it up to you soon."

"That sounds dangerously like a promised favor, *human*."

"I'll keep Myra out of your hair this weekend."

His muffled curses trailed me as I left the graveyard and headed for home with sadness weighing on me but a renewed sense of purpose.

I'd find not only my mother's necklace, but the one who'd killed her along with it.

And once the spell was broken, I'd get power and vengeance all my own.

I threw open the door to my apartment, the details of Yael's visit to my mother's grave on the tip of my tongue, ready to report to Volker. But when I flipped on the lights and barged into the room, I found it empty. No fae assassin lurking in the corner. No painfully handsome ally awaiting the news. Disappointment shot through me, but I quickly rationalized it away.

Emotionally frazzled and covered in dirt, I walked to the bathroom and turned on the shower. I stripped off my clothes while I waited for the water to heat up, then stepped in front of the mirror for a quick look. Staring back at me was a completely exhausted version of myself.

The stress of everything going on had taken its toll physically. Dark circles lined the bottoms of my eyes, and my cheekbones looked sharper than usual, looming above the gaunt hollows just below them. Had I eaten that day? The day before? It was all a blur of chaos and adrenaline—one I couldn't sustain forever.

I let out a breath and pulled the shower curtain back, metal rings screeching along the rod. The scalding water pelted my leg as I stepped in, and I sucked in a breath as I quickly adjusted the temperature to one that wouldn't cook the flesh right off my bones. That was definitely not a problem I needed to add to the list.

"Fucking water heater," I mumbled as I cranked the cold water knob.

Once the temperature evened out, I grabbed the soap to wash away any reminder of the grim ordeal. As my hands swept across my skin, scrubbing it clean, I thought of Volker. The intensity in his eyes as he'd gently taken the shovel from my hand. His soft touch while wiping my tears. The strange expression he'd worn as he'd let them run along his fingertips. Even amid all the mystery and confusion, I was certain I hadn't imagined that look in his eyes—the humanity lurking in their depths.

The longing.

My hand passed over my stomach, and a rush of heat pooled between my legs as the image of Volker touching me in the same way overtook my mind. Lower and lower it sank, until it neared where that sudden sense of throbbing need now consumed me. My hand —*his* hand—pressed against it, and a moan escaped my lips.

One that soon turned to a cry of surprise when the water suddenly ran ice-cold, sending me scrambling to escape the shower. I tripped on the tub's edge and keeled forward into the bathroom door, slamming it shut. The rug gave way beneath me, and I collapsed to the floor by the sink in a naked, panting heap. And not the good kind.

Flustered and freezing, I grabbed a towel to dry off, then slipped into shorts and a tee for bed. Clearly, I needed sleep after what had just transpired. If ever I'd needed a sign that my mental wanderings were far off course, that had been it. *Message received, universe. Message received.*

Too tired to rummage the fridge for edible leftovers (if they even existed), I schlepped over to the bed and flipped off the light. My phone screen sprang to life as I flopped down on the mattress and pulled the covers over me, my mind still playing the fantasy of Volker on repeat like it hadn't gotten the not-so-subtle hint in the bathroom.

"Ugh . . . I hate me sometimes," I groaned as I checked the phone to see who'd messaged. Andreas' name popped up on the screen, and I stared at it for a moment before tossing it down on the nightstand. I could deal with his party taunting in the morning. For now, I needed sleep to get control of my traitorous mind so I could refocus on my mother's killer in the morning. But as my eyes closed and slumber loomed, my thoughts drifted back once more to the fae assassin who'd bulldozed his way into my life and taken root in a way I couldn't explain.

There would be no plucking him from my mind, no matter how hard I tried.

CHAPTER 18
ROWE

"How was your little fae friend?" Volker asked from the shadows. "Did he take care of everything?"

I leaned against the kitchen sink and waited for him to emerge from the darkness like a bad omen. His skin gleamed in the scant light of the room, and it was all I could do to keep myself from touching it. "He did."

Volker's gaze raked over me as I stood there in my black shorts and cropped shirt, bare legs locked out a few inches in front of me. "Everything?" he asked again, his eyes lingering on the skin-tight shorts barely covering me.

"Everything you and I discussed." I stood up straighter to face him, wondering why in the hell he sounded so jealous—and why I liked it so much.

"Good." His eyes slowly made their way up the rest of me until they leveled on mine. Mischief sparkled in the dark depths, and I sucked in a breath as he leaned in closer. "I wouldn't want to have to kill him."

"Save that for the queen," I whispered.

His hand trailed up my thigh to my hip, then along my side, skim-

ming my breast before it reached my collarbone. "Oh, I plan to." He traced it with painful slowness until his fingertip caught the chain of my necklace. "It's only a matter of time until she gets what's coming to her." I swallowed hard, my heart slamming against my ribs as he stared down at me. "Does that scare you, little queen? That I'm capable of such cold, calculated murder?"

"No . . ."

That wicked smirk that made me insane graced his expression as his face drew closer to mine. "I think you're lying."

"I'm not—"

"I think, deep down inside, I scare you—"

"No—"

"—not because of what I am, but because you like it. Because it does something to you that you don't want to admit."

I inhaled sharply and let it out slowly, trying to calm myself. Because he was right. There was a small part of me that reveled in his darkness—was excited by exactly what he was.

Instead of admitting as much, I notched my chin higher and stared back. "I'm not scared."

His finger trailed along my necklace, catching on the gabbro stone pendant. "Not yet . . ."

He toyed with it for a moment, and I tried to keep my pounding heart from giving me away. Blood thundered through my veins and pulsed between my thighs, the need building to an unbearable level. Maybe I liked what he did to me way more than I should have.

But at that moment, I didn't give a shit.

He lifted the black stone and delicately ran his finger along the craggy edges. "It's strange that something so small could contain so much power." He placed the gabbro back in its spot at the notch of my throat and stared at me like he was looking right into my soul. "It seems like such a fragile, breakable thing."

"But it isn't," I said, my voice low and breathy and as traitorous as my devolving thoughts. "It's stronger than you imagine—more than you expect."

"In so many ways." His fingers continued down along my sternum, snagging on the v-neck of my shirt. "It is a puzzle I can't yet solve, but I don't care. I must have it regardless." The cotton of my shirt stretched as he dragged that finger lower still, the collar finally giving way so his hand could slide between my breasts. "It must be mine."

"But you can't have it without me."

His head dipped lower, his tousled hair tickling my face as he whispered in my ear. "Perhaps that's exactly what I want . . ."

The cold touch of his palm against the bare strip of exposed skin on my stomach sent a shiver through me that I couldn't contain, and the look of amusement in those endless pewter eyes did nothing to help. He stared back with wicked delight at what he'd done—what he planned to do.

With painstaking slowness, his finger traced along the waist of my shorts, teasing me as he tugged gently at the elastic. I held my breath, paralyzed with anticipation, as his fingers ventured beneath the satiny fabric. The second they met the soft flesh of my core, I sucked in a breath.

His mischievous smile widened at my reaction. "Perhaps I want both." I struggled to control my breathing as his finger teased between my legs. "Would you like that, little queen? To be mine?"

"Yes . . ."

"Would you bind that power to me?" he asked as he drew his nose along my cheek. "To save yourself?"

"Yes . . ."

"Will you bring me vengeance against the queen as I bring you pleasure now?"

I swallowed hard. "Yes."

With lightning speed, he spun me around and pressed me against the wall, his hand quickly finding its place again. "Then I will bring you both to your knees," he growled in my ear as he slipped his finger inside me.

Warmth exploded through my core, and I threw my head back as an animalistic cry ripped from my throat.

One that woke me from my dream.

I shot up in bed, panting and sweating. It had all seemed so real—the tingling and throbbing between my legs could attest to that—and yet there I sat in the darkness, very much alone. With a heavy exhale, I flopped back on the bed and pushed the hair stuck to my sweaty face aside. In just a few days, I'd gone from learning of my necklace's power, to digging up my mother's grave, to having sex dreams about the surly fae hell-bent on using me for his revenge. I scrubbed my hand over my face and wondered what else could go wrong.

Then I heard a floorboard in the corner creak.

I launched to my feet, my crop top and tiny skin-tight shorts on full display for said surly fae as he emerged from the shadows, smiling.

Not a smug smile. Not an all-knowing smirk. An honest-to-gods amused smile, which was far more unnerving than I could have ever imagined. His eyes raked over my barely covered bits as I stood there, still breathing hard. "What are you doing here?" I asked, desperate to yank the blanket off the bed and cover myself under the weight of those steely eyes, but I held my ground. And that fact seemed to amuse him more.

"Has anyone ever told you that you make the most . . . *interesting* noises when you sleep?"

"Has anyone ever told you that breaking into someone's apartment to watch them sleep is as disturbing as it is illegal?"

"Do I look concerned about that?" he asked as he stepped closer.

"Not a damn bit." I folded my arms under my chest, and his eyes dropped to the V of my shirt and the cleavage peeking out of it. Heat shot through me at the memory of my dream. Where his hands had gone. What I'd wanted them to do. "But maybe *I* am."

"Oh, I don't think that's what concerns you right now." He advanced another step. Then another. Then another, until there was only a few inches and the tension in the room separating us.

"What concerns me?" I asked, my husky, sleep-filled voice doing all it could to give me away.

"Many things, I imagine, but a few in particular."

"Like what?"

"Like who killed your mother," he said, staring down at me. "How you'll get her necklace back. If I can be trusted . . . " His heavy gaze shifted to my lips, then slowly made its way up to meet my eyes. "What I'll do with you once you give me what I want."

"That might have crossed my mind."

The corner of his mouth hitched at my words. "I'll just bet it has."

"But none of that matters if we can't get the necklace back," I said, straightening my spine.

"So very true, little queen, which is why I'm here. I plan to take it from her soon. She's at the embassy now; I merely have to verify her routine there, then I can make my move. It's the next logical step."

"How in the hell are you going to do that?" I did little to hide my incredulous tone. "It's not like you can just roll up there, waltz in, and snatch it off her person. Especially if your power is wonky."

"That's not a matter you need to concern yourself with."

"When are you planning to do this?"

"I'll go tonight."

"Great, then I'm coming with—"

I cut myself off, realizing what day it was: Andreas' party. There was no way I was getting out of that.

"You most certainly are not," Volker said, pulling me from my frustrated musings.

"I know," I groused. "I have to go to a party at Andreas' tonight."

Volker's devilish expression quickly fell away, leaving the true visage of the Moonlight Wraith in its wake. "So you'll be busy with the little wolf while I'm gone?"

"I'll be hating life at his party, yes," I said, correcting his assessment.

"I'm sure he'll keep you occupied in my absence." Anger simmered in his eyes before his smirk returned with a vengeance. "Or he'll try to, at least." He leaned closer to me, and that damned heat surged through my body again. "I'm not so easily replaced."

I ignored the implication of his words, clearly meant to tease me, and stayed focused on the danger he faced. "No," I said, pushing past him to pace the room. "This is a stupid plan."

"There is only one way to get your mother's necklace. I need to assume the identity of someone close to the queen, then steal it. Now that she is here in Portland, her routine has changed slightly, and I need to get closer to confirm a few things."

"And if you get caught on this mission?" I shouted at him. "How effective will your vengeance be then?"

"I won't get caught—"

"You don't know that—"

"Yes, I do."

"Ugh . . . fucking arrogant fairy," I groaned, fisting my hands in my hair. "If you screw this up, you're not just messing things up for yourself, you know? My chance at getting my power hangs in the balance, too. It's not all about you!"

That cold, hard stare met mine, and the reality of who I was yelling at pierced my gut. "I am well aware that this is not all about me, little queen. I am not doing this for myself alone." He closed the distance between us in a blink, his body nearly flush with mine, and I flinched, prepared to weather his anger as I had when he'd first come to my home making demands. But instead of violent hands around my arms, pinning me to the wall, I found narrowed, angry eyes boring holes through mine. "I am not the only one seeking vengeance anymore. I am not the only one who wishes to see the queen take one final, labored breath. If she was indeed the one who killed your mother, then you and I share the same goal, and my mission is to make that possible. Do not forget that."

Moonlight spilled in through the window and framed his silhouette in a gloriously terrifying way. He was pale death; an ethereal killer. I stared up at him in fear and awe. "You really are an angel of death," I said, the words escaping without thought.

"Yes . . . " he replied, those dark eyes glowing silver from deep within. "But not for you."

He stood there for a moment, body stiff and jaw tight, before he turned on his heels, headed for the door. The screech of the metal echoed through the room, nearly distorting his parting words as he stormed out of my apartment.

But I'd heard them nonetheless.

'Never for you' echoed through my mind, sending that warm feeling through my veins yet again—until my brain stepped in. Volker couldn't exactly use my power if I were dead. And once he was done, I was willing to bet he'd want me to do exactly what my dream had prophesied: bind that power to him.

His sentiment wasn't a romantic notion. It was a tactical move to keep him from ever meeting that same fate again.

I flopped back down on the bed, my lips flapping as I exhaled hard. My fantasies were muddying my reality, and I needed to get a handle on that ASAP. Before I let my guard down.

Before I did something really stupid.

CHAPTER 19
ROWE

I woke up later that morning nervous and edgy, knowing that I'd be hanging out at a party while Volker was off putting his skulking skills to good use. I knew he shouldn't be in any real danger on his reconnaissance mission, but still, the tightness in my chest wouldn't abate, no matter what I did. I needed a distraction, and unfortunately, I didn't even have work to help out with that; Shade had given me the day off, and Myra hadn't called in a crisis courtesy of Sasha's absent ass, so I spent the better part of the morning getting caught up on laundry until I couldn't stand it any longer.

Before too long, I was standing outside Shade's office. "Hey," I said, knocking on the open door. "I know I'm not supposed to be working today, but I was getting a little squirrely over at my apartment, so I thought I'd come see if you needed anything?"

"Other than something to unite the House again?" he asked, an unexpected hopelessness in his voice. It caught me off guard, which must have shown on my face, because he quickly forced a tight smile. "No, Rowe. I'm good." He propped his elbows on the desk and leaned his head against his hands.

"You don't look like you're good," I said, edging into the room. "You look like someone kicked you in the nuts."

"Well, that's about how I feel. Fire and Fluorite is in a real mess, and I'm not sure how to fix it."

"Is it possible?"

"It is . . . I think. But it will take something big to unite us."

"Well," I said, smiling tentatively, "if anyone can pull it off, it's you."

He lifted his head enough to smile back, but it didn't reach his eyes. Didn't wrinkle the corners like it normally would. "Andreas was adamant about you having the day to yourself—the night, too. Anything I should know about there?"

His parental tone was duly noted.

"He's just trying to do something nice for me. He's worried about me working so much and being lonely."

He nodded lightly. "Well, you've earned some time off, Rowe. I hope you enjoy it."

"I will, but don't worry, I won't get too used to it. I'll be pulling a double at the restaurant tomorrow. Probably Sunday, too," I said with a shrug. "Fucking Sasha . . . "

"Then I'd recommend against a repeat performance of last weekend," he said with a mischievous grin.

At that, I laughed. "You might want to tell your son that. I think he has BIG plans . . . "

"He always does, Rowe. Proceed accordingly."

"I will," I said as I turned to leave. "And I hope you find the solution you're looking for, Shade. Really. I don't like seeing you this way."

"It'll all work out somehow," he said under his breath as I swung the door open.

I looked back over my shoulder and winked at him. "It usually does."

I stepped out into the hallway and nearly slammed into Andreas, who stood just beyond the door. I jumped back, stifling a scream—

much to his amusement—and he slung his arm around my shoulder as I headed toward the back entrance. "You're not trying to get out of tonight, are you?" he asked as we walked down the dimly lit hall.

"Like you didn't just overhear our entire conversation," I countered.

"I did indeed. I especially liked the part at the end where you tried to throw me under the bus for being a bad influence."

"You mean when I *did* throw you under the bus?" I corrected.

He let out a laugh that rang through the narrow way. "I remain unfazed by your slander, Rowe. Now, about tonight—"

"I'm coming, I'm coming," I said, cutting him off, "calm down. I have to finish up my laundry and get some groceries. Other than that, I'm all yours."

He stopped short and stared down at me with a strange intensity in his eyes. "Just like I planned."

Maybe I was tired and horny from the night before, or maybe I was just stressed and my brain wasn't functioning correctly, because it felt a lot like Andreas was standing in the hallway of his father's home flirting with me, which, unless hell had frozen over, couldn't possibly be a thing.

Right?

My heart sped up and my palms began to sweat like I was still a sixteen-year-old girl whose crush had just asked her on a date. But the longer I stood there, the more I remembered that I wasn't that girl anymore. "I should probably go finish those things so I'm not late tonight," I said, slipping out from under his arm. "I forgot that I also have to pick up my pay from Ravi before that place gets crazy and he tries to make me stay."

"I wouldn't let him," he replied, body tensing at the promise of a fight.

"Down, boy. It'll be fine." His intense stare made me squirm a little as I turned to leave. "I'll see you tonight, Andreas."

He watched me as I walked away. "Yes, you sure will."

I snuck through the kitchen to Ravi's office, where he kept our payments locked in individual black lockers on the wall. It only took a second to unlock mine and grab the tiny vial of what appeared to be vampire venom, and I turned to leave, hoping I could get out of there without anyone noticing me. The roar of the crowd out front didn't bode well for the waitstaff, and I had no intention of getting roped into helping.

Doing my best to be invisible, I shuffled behind the cooks, who were working like madmen to fill orders, until I reached the back door: my portal to freedom. I pushed it open, but soon found my arm hijacked by one pissed-off-looking mermaid.

"Outside. Now," she said by way of greeting, then hauled my ass through the door like I was incapable of exiting on my own. Before it slammed shut, I heard footsteps behind us, and I turned to find Yael hovering near the closed door. "What happened with your mom?" she asked, her eyes darting from me to Yael. "I know this asshole knows something, but he wouldn't talk, so I expect you to."

"There's not much to tell. The necklace wasn't in the casket. Whoever killed her must have taken it."

"How are you going to find them?" she asked, her arms folded across her chest. "Didn't she die years ago?"

I let out a breath. "I'm pretty sure I know who has the necklace."

She spread her hands wide and made the 'then fucking tell me' face I'd seen too many times to count.

I steadied myself, then let the facts fly. "The queen of Air and Amethyst has it."

Boy, did that little tidbit knock the wind out of her sails. "I'm sorry, what did you just say?"

"I said, the queen of—"

"Oh, I fucking *heard* you," she said, cutting me off, "but your words don't make any sense. Because if the queen of Air and Amethyst did, in fact, kill your mother and now has that necklace in her possession, there's no way you're getting it back." Her disbelief was plain in her tone, but it was edged with concern, and I was starting to wonder if I understood my outcast coworkers at all. Neither she nor Yael was exactly the caring sort, and yet . . .

"I don't think her plan is to get it back from her, exactly," Yael replied for me. "Is it, Rowe?"

"What's that supposed to mean?" Myra asked, her irritation spilling over.

My lack of response tipped my hand.

"It means that I think our little human here is planning to kill the queen."

Myra's blue eyes went so wide they nearly popped out of her skull. "*Kill her*? The queen of Air and Amethyst? The fae who murdered the Moonlight Wraith? Are you fucking *high*? Is the human part of your questionably-human brain malfunctioning? Because you cannot possibly go after the queen, Rowe. It's a suicide mission."

"For once, I agree with the mermaid," Yael added, "though it pains me to admit it."

"You guys—"

"You'd need an army," Myra continued, "which you don't have, by the way. All you have is the puppy-dog, bad-boy wannabe that comes in here, and he isn't enough by a long shot."

Yael nodded in agreement. "As much as I'd love to see the queen fall, my money wouldn't be on you in this fight."

"Seriously, you two, just shut up for a minute—"

"Not until you promise not to go after the queen without a whole lot of backup," Myra shouted over me.

"I'm not going to go after her without an army, okay?" I yelled back. Silence fell between the three of us for a moment until Yael broke it.

"Then tell me where you're going to get an army to bring her down, because I don't want to miss this."

"It's not an army *per se*," I said, hedging slightly.

Myra's shock wore off, releasing her tongue. "Then what is it, Rowe?"

"A formidable force . . . how's that?"

"A tornado is a formidable force," she countered, hands on hips, prepared to do verbal battle. "My great aunt Myrtle is a formidable force. And neither of them is bringing down the queen."

"Perhaps you should go with her, Myra," Yael suggested—unhelpfully. "That resting bitch face of yours could surely do some damage."

"You guys—"

"Come closer and I'll show you damage, pretty little fairy boy."

"C'mon, you two—"

"You're out of your element, Myra. I, unlike you, haven't lost almost all connection to my magic—just my House."

"I don't need magic to bury my fist in your face," she said, lunging at him. I jumped in her path to intercept her, but she bulldozed right through me like I wasn't even standing there. She collided with Yael and drove him back against the door, fists swinging wildly. I knew they wouldn't stop until Myra beat him to death or Yael fought back with magic and did irreparable damage to her body—and pride.

"Stop it!" I screamed, trying to pry her off of Yael, who stood there, arms at his sides, dodging punches like a champ. "Myra, stop!" I managed to spin her around and nearly got decked for my efforts. Yael pinned her arms at her sides from behind her, and she struggled like a wild animal to get free.

"You need to calm down," I said, realizing how unhelpful that was as I said it, but the words were out, and her reaction was all I thought it would be.

"Get off of me!" she snapped at Yael.

"I'll let go of you when you get hold of yourself."

"All I'm going to get hold of in a minute is your fucking face—right before I break it."

"Enough!" I shouted at her. "That's enough."

"Says the girl who thinks she can kill the queen of Air and

Amethyst," she scoffed. "You and your imaginary *formidable force*." She stopped struggling for a moment to glare at me. "You don't have anyone to help you, Rowe, and you're going to die because of it." She shrugged out of Yael's hold and shoved past him to go back inside.

"I have the person I need to take her down," I clapped back at her, fear and anger and the tension of the moment driving my words.

Yael stared at me for a moment, eyes narrowed and shrewd and a little too focused on me. "I told you, there was only one that could stand against her," he said calmly, "and he's dead." I steadied my face, doing all I could to keep it from giving anything away. "You want to know a secret, Rowe?" I stood silent, not answering his rhetorical question but fearing the answer. "Something never sat well with me about the Moonlight Wraith's death," he continued. "The body was never seen by anyone who inquired about it."

Myra, breathing hard and lingering by the door, turned with eerie slowness, her angry expression now replaced by a dubious one. "Rowe . . . who told you about your magic?"

"Magic?" Yael repeated with disbelief of his own.

"That's what started this all," she explained. "Someone told Rowe she had magic, but she never said who—or wouldn't say."

Yael's eyes widened for a second before narrowing to slits. "I wonder if it's the same being who helped her dig up her mother's casket? Because as hard as you tried to sell that lie, there was no hint of your energy in the ground last night—I checked after you left me to clean up your mess." *Shit.* "But there was other energy . . . faint fae energy, as I recall. I couldn't tell whose because they did not use magic to disturb the earth, but their mark lingered all the same."

"Who was it?" Myra asked, stepping closer.

"Guys, listen, I know you're worried about me, but I promise you, I have things under control. You don't have to worry—"

"Because you have the aid of the one being who can kill the queen," Yael said, cutting me off. "Right?"

I swallowed hard, but said nothing.

The two of them shared a look of concern, as though Myra hadn't just been about to beat Yael to death, then turned to me. Myra took another step, and I backed away.

"Rowe, are you saying that—"

"I have to go!" I shouted, turning to run. "I'm sorry . . . "

I hauled ass down the alley until I hit the street, then kept on going. By not refuting Yael's insinuation, I'd fucked up big time, and I had no way to undo it. In my panic, leaving before I could make things any worse had seemed like my only course of action, because I surely would have caved under their scrutiny.

But as I ran through the streets, praying I could trust the two of them with the knowledge they'd inferred, I knew that my fuck-up could cost Volker and me both.

And if he found out, it would surely cost Myra and Yael their lives.

CHAPTER 20
ROWE

Volker didn't show for the rest of the afternoon. By evening, I was a jittery mess for more reasons than I could count, so I did what any unreasonable twenty-something would do—I started drinking early to take the edge off. Two or three shots and a grilled cheese later, I was ready to head over to the party. I'd waited as long as I could, hoping Volker would appear so I could try to do damage control somehow. Telling him that I'd spilled the beans, in a sense, wasn't going to end well, but him being ambushed by that information later seemed even worse. If Yael decided to go to the queen and warn her of the Wraith's reappearance in order to earn a reprieve from his House banishment, then Volker was potentially walking into a trap.

Did I think Yael would do this, based on his apparent hatred of the queen? No. But he hated his exile just as much, as far as I could tell, so I couldn't rule it out. I knew there had to be a way to avoid fallout from what I'd inadvertently done, but the solution hadn't come to me, not that it would have mattered if it had.

Volker didn't exactly have a cell phone, and I didn't have a bat signal to summon him.

I took a deep breath before I headed out for the night, lingering at the door in the hope that he'd slip out of the shadows behind me, but he didn't. And so my anxiety grew.

By the time I arrived at Andreas' house, the party was clearly in full swing. The music could be heard down the block, and it sounded like half the pack was there, at least. In truth, partying was the last thing I wanted to be doing, but with no way to reach Volker, I hoped it would prove to be a solid distraction until the fae assassin showed up in my room tonight to report on his evening—or maybe kill me for outing him. If he survived.

I walked around the side of the house to the back yard, where the firepit was roaring and bodies surrounded it as if they needed the heat to stay warm. Music blared through the outdoor speakers, and the deck and patio were filled with more familiar shifters—some I liked, others I didn't. I scanned the crowd, hoping to spot Andreas, but it was he who found me. He stepped out onto the deck with drinks in hand like he'd seen me coming and smiled.

"Now the party can start!" he shouted over the din. Some of his friends turned to see what he was talking about, then quickly went back to whatever they were doing.

Ah yes . . . a warm welcome.

He descended the steps and made his way over to me through the crowd. "I made you a margarita," he said, handing me the drink. "Lots of salt."

"You're a good friend," I replied as I took the offering and swallowed back a few gulps.

He laughed at my antics. "So it's gonna be that kinda night, huh?"

"I'm already in deep. No sense in stopping now."

"Was the thought of partying with me so bad that you had to pregame?"

I swatted his arm, then flapped my hand, trying to ease the sting. "Owww . . . is your tricep made of stone or something? That hurt."

"Instant karma—she can be a cruel one, Rowe."

"I don't need any more cruel women in my life," I replied, taking another sip. "I have Myra."

As we stood on the perimeter of the crowd, someone yelled something about the fights starting on TV in a few minutes. Like clockwork, virtually everyone in the yard filed into the house, riled up at the promise of violence. Andreas took my hand to lead me inside, but I pulled back. He looked down at me, and I shrugged. "I believe I was promised my favorite song no less than four times tonight," I said, feigning irritation. "And I'm going to need a few more drinks before I can watch fights with that crowd."

Andreas smiled. "You were indeed promised that. And I didn't have any plans to watch the fights with those assholes tonight, but I can get those drinks ready for you all the same. Come inside with me, and I'll get that taken care of right away."

"I'll hang out here while you do that," I said. "Enjoy the stars in peace for a few minutes."

"You're not thinking of making a break for it, are you? Because a house full of shifters will make it hard for you to get very far."

"Song. Drinks. Now," I replied before I downed the rest of my drink and handed him the empty.

He laughed as he took it, then turned to jog back to the house. His commitment to me having a fun night was admirable, especially when it seemed pretty clear that some of the others weren't thrilled with my presence, the backlash of still being friends with Danni and Adora—and a human in their midst.

At least as far as they knew.

I stared at the brightly moonlit sky and smiled as I took a deep breath, soaking in the unseasonably warm night and the smell of the campfire. A light breeze tickled my bare arms, and I tipped my head back to gaze at the starry night sky above. The moon's silvery face seemed to smirk at me in amusement, and thoughts of Volker immediately came to mind—both welcome and not—followed by the worry the alcohol had temporarily eclipsed.

It was clearly the solution to my problems.

"You might want to pace yourself better," a sultry voice murmured in my ear. I nearly screamed in response, but Volker, smart son of a bitch that he was, knew that was likely and slipped his hand over my mouth to silence me before I caused a scene.

In one smooth motion, he pulled me into the massive trees that lined the back of the yard, completely out of sight from anyone in the house—like Andreas. Terror shot through me, but it quickly turned to heat the second my back pressed against his hard body. I bit my lip to stifle the gasp (or moan) that threatened to sneak past my lips and balled my hands at my sides to keep from grabbing his strong legs.

His chest reverberated with a faint rumble that carried through me in the most scandalizing way. "You seem jumpy tonight, little queen," he whispered in my ear. "Is there a reason for that?"

He slowly released my mouth but made no effort to put distance between us. Instead, he dropped his hand to my waist and drew me further back into the shadows of the trees. The thrum of desire pulsated through me like a living thing, and I took a deep breath to try to clear my mind of the thoughts bombarding it. Memories of the dream I'd had.

"Maybe it's because you snuck up on me," I replied with all the forced sarcasm I could muster, still trying to steady my breathing.

Then a completely different train of thought permeated my drunk and horny haze—one involving Myra and Yael and a secret they most certainly weren't supposed to know. Through that filter, Volker's surprise visit took on a potentially different meaning.

"I wanted to see you before I left," he said, fingertips pressing against my stomach, "and I didn't think strolling into the yard while your wolf cub stood watch was the best idea."

"Why did you want to see me?" I asked, trying to focus on how to deal with the issue of Myra and Yael in a way that wouldn't get them hurt or killed, but that was nearly impossible while Volker's fingers stroked my belly and the strength of his body caged me in from behind. "Is something wrong?"

"I don't know . . . *is* something wrong, little queen?"

The way he said that word set my nerves on edge, and my tongue took off without my brain's approval. "I think my friend from work knows you're alive."

I tried to turn in his arms to face him, but his grip was like iron. "And how would he know that?"

"Because I said something tonight—something that aroused suspicion in him. Combined with the suspicions he already had from the graveyard and my previous questions about the queen, he kinda put it together," I said, fear snaking up my spine, "but I never said your name to confirm anything—and neither did he."

"Semantics, little queen—"

"I don't want you to hurt him."

"Then you probably shouldn't have told me—"

"I didn't really have a choice," I argued, wriggling in his hold. But that damn hand pressed against my belly harder and pinned me in place. I let out a frustrated sound, then said, "I had to tell you before you went tonight."

Silence. "Because you think he might warn the queen somehow?"

I shook my head. "I don't think so, but I couldn't risk it."

"So you risked him instead?" he asked, his lips at my ear. His firm hold was unrelenting, so I craned my head to see him. I found his piercing stare looking back at me, magically illuminated from within and assessing my expression in the darkness.

"I don't want to risk *either* of you."

His eyes flared brighter for a moment. "Are you worried, little queen?"

"Well, I'm not *not* worried," I argued. "I don't want you to hurt Yael. I don't want you to walk into a trap, either. But if I ever want to get these powers of mine, I need you to get my mother's necklace back, so . . . "

His fingers relaxed a bit, then flexed against my belly ever so slightly. "Are you worried I won't?" he rumbled in my ear. "Or is it something else?"

The back door flew open, and Andreas stepped out into the

seemingly empty yard. Volker's arm tensed around me. "Rowe? Are you out here?"

Volker's lips brushed my ear. "*Shhhhh.*"

"*Rowe?*" Andreas called again as he scanned the back yard for any sign of me, eyes narrowed and ears perked. He hovered there for a while, gaze focused on the trees that offered us shelter, but I knew he could see in the dark with relative ease, and panic quickly set in. The second he laid his sights on me—and the assassin at my back—all hell would break loose for sure. And with his pack just inside, drinking and ready to brawl, there was no way it would end well.

I took a deep breath to steady my nerves, then prepared to step from the shadows, alone. Volker's hold on me tightened like a vise, securing me in place.

Andreas lingered for a moment more, then turned back to the house, calling my name as he walked through the door.

Seconds passed in silence as Volker held me still until he finally broke it. "It's almost as if he senses my presence in his territory," he whispered in my ear. Every nerve in my body came to life at the feel of his soft breath tickling my ear.

"Maybe he can," I replied, heart pounding and breathless.

"As if he knows a threat is near."

"But you're not threatening his territory," I said, pointing out what seemed obvious.

He pressed his hand harder against my stomach. "Aren't I?" My mind scrambled to sort through the potential subtext in his words. "I should go before he returns," he said, releasing me as he backed away. "I'll see you soon, little queen."

I turned to find that smirk staring back at me in the darkness. "Be careful."

It widened at my words. "Always."

In the blink of an eye, the darkness enveloped him, and he disappeared from sight.

I was getting kinda tired of that routine, but my irritation was cut short when Andreas came barging out onto the porch again, worry furrowing his brow. "Rowe? Are you out here?"

"Yes," I called from the trees. I stepped out into the moonlight just as he jumped over the deck's railing and landed gracefully in the middle of the yard. He hurried over to me like I was bleeding to death, and I forced a smile to calm him.

"Where were you?"

In the woods with a gorgeous fae assassin.

"Emergency pee," I lied, hoping he'd buy it. "My pre-party whiskey hit me hard, and I didn't feel like running into the house like my pants were on fire so the guys could give me shit about it."

The tension in his expression eased a little. "Didn't you hear me calling you earlier?"

"I did, but I didn't answer because, well . . . let's face it. It wasn't one of my better ideas, but I was in deep at that point, and I was hoping I could get away with it somehow. But here I am, totally busted." I shrugged my shoulders, my arms splayed wide. "Probably should have just endured the boys' razzing—it might have been less humiliating."

At that, he smiled. "Pretty sure we've all peed in the woods before, Rowe. It's not a big deal."

"Maybe not for shifters," I countered, "but humans generally try to use the bathroom whenever possible. It's an unspoken expectation."

"I'll try to remember that. And if you give me a heads-up next time, I'll wait until you're done to queue up your song so you don't miss it."

Dammit. I hadn't even noticed it was on. The distraction Volker provided had been too strong to ignore. "That's okay. You owe me three more anyway . . . "

He laughed as he looped his arm around my shoulders, bottle of booze in hand, and led us over to a bench near a beautifully landscaped patio close to the house. I took a seat near the end and he sat down right next to me. Together, we stared at the night sky for a while, passing the bottle back and forth between us while we bantered about work, life, and the apparent shenanigans going on inside the house, given the ruckus we could hear all the way outside. But about ten or fifteen minutes into what seemed like a fun, light conversation, his warm brown eyes met mine as I looked over at him, and I found concern etching his brow yet again. But this time an unknown sadness lurked behind it.

I stiffened at the sight.

"I'm worried about you, Rowe" he said softly. "You're not yourself lately, and I think I know why."

Oh. Shit.

"Why?" I asked, doing all I could to remain neutral and passive with just the right amount of curiosity to avoid suspicion. Andreas was like his father—keen and smart—a deadly combo if you needed to lie your pants off to that person.

"I know you miss the girls," he said, straining to mention them without growling out their names, "but I think it's more than that."

"Oh . . . ?"

He shifted on the bench to better face me. "The anniversary of your mother's death is coming up soon . . . " His words hung in the air —both spoken and unspoken—as he watched my response.

Shame washed through me and I hung my head. In all the craziness, I'd forgotten all about that fact, which was ironic given that I'd just helped dig up her grave. My focus had been solely on the necklace, so much so that I'd all but forgotten about the person who'd worn it.

Not one of my finer moments.

I grabbed the bottle of whiskey from his hand and tossed it back, not sure what to say. Unable to swallow anymore, I had to answer. "You're right. I'm not myself lately, and Mom definitely has something to do with it," I said, absentmindedly pulling out my necklace to rub the gabbro stone. "It's all still so unsettled, and the older I get, the more I want answers. The anniversary of her death just brings attention to that fact."

"I know Mathis and Dad did all they could to find who killed her, but there was nothing to work with. I remember eavesdropping on their conversations about it. The killer was all but a ghost."

"Yeah, I know. But it's not just that."

I stole a glance at him to find a pensive look on his face. "What else?"

My gaze dropped to the stone between my fingertips. "Mom gave me this when I was little," I said, letting it drop against my chest. "When I was older, she told me that it was special—that it would protect me—but . . . I think she lied."

His soft brown eyes met mine as concern furrowed his brow. "What makes you say that?"

"Because she had one just like it that she always wore, but no one ever gave it to me after she died. I think that whoever killed her took it." Pain ripped through me at the thought, and I put the bottle of whiskey dangling in my hand back to my lips, hoping to wash away the swell of emotions rising within me. "Murdered over a 'protection' stone . . . if that wouldn't be irony at its finest, I don't know what would."

"Where is all this coming from?" he asked as his eyes fell to the gabbro stone nestled in the notch of my throat.

"It's just something I realized recently—something I never thought much about because I was basically still a kid when she died."

"Maybe your Mom's stone did something different? Maybe hers wasn't for protection."

I shook my head, my wild waves dancing around my shoulders. "I spoke to Myra about it, and she said that if Mom had a matching gabbro, they had to be related—they're too rare for them not to be."

Andreas sat back a bit to better take me in. I could see that he wanted to believe me, but doubt plagued his expression. I was sure the fact that there was no love lost between him and the mermaid didn't help at all. "Okay . . . let's suppose she's right. They were tied together somehow, and they weren't charmed for protection. Then what did they do? And what does yours do now, if your mom's is missing?"

I threw back another sip from the bottle. I was going to need it before I dropped that particular bomb on him.

"I think maybe it suppresses something," I said, leaning in closer to whisper, "like power."

I pulled away to find shock had overtaken his expression. "*Power*? Why would your mom suppress her power? And how could it suppress power you don't have?" he asked, muddling through the implications until the obvious one hit him hard. "Or do you . . . ?" I waited for a moment to let him catch up, my lips pressed to a sympathetic smile of sorts. "You think your mom suppressed power you've never known you have since you were young?"

"Mhm," I mumbled against the mouth of the bottle before I took another sip.

Andreas quickly snatched it back from me and took a massive swig. "So you're saying you think you're a witch too—like with *active powers*, not just by genetic ties?"

"No," I said, hesitating slightly. "I think I'm something else altogether. Something special."

His tense expression softened. "You're already special, Rowe—"

"No," I said, trying to keep him focused, "that's not what I mean. Something one of a kind. Something filled with unique magic."

"Or endless whiskey, at the moment," he countered, pulling the bottle away from my grasp with a playful smile.

"I'm serious, Andreas," I said, lowering my drunken volume. "It's supposed to be a secret . . . but maybe I can tell you." I thought about all the times I'd confided in him after my mother had died. How, for a long time—before I'd gotten to know the girls—he'd been the only person close to me that I'd truly trusted. The one I'd shared everything with. The one I'd always turned to. Things had changed a bit as I'd gotten older and his importance in the House had grown, but sitting there with him in front of me, it felt just like it had years ago, and I wondered . . . . "Maybe it'll be just like old times, like when I was a goofy teenager and you hung out with me for some unknown reason."

He edged in closer, voice soft and low as he spoke. "You were never just a goofy teenager to me. And like old times or not, I'm going to need you to tell me, because I may look like I'm totally calm, but I'm freaking out a bit inside," he said, before taking another sip.

I sheltered my mouth with my hand, as though that could do anything in a property full of shifters, and leaned in so close our noses nearly touched. "I think I'm the *wellspring*," I whispered.

I pulled away enough to see his eyes go wide with surprise—or disbelief. I was rapidly becoming too drunk to tell. "Rowe . . . I don't want to be a dick about this, but I'm pretty sure someone in the entire House would have noticed if you were the wellspring. Who put that idea in your head?"

"Not if this suppresses my power," I argued, holding up the gabbro stone, ignoring his question entirely.

"Is that what Myra told you it does?"

"I mean, not exactly, but kinda? She said I'd need my mom's stone to find out—and to break the spell."

He sat in silence for a moment, scratching his upper arm—a nervous tell I think only I'd ever noticed—which was a bad sign to be sure.

"Rowe," he finally said, sounding painfully serious, "did it ever cross your mind that she might be fucking with you?"

I immediately shook my head. "She's not. She's trying to help. Yael, too. We're going to find my mother's necklace so we can break the spell and find her killer."

He pressed the bottle to his lips again and tossed his head back, draining way more of its contents than was safe for a human. When he came back up for air, I snatched the bottle back and cradled it to my chest so he couldn't pilfer any more.

"So the three of you are going to find the necklace, break the spell, and release your wellspring powers so you can use them to avenge your mother's death?"

"I mean, I hadn't planned to involve them in the killing part." Because I had Volker for that. But that was a tiny detail I couldn't share with him.

"And then what? Run away and live a life of solitude until you go insane?" he asked, concern in his voice. "You do know that's what happens to the wellspring, right? They go mad at some point."

"I might have heard that rumor, yes—"

"Rowe, this is crazy, even for you, and I say that in the most loving, non-gaslighting way possible."

"Um . . . thanks?"

"Let's just say that you're right, that you're the wellspring and that someone killed your mother to get her necklace. How will you avenge her?" He leaned forward, pity simmering in his stare as he rested his hand on my knee. "The wellspring doesn't have offensive magic, Rowe. They're just a source of power for those that do. You can't use that power to avenge your mother on your own . . . you'll need help."

"I'll have help—"

"From who? Yael? Myra? Because you just said you wouldn't involve them."

"I guess I didn't really think that part of my plan through yet."

"You need to be careful," he continued, desperation in his tone. "If you *are* right, and you somehow get your power back, you'll be a target for just about every supernatural out there looking to bind that magic to them."

"But I'd have to do it willingly," I said, the statement coming out far more like a question than I wanted it to. "They can't *make* me . . . "

The longer he stared at me in silence, the more my nerves frayed. Even the whiskey wasn't helping calm them. "We need to talk to Dad about this—"

"No!" I shouted before lowering my voice. "Not until I know more. I don't want him to think I've lost my mind. It's bad enough having you look at me like I have."

He pushed a stray hair from my face and tucked it behind my ear. "I don't think you've lost your mind. I'm just worried about you."

"That's basically the same thing."

"No," he said, resting his hand on my knee, "it isn't. I believe that you believe this, which is enough for me. You know I loved your mom. If someone killed her to get her necklace, then I want justice for her too." He stared at me for a moment, any earlier shred of doubt now absent from his expression. "And if you need my help to avenge her, I'm in."

I lifted my eyes. "You'd do that for me?"

"That and more—but I'd definitely feel better about that agreement if I knew who I was up against."

"What if I told you that I think I know who did it?"

His deep brown eyes narrowed. "Who?"

I took a steadying breath. "The queen of Air and Amethyst."

"*What*? Why do you think that?"

Shit. "Umm . . . someone at the restaurant saw my necklace and said they'd seen the queen wearing one just like it."

He let out a long breath. "That's not good, Rowe—"

"I know—"

"—but it doesn't change anything." My mouth hung open and my prepared arguments fell dead on my tongue.

"It doesn't?"

He shook his head. "It's you and me. Always."

His intense gaze pressed down upon me, full of something I'd never seen from him before. Something I would have given my left arm to see from him when I was fifteen.

But I wasn't that kid anymore. And as he leaned in closer, his eyes focused on mine, all I could think about was the mystery behind my mother's death, the stone at my neck, and the fae assassin risking his life at that very moment to figure out how to get the stolen necklace back—even if it was as much for his benefit as my own.

The longer my thoughts lingered on him, the more the memory of his hand on my stomach, his lips at my ear, and the way he'd looked at me when he'd stolen the rogue tear from my cheek the night before became muddled.

My mixed emotions swirled uncomfortably in my gut, driving me to my feet. "I don't feel so good," I said, swaying a little. "I should probably go home."

Andreas was on his feet in a second. "Rowe, I'm sorry if I upset you—"

"It's not that," I said, waving him off with the bottle of whiskey still in my hand. "I'm just—I shouldn't have said anything about this. It's my problem to deal with. You and your dad have enough going on with the House. Just forget I said anything—write it off as crazy drunken Rowe ramblings."

"You're not crazy—"

"I feel pretty crazy," I muttered under my breath.

"I heard that," he said, reaching for me as I staggered back a step and nearly fell. "Why don't you stay and sober up a bit?"

"Staying will one hundred percent *not* help with that," I argued.

"Fine. Then let me drive you, at least." He reached to take my arm, but I ducked out of his grasp. I smiled at my sly maneuver until I tripped on a paver and nearly ate shit. I managed to right myself, narrowly avoiding disaster—especially given that a bunch of the guys had made their way out onto the deck to watch the entertainment provided by the inebriated human.

"This isn't my first drunken walk home, my friend."

"I'm confident about that," he deadpanned, "but it's a solid thirty minute walk when you're sober, Rowe—"

"I'll be fine. I promise." His frown said he didn't agree, but he didn't push the issue. Probably because he knew I was a stubborn mule when it came to things like that. Human things. "I'll text you once I get there." I waved the bottle at him and smiled. "I hope you have another of these, because I'm taking this guy on the road with me."

He shook his head and let out a nervous laugh. "I've been turned down for Jack Daniels. I have no idea how I should feel about that."

"Don't take it personally. Jack and I have always had a good thing going."

I turned to leave just as the song I'd been promised played for the second time that night. Bowie's lyrics to "Rebel, Rebel" nearly eclipsed Andreas' 'I thought we did, too' that trailed me as I rounded the side of the house.

I should have been elated at the sound of them.

Instead, all I felt was confused.

CHAPTER 21
VOLKER

I lingered in the shadows near the Air and Amethyst embassy, watching. Waiting. Whatever reconnaissance I'd done prior to finding Rowe no longer applied, given that the queen had left her Canadian estate to come to Portland in the last few days. There were only two reasons why she would have done so: knowledge that Fire and Fluorite was struggling, or word of my existence. Since she'd arrived before Rowe's fae friend had inferred that I was still alive, it wasn't because of him.

But that didn't mean he didn't still pose a threat.

If he did indeed decide to trade information for his reinstatement, then I'd lose the element of surprise, which I sorely needed to get what I wanted. So my plan for the evening had changed.

It was no longer a reconnaissance mission.

I was going to get the necklace.

Watching the guards from the darkness of an alley across the street, it became painfully clear that Nyssa was every bit the amateur I'd expected her to be. During her short reign, her arrogance had blinded her to the importance of a varied routine, and that would be her undoing. Her predictable schedule would provide me all the opportunity I needed to slip into her room under the glamour of one of her trusted inner circle. Fae I knew well enough to imitate with the help of magic.

A risk I'd have to take to secure my revenge.

My gaze cut to the moon above, and I muttered a prayer to her under my breath. That she would not fail me that night. That my power would be stable long enough to get what I'd come for.

And that my suspicion about the necklace would be true. If it was, my mission that night would not be solely to take it.

At precisely midnight, the guards standing watch out front stepped aside to let a new watch exit. With military efficiency, they switched places, and the retiring guard slipped inside. One of them would be sent to rest for the night; the other to retire to Nyssa's room. Taking a lover from those who protected you was dangerous for many reasons, not the least of which was that they could get close to you—intimately close. Close enough to steal what was most precious.

Close enough to kill.

As I materialized in an alcove of the embassy near the top floor living quarters, I smiled to myself at the thought of turning the tables on her and finishing what she could not. I would make her bleed.

I would make her pay.

The soft footfalls of the tall, handsome male heading to her room announced his approach. I counted them as he walked, waiting until the last second to strike. *Fifteen, sixteen, seventeen . . .*

I launched from the shadows, calling my blade as I wrapped my arm around his neck and pulled him into my sword. It impaled his heart, killing him instantly, and I dragged him into the shadowy alcove as I released my blade. It disappeared, and the hall went dark again.

"You should never have helped her," I whispered to the wide-eyed corpse at my feet.

After adopting his likeness, I continued on his intended path to the queen's room and knocked lightly on the door.

"Come in," she called from within.

My skin crawled at the sound of her voice.

I opened the door and stepped into the opulent room I'd once called my own. She hadn't even had time yet to change the décor, and I tried to keep my raging emotions from my face as I slowly walked toward where she stood before the full-length mirror, admiring herself as she slipped out of her black dress. It puddled at her feet as it hit the floor, and her reflection stared at me with hungry eyes. And there, hanging at the notch of her throat from a chain identical to Rowe's, was the gabbro stone.

Fury burned in my veins.

"You're late," she said, feigning irritation as she turned to face me. "I wonder how I should punish you . . . "

"However you like," I replied, my voice not my own. I spread my arms wide and gave a small bow. "I am yours."

As her laugh trilled through the air, the desire to crush her throat and cut off that horrid sound ran through my mind. But my expression remained impassive as she slowly walked toward me, her naked body meant to tease me. All it was to me was a canvas for bloody revenge.

She stopped just out of reach and crossed her arms beneath her breasts, accentuating them. "Take your clothes off."

I didn't hesitate, though concern eclipsed my anger for a moment. Holding glamour in place on your person was far easier than maintaining it on things no longer connected to you. And with my erratic abilities, I feared that the moment my coat hit the floor, the illusion would fail.

I unfastened the coat and took a step closer. "And then what, my queen? What would you have me do then?" I took another step. And another. And another, until she was only inches from me, her breath hitching at my proximity. Her act of dominance fractured with that traitorous tell, and I pressed closer still, so close that her chest brushed against my open coat. "Shall I touch you?" I asked, my hand moving slowly between us, headed for my target.

I could practically feel the unpolished stone biting into my palm

—could practically feel its power coursing through me as it had when the former wellspring's blood had seeped into my moonlight blade, then into me. For that fraction of time, I had known what it was like to be connected to such a source of power. And soon, I would know again.

"You're still dressed," she said, eyeing my hand as it traced its way along her stomach and between her breasts.

"You look cold." My hand continued its slow ascent to the gabbro near her throat.

Her hand caught mine just before it reached its target. "And you look warm," she said, leaning in closer. "So Take. Your. Clothes. Off."

She pulled away, taking a step back, and I felt the strange sensation I always did before my magic wavered over my skin.

The time to play her game was gone.

Knowing the glamour would soon fall, I shrugged off my coat and closed the distance between us as though I couldn't stand to be apart. I reached for her face to kiss her while my other hand slid up to that cold stone and closed around it. With a silent prayer and a violent pull, I yanked the necklace until the chain snapped. Nyssa, unlike Rowe's mother, had not taken steps to magically lock the necklace on her person—a grave oversight, given her current predicament.

I stumbled back a step and called my blade as her eyes went wide with surprise and rage. She growled as my glamour fell, then realized what I'd done. The power of the wellspring pulsed in my palm as it entered my body, renewing my own—stabilizing my magic—which meant that my suspicion about the gabbro had been right.

The necklace had never suppressed Rowe's power.

It had siphoned it.

"How?" she asked as anger simmered in her eyes.

My grip on the moonlight blade tightened in anticipation. "You should have killed me faster, Nyssa. This is the price to pay for your arrogance."

She took a defensive stance as she screamed for her guards—for anyone that could help her. She knew she could not take me alone;

not anymore. But as that sense of smug satisfaction settled in, knowing that she'd die before they arrived, the initial thrum of magic from the gabbro dissipated, leaving only an echo of power—a fraction of what I'd felt the night the previous wellspring had died.

I squeezed it harder, but nothing happened.

My confusion must have played out in my expression, because her annoying laughter filled the room yet again. "You are not as smart as you like to think you are," she said as the air in the room began to twist and swirl into a gale that blew me backward toward the windows.

I braced my shoulder against the frame to keep from flying through it. "And you are no match for me now," I replied, raising my blade again. "This will be your final hour, Nyssa." I lunged forward as she fired her winds at me, and we collided like a wave against rock. But her power couldn't hold against mine as I pressed forward, gaining ground against her magic with every passing second.

The door crashed open and guards spilled in, distracting me for a moment, and she used that moment to drive me back. I crashed into the window, my limbs fanned out to keep me from defenestration. I had only seconds to choose a course of action. "I'll see you soon," I shouted over the din before I disappeared into the night air, my vengeance slipping through my fingers with every passing moment.

Seeking vengeance without the full power of the wellspring would be dangerous, especially now that Nyssa knew of my survival, and the paltry amount of power coursing through it into me would not suffice—not against an army of fae. I would need the rush I'd felt when the former wellspring had impaled himself on my blade to accomplish that task.

I'd need all of Rowe's power.

Frustration coursing through my veins at this twist of events, I returned to Fire and Fluorite territory to find her at her party. My jaw clenched as I wove silently through the trees behind the house. She sat next to the wolf on a bench in the yard, their bodies close together. Too close.

That frustration quickly turned to something far darker.

Under the cover of shadow, I dared to move closer, listening intently.

"You'd do that for me?" she asked, looking up at him with those beautiful green eyes, so pure and full of innocence. His hand brushed against hers, and the flames of rage licked up my spine.

"That and more." He leaned closer as she sat there, unmoving, awaiting his kiss with bated breath.

I squeezed the gabbro in my hand until it bit into the skin, the pain and magic reminding me of my true mission—my future. One that didn't involve the little queen.

Then I disappeared into the night once again.

I did not need to see how her story would end.

I wrapped the night's darkness around me as I waited for her to return.

The prickling sensation that arose when I thought about her and the wolf together set me on edge. The way she'd looked at him on that bench . . . I'd known he wanted her, but before that moment, I had not believed she wanted him, despite my taunting.

He had most definitely become a problem—but not in the way I'd originally imagined.

And I liked this way even less.

Frustration drove me from my spot, and I stormed down the alley, trying to clear that image from my mind. But there, in the distance, wobbling around the corner, came the object of my spiraling thoughts, a bottle dangling from her hand. Relief washed over me, followed by a wave of anger. "Is the party over already?" I called to her.

She yelped at the sound of my voice and staggered back a step. "You scared me!" she yelled back as she made her way toward me in a less than linear fashion.

"That's an easy task when you pay so little attention to your surroundings."

Even from that distance, her frown was plain. "I'm nearly home, in Fire and Fluorite territory," she argued, jabbing her finger at me to drive her point home. "What could possibly happen here?"

"Perhaps a fae assassin could sneak up on you."

She stopped to contemplate my reply, swaying on her unsteady feet. "Like, another one?"

I inhaled slowly to calm my anger. "No. Not another one."

"Okay . . . then I'm good," she said, resuming her approach, "because you're not going to kill me, right?"

Never . . . "Not at the moment, no."

"Ugggh, you're so grumpy. Did your
recona . . . reconasinz . . . *recon* mission not go so well?"

"It went well enough." I stared at her as she grew closer, wild red hair blowing around her in the breeze. Her cheeks were flushed from the alcohol in her system—or something else entirely. Something that made my anger return at the thought. "Was your party all you hoped it would be?" Her shoulders slumped at my question, and she pressed the half-empty bottle to her mouth in response. "Shall I take that as a 'no'?"

"It was fine, just—" She cut herself off, and that darkness inside me stirred again.

"What happened?"

"Nothing *happened*," she said with a shrug. "The night just took an unexpected turn, and I wanted to leave." She stopped before me and lifted those big green eyes up to me—the way she had to him. "Everything's fine."

I balled my hands into fists to keep from touching her. "It doesn't look fine." The sadness in her tone had violence coursing through my veins. If the wolf had hurt her, I'd carve him into pieces so small, there would be no way to identify him.

"It is. I just—"

Silence. "Just what?"

She shrugged, and the liquor in her bottle sloshed wildly. "I just realized tonight that even if I am the wellspring, it doesn't change anything."

"It changes everything," I argued, but the slump of her shoulders said otherwise.

And the darkness in me raged.

CHAPTER 22
ROWE

I did my best to meet Volker's heavy gaze. "I still won't really belong," I explained. "Having that power won't make my life in this world better." He opened his mouth to respond, but I waved him off with a drunken flail of my arm. "Never mind. You clearly wouldn't understand."

"Wouldn't I?" He closed the distance between us, not a hint of malice in his approach. "Was I not usurped by my own House? Was I not betrayed by someone close to me?"

"That's not the same thing."

He canted his head, and the light reflected in those dark eyes. "Isn't it?"

"Massive coup aside, you belonged there at some point . . . were accepted. Respected."

"I was *feared*," he corrected, "until I wasn't. Until someone grew bold enough to try something others had never thought possible."

"Well, I guess you have all that supernatural power to comfort you," I said sarcastically, "or you will soon enough."

"As will you."

I choked on a laugh. "Yeah? I guess we'll see how that works out for me."

His expression soured. "Poor little queen . . . so desperate for acceptance, for affection. For love."

"Everyone wants to be loved, Volker. There's nothing wrong with that. It's a normal human emotion."

"Exactly," he said, leaning in closer, "and it is one of their greatest weaknesses."

"And you couldn't possibly afford that," I countered, anger simmering in my veins along with something far more uncomfortable. Something that tugged at my heart, roiled in my stomach, and tightened my throat. An emotion I didn't dare name for fear of what it might mean. Because it felt dangerously close to disappointment mixed with sadness, and that was a combination I had no intention of unpacking right now, in front of the Moonlight Wraith. Maybe ever.

He said nothing in response; just stood and stared back with narrowed eyes and a tense jaw.

"Poor little Moonlight Wraith," I mocked in return. "Too strong and callous to love anything but the power that consumes his every thought."

"Not my every thought," he said as he lifted his hand and took a stray strand of my hair between his fingers.

I quickly batted it away, nearly losing my balance in the process. "Don't touch me."

"I touch what I want."

"Of course you do," I said, resting the whiskey bottle against my lips. Volker's eyes studied it with great intensity. "Why would you be any different than every other powerful man? But for your information, consent's a thing—even for surly, heartless fae like you."

"I am nothing like the other men you've known," he said, leaning in close to emphasize his point. "And I am not entirely heartless . . . " His piercing eyes bored right through me, as though their intensity alone could convince me.

I shrugged. "I wouldn't know."

"And *surly*?" he repeated. Even with drunk vision, I couldn't miss the slight upturn of his lips as he spoke the word.

"Yes. Surly. It means ill-tempered and unfriendly—"

"I think 'sexy' was the adjective you were looking for," he replied, his amused expression turning to something far more intense and hungry.

Heat surged through me, and I took a long sip from the bottle, enjoying—a little too much—how he watched me like a hawk as I did. Baiting him was a distraction I could manage, so I kept the game alive. "Nope. I landed on the right descriptor."

"Then your alcohol consumption has clearly clouded your mind."

I shook the bottle between us. "Not even whiskey can eclipse your true nature, *Moonlight Wraith*."

"No better than your alcohol consumption can hide your true feelings, *little queen*."

"Oh yeah? And what exactly are those?"

He leaned in so close that his legs brushed the skirt of my dress and his chest pressed the bottle into mine. "That you want to be touched . . . " My breath hitched as his lapels gently grazed my breasts. "Kissed . . . possibly more."

I closed my eyes as visions of him doing just that assaulted my mind. Swaying on my feet, I caught his arm and steadied myself against my traitorous mind and his intimidating stare. Embarrassment flooded my cheeks when I opened my eyes and saw the amusement in his.

I squared my shoulders defiantly. "Maybe I do," I said, pressing back against him, "but not by you."

A sultry laugh escaped him, and the sound stroked my insides. I tried to play it cool, but the gasp I let loose gave me away. His laughter rumbled on. "By who then, little queen? The wolf?"

"No," I snapped. "I told you, it's not like that with him—"

His laughter stopped cold and his eyes shone bright silver for a split second. "Strange . . . it did not look that way this evening."

"Wait, you were watching us?" I staggered back a step. "I thought you were supposed to be at the embassy."

"I was. I came to find you afterward and saw the two of you rather cozy on a bench together."

I swallowed hard, nerves rising within me, even though I didn't fully understand why. The sting of his implication pulled me from my horny haze, and I pushed him back a pace.

I suddenly needed space.

"Why do you even care?" I asked, anger bubbling up in my voice. "Are you jealous?"

"I don't care," he replied with a sudden indifference that cut me to the bone. "I merely made an observation. I notice you haven't refuted it."

"And I asked a question. I notice you haven't answered it."

"I don't get jealous, because there is nothing in this world I cannot have if I want it." The intensity of his eyes as they drifted down my body to the plunge of my neckline sent fire through my veins. His gaze met mine again, and his eyebrow quirked slightly in challenge.

"Has anyone ever told you that you're an arrogant fucking prick?" I asked, flustered and frustrated by his antics, his charms, his presumptions.

His expression never faltered. "Yes," he replied, voice cold as ice, "and I plan to kill that bitch very soon."

He held my gaze until I couldn't stand it any longer. The hostile tension growing between us was more than I could bear. "Vengeance mode re-activated!" I said, throwing my arms up in the air. "But I guess that implies that it ever went away . . . " My eyes fell to the bottle in my hand, and I slowly extended it to him. "Maybe you need this even more than I do."

He looked at the bottle like it was filled with poison, then turned those grey eyes back to me. He held my gaze as he took my offering and brought it to his lips. I stared as he downed most of the rest of the night's provisions. I watched his throat bob as he swallowed, then handed what little was left back to me.

"Maybe it's better you not drink any more of that tonight," he said, leaning in so close I could smell the alcohol on his breath. "We wouldn't want you making any terrible decisions, now would we?"

"Would I do that?" Instead of fear and panic, something else entirely filled me—something warm and consuming and altogether dangerous. Even drunk me knew the need building deep inside was a lit match near a canister of gasoline.

Unfortunately, drunk me didn't care.

Visions of Volker pressing me up against the wall assailed my mind, only this time they took a very different turn than the events of that night had—ones that involved his hands sliding up my thighs, my skirt at my waist, and the feel of his fingers between my legs. I hated him so much for being right about what I wanted.

Luckily, the smug bastard couldn't read minds.

I glanced up to find him staring at me with wild eyes, as though he'd just shared my vision. I held my breath, waiting to see what he might do. If he might bend down and kiss me, or pick me up and carry me home, or slam me against the nearest building and fuck me sober. The thought of any and all had me pressing up onto my tiptoes while I held his arm for balance, until my face was only inches from his.

But when nothing happened, I dropped back down and took a defiant swig from the bottle, then started off toward my apartment. He fell in step at my side, hand resting on the small of my back to keep me on target.

"So, did you get whatever intel you needed at you-know-who's place?"

"That's a conversation better had in your apartment," he said as he ushered me to the back door, "but yes. I got what I needed . . . "

Something about the way he said those words niggled at my drunken mind, but before I could ask him anything, I tripped on the final step and lurched forward. I would have smashed my face on the door if Volker hadn't caught me around the waist. I turned in his arms and looked up at his beautiful face, his features tight with concern.

"I hate to admit it, but it seems you're pretty useful to have around sometimes."

"I'm useful all the time," he countered, staring back at me.

I sucked in a breath, then pulled away from him and walked into the apartment—and to the far side of the room. "If you say so . . . "

"I do. Now, tell me what happened this evening that sent you home so early—and don't include the word 'fine' in your explanation."

I could tell I was in for a long night, but maybe it was for the best. One way or another, we needed to get some things sorted out between us, and I was just drunk enough to do it. I leaned against the far wall, my arms crossed over my stomach in challenge, the bottle still in my hand, and smiled like the devil.

"Fine."

CHAPTER 23
VOLKER

"Andreas and I were talking about my mom and her necklace," she said, staring back at me, arms folded across her chest, "and I might have mentioned that I thought I had power—"

"You did *what*?"

"—and then things got all weird, so I bailed. That's it. That's the big story."

"You told him you thought you had power?"

"I did."

"Because you thought that was a good idea?"

"I mean, Myra and Yael know, and you didn't pitch a fit about them," she argued. "Not sure why Andreas knowing about it is such a problem."

I clenched my teeth to bite back my anger. "You cannot tell anyone else," I said, taking a step toward her. "You are an outsider in their world, and it's best to allow them to think that—for your safety."

"Maybe I'm wrong . . . .maybe they will want me once they learn what I really am," she muttered against the bottle's mouth.

"They'll want to *use* you," I said, correcting her statement, though the way she flinched when I spoke those words made me wish I hadn't.

Her expression and body tightened as if preparing for a fight. "Maybe. But technically, so do you, remember?"

My jaw flexed as I inhaled hard to calm myself. "Not in the same way. You cannot trust them."

She choked on a laugh, then took a sip from the bottle. "But I can trust you?"

"I have never lied about what I want."

"Neither have they. They don't exactly hide their agendas."

"Does the wolf? He appeared rather enamored with you tonight . . . " I let my words trail off to leave the unspoken hanging in the air between us.

"He's worried about me."

"Is that what you think?" I asked, stepping closer. "That wasn't worry I saw in his eyes when he leaned in to kiss you."

She frowned at my words. "Maybe your spying skills aren't as good as you'd like to think." She planted her hands on her hips, the bottle dangling awkwardly from her hand. "And you sure seem pretty hung up on this subject for someone who says he doesn't care." Her implication that I had an ulterior motive for checking up on her was clear, and I opened my mouth to refute it, but the look of drunken indignation on her face gave me pause—as did the way I had felt when I'd observed their interaction. Perhaps her observation was far more astute than I wanted to admit.

Perhaps I cared far more than I should have.

"I guess none of it really matters," she continued. "Once you get what you want, you'll disappear in that super fucking annoying way you always do, and my life won't matter to you at all anymore. You'll be too busy getting revenge and retaking your throne to care who I'm hooking up with." She shook the bottle at me and stumbled a little as she leaned forward. "But don't worry, Jack is all the man I need." She stared at me for a moment, fiery anger in those emerald eyes, and I wondered what was really driving it—if even she fully understood.

"Why did you even come here tonight, Volker? You could have told me that your mission was successful tomorrow."

"I told you, I came to check on you," I said, meeting her stare with my own, "but it appears that might be beyond your comprehension at the moment."

"There it is," she shouted, throwing her arms up in mock victory. "I was waiting for your judgment to kick in. I'm so glad I didn't pass out before it showed up." She kicked off her shoes, launching them toward the closet. They crashed against the wall, leaving black scuffs in their wake.

"Did you wish to further my point?"

"I'm drunk. I get it. But that doesn't mean that I can't see what's going on," she said, waving the bottle at me. "That I don't know that you're holding back."

Ice slid down my spine. "Holding what back?" I dared to ask.

"The truth," she replied, staring right through me with wide, wild eyes.

"And what truth is that?"

"That you care." She took a wobbling step toward me. Then another. Then another, until she was standing right before me, staring up at me with determination in her narrowed eyes. "About me." Her gaze dropped to my lips, and my body tensed. "Would it be such a terrible thing to admit that?"

I wanted to answer her—to give her some shred of what she so desperately wanted—but to do so with her in that state would have only clouded her judgment further and driven her to do something she'd undoubtedly regret in the morning. She had already suffered so much at the hands of supernaturals who wanted to use her for her power—including me—and I would never want her to believe I'd used her for anything else. She deserved better than that.

Better than me.

"You know what I care about," I said, staring back at her.

The sting she felt at my words flashed in her face, and she backed away slowly. "I guess I do. Now, if you'd be so kind . . . " She gestured to the door. "I want to get to the passing out part I just mentioned. Maybe the forgetting part, too." She walked over to the edge of the bed and flopped down inelegantly, booze sloshing out of the tipped bottle.

I took a slow, calculated step toward her. "Despite what you think, I did not come here tonight to fight with you, little queen."

My words cut through her drunken haze like my moonlight blade, allowing her true feelings to surface. The hurt in her eyes when she looked up at me was almost more than I could bear. "Then why does it feel that way?"

"Because you affect me in unexpected ways, and I don't always handle it well."

She looked up at me as I hovered near the foot of her bed. "I must be even more wasted than I thought, because that sounded a lot like an almost-apology, Volker—"

"It is the truth. Nothing more."

She forced a smile, but it did little to hide the sadness she clearly felt. "If you say so."

I bent down before her, planting my hands on the bed next to her hips, caging her in. With my face in hers, angled slightly to the right, I whispered in her ear. "You've forgotten one small yet important detail in your alcohol-induced stupor, little queen. I can't lie."

My hair fell into my eyes as I pulled away to look at her face once again, and I saw her hand drift up toward me, her delicate fingers outstretched to brush it away. My body went rigid at her approach, and she stopped just before her soft touch grazed my skin.

With an exhale, she lowered her hand slowly but held my gaze, and the darkness within me went deathly still. "I really want to touch you," she whispered, the words so faint I wasn't sure she'd meant to say them aloud. She licked her lips, and I tracked the subtle movement intently, my throat suddenly dry as I followed her tongue's path. "Maybe one day you'll let me . . . "

The tension in the room was eclipsed only by the penetrating, unbearable silence filling it. Every second that passed seemed to press down upon us like a growing weight, crushing us slowly. Painfully. Never in my life had I felt discomfort like this. Never had someone had such power over me. And as I stared at her pale face, her lips slightly parted and her cheeks flushed, fire consumed me.

All I wanted to do was unleash it upon her.

Then, without warning, she flopped back on the bed and laughed nervously. "Or maybe you'll just kill me once you get what you want. Guess I'll have to wait and see how it all plays out."

I stood and looked down upon her, hair splayed around her as her eyes drifted shut. "I thought we had that matter settled."

"I'm not sure it ever will be," she said, sleep muffling her voice. "Mom always said 'never trust the fae' . . . " The bottle slipped from her grasp as sleep overtook her, and I caught it before it shattered on the floor.

"But your mother lied to you," I said as I pulled the blanket over her legs. "I have not."

But as I walked to the door to make sure it was locked, I could feel the untruth of my words pressing down upon me. I hadn't directly lied to Rowe, but like her mother, I'd willfully omitted information. If I didn't tell her about the necklace the next morning when she was sober enough to process it, I knew it would not end well. Her mother had hidden the truth from her to keep her safe, but her untimely death had left her daughter ill-prepared for the consequences.

I would not do the same.

CHAPTER 24
ROWE

I woke up the next morning seriously rethinking my life choices. Jack Daniels was not, in fact, all the man I needed. He was the devil wrapped in a black label, with the false promise that he'd make all my problems go away. Lying bastard.

I didn't need to look at my phone to see that I was late for my double, so I peeled myself off the mattress and rushed around on wobbly legs in search of something to wear. I managed to find a pair of black pants in my pile of clean laundry, along with a top that I was pretty certain was black. I threw them on quickly, grabbed my jacket and phone, and ignored my rumbling stomach as I chugged as much water as I could bear before hurrying out the door.

I knew I was going to be at least an hour late, which meant Ravi would be livid when I arrived, Myra would have already plotted my death, and Yael would be delighting in the promise of a fight the second I walked in the door. Not exactly the welcome I was looking forward to.

But it was definitely the one I got.

I rushed through the back door to the kitchen, apologies flying as I made my way past the line, screaming "behind" until I got to the coat rack in the employee space. Before I even let go of my jacket, Ravi was there, his dark brown eyes glaring at me.

"You're late."

"I know—"

"Do I need to explain how inconvenient that is on a Saturday afternoon?"

"Do I need to explain how I'm doing this double to help out and that your rage should be unleashed on Sasha when she comes back instead of me?" I propped my hands on my hips and glared right back, my hangry hangover driving my irritated mood. "Would you prefer I just leave? Maybe disappear into another realm and not return, too?"

His lips pressed to a thin line as he carefully crafted his response. "No, I wouldn't."

"Cool, then I'll get to it." I pushed past him, headed for the dining room, when Yael caught my eye from the prep area, the note of suspicion plain in his expression. Not wanting him to start, I quickly pushed the right side of the double doors open and nearly walked right into Myra.

Her blue eyes raked over me once, then she grabbed my arm. "Come with me," she said as she hauled me back into the kitchen. " Ravi, I'm going on my break. Rowe is too—"

"She just got here!"

"And she already needs a break because this place is a toxic wasteland that sucks the very marrow from your bones, along with your will to live."

To that, Ravi had no response.

"I'm taking mine now, too," Yael called out with glee as he abandoned his station and fell in line behind us.

Ravi's protests followed us out, but the slamming of the heavy metal door managed to cut them off, which was impressive given the volume of his voice. But I didn't focus on that for long, once Myra pinned her assessing gaze on me, arms folded across her chest for added effect. She was pissed, no doubt about that.

Getting hammered the previous night only seemed like a worse idea when facing her rage.

"You look like shit," she finally said.

Couldn't argue with that. "The outside accurately reflects my current internal state."

"Rough night with your boy toy—"

"Still not my boy toy, Myra—"

"—or were you up to something worse than that?" she continued, undaunted by my interruptions. "Like, I don't know, maybe breaking into the Air and Amethyst embassy?"

"I'm sorry, *what*?"

"Where were you?" she pressed, unwilling to explain.

"I was at a party trying to bury myself in a bottle of whiskey to avoid the growing awkwardness between Andreas and me—which didn't work, in case you were wondering. It made it worse, and now I'm wicked hung over." Her eyes narrowed and her brow furrowed, and I wondered just what I'd walked into. "Wanna tell me why you're low-key accusing me of some crazy shit?"

"What would she know about the incident at the embassy?" Yael asked, sounding as though Myra's suggestion was the most ridiculous thing he'd ever heard. "She wouldn't be standing here if she'd done something that stupid—nobody would."

My tired, hung-over mind was too grateful for Yael's words to be offended by them. I needed food and sleep, STAT.

"What *incident*?" I asked, still confused. Though I knew it undoubtedly had something to do with Volker—given the timing, there was no way it could be coincidence—he'd returned unscathed and unalarmed from his recon mission, with nothing memorable to report. Or at least I didn't remember anything memorable.

Alcohol might have had something to do with that, though . . .

"Any news on the necklace front?" Myra asked, pulling me from my thoughts as she edged closer.

"Sort of," I said, covering my mouth as I yawned. "We have a plan in place. Vol—" I cut myself off as my brain caught up to my tongue and choked off the rest of his name. Panic shot through me, and I knew the longer I remained silent, the worse my faux pas would be. *Words* . . . I needed words. Fast. "I've got someone who can retrieve it —I think."

Myra stared at me expectantly, unfazed by my stumble. But Yael was not. His entire I'm-just-here-for-the-entertainment demeanor changed in a blink. His body went rigid and his gaze sharpened, and every inch of my skin prickled with fear. He'd most definitely caught my mistake. "You said 'Vol'—"

"No, I didn't—"

"—which confirms my suspicion that this one who is helping you is none other than the former leader of Air and Amethyst. The one whose death landed me in No Man's Land." His expression soured. " The question is how . . . and why? How is the Moonlight Wraith alive? And why would he come to you?"

"Because he wants the necklace," Myra said without an ounce of doubt.

Yael stepped closer to loom over me like Volker loved to, and I couldn't help but wonder if I'd underestimated Yael. If he wasn't more like the assassin than I'd imagined. "You asked for my help the other night and I gave it without question—without requiring a favor in return—but now I want answers. Especially if they can possibly reinstate my position with Air and Amethyst." His tight expression slackened for a moment, and he leaned away as some sort of realization dawned. "That's why you said what you did at your mother's grave . . . about my return to the House. You knew it could happen because you knew he was alive . . . " He trailed off, beautiful green eyes wide. "And he's planning to overthrow the queen—"

"No!" I said as panic shot through me. I frantically shook my head, but I could see the damage was done. I was officially screwed. There was no way out of this mess that my hung-over brain could see.

Fear paralyzed me. Fear for them. For me.

And for Volker, too.

"Rowe," Myra called, her voice far softer than it had been before.

"I can't tell you anything," I said, my voice shaking.

"And in not doing so," Yael said, "you have."

I clutched his arm, desperation driving me at this point, for his sake and everyone else's. "You can't tell anyone about this or he'll kill you, Yael." I let the panic I felt taint my words. "He knows you already know about the necklace. Who do you think he'll come for if he's suddenly rumored to be alive?"

"He won't say anything," Myra said as she shot Yael a warning look. "Neither of us will, but tell me something: why *did* he come to you?"

I took a deep breath, preparing to spill the proverbial beans. "His power is unstable right now. According to him, there's some kind of disruption to the night's magic, so he needs me to help restore his power so he can overthrow the queen."

Silence.

Yael looked at me as though I'd lost my mind. "You have no power. Your mother was a half-witch with no real magic to speak of—"

"But her father," Myra said, cutting him off, "could have been something more powerful than any of us could imagine. Powerful enough that her mother thought it best to hide whatever Rowe inherited from him from the world by suppressing that magic."

"Like what?" Yael asked, unable to hide the note of concern in his voice. Concern Myra clearly shared, given the look on her face.

"Rowe? Do you know?"

I worried my lip between my teeth. "Maybe . . . " The two of them stared at me, anticipation in their wide eyes. "He thinks I'm the wellspring. He thinks my necklace is somehow blocking my ability."

Both swore under their breath at my response. "No," Yael said with a shake of his head. "It's not possible. We'd know. Not even gabbro could withhold that kind of power."

"He's convinced it's true," I argued. "I don't know why, but he's certain. He's gambling his entire vengeance on it."

Yael went rigid. "And he is not the gambling sort." His cruel stare cut to me, and I withered under the weight of it.

"This is why he needs your mother's necklace," Myra said, words barely a whisper. "He needs it to break the spell and use your power." She stared at me with genuine fear in her eyes. "You're the key to his revenge."

Yael leaned forward and pulled my gabbro free. He rolled it over in his palm, admiring the way it reflected the light. "I said her necklace must be powerful if someone was willing to kill for it."

A sharp pounding sounded from inside the back door, followed by Ravi's muffled voice threatening us all to come inside.

None of us moved.

"He's the one who went to the embassy last night," he said, letting the pendant drop to my chest.

I nodded. "But I don't know any details. He might have told me when he came to my apartment afterward, but I was too drunk to remember."

"I've told you the queen isn't to be trifled with, Rowe. If she learns of his return and your involvement, she will come for you both."

"Something is off about this," Myra said right before the back door slammed open, exposing an angry Ravi glaring at us, actual flames burning in his stare.

"If you three don't get back in here right now, I will incinerate the lot of you, understood?"

"And start a war?" Myra countered, turning that cool-as-a-cucumber attitude on him like he was bluffing. To be honest, I wasn't so sure about that. "I don't think so."

"Your Houses don't care about you, Myra. The sooner you realize that, the easier it'll make my life—and yours." He slammed the door shut, punctuating his harsh observation.

Silence descended upon us again, and nobody moved; we just stared at one another, mulling over everything in our minds, until Myra finally broke the oppressive quiet. "I believe you, Rowe. I do.

But something about all this doesn't add up for me, and I don't like it."

"How so?" I dared to ask.

Her mouth pressed to a thin line. "I get why Volker would want the necklace if he needs to break the spell to release your power, provided he's even right about that, but . . . " Her hesitation did nothing for my rising anxiety. "Why would the queen possibly kill your mother for a necklace that suppresses your power? It just doesn't make sense."

"I . . . I don't know." Which was true. I didn't know, because I hadn't thought about that. Volker had seemed so convinced that it was suppressing my ability that I'd never questioned it. And I had been so blinded by the idea that the queen had killed my mother to get it that I had never bothered to ask why. I'd been too consumed by revenge to care.

Yael and Myra watched me as my thoughts undoubtedly played out in my expression. "Maybe Volker doesn't want it so he can break the spell," Yael said gently. "Maybe he wants it for the same reason the queen did."

"And maybe Rowe needs to figure out what that reason is really quick," Myra added, her brow furrowed with concern.

Something heavy slammed against the back door, and smoke billowed out from the cracks. "I don't think Ravi was kidding," I said, leading the way to the ominous entrance. "We should go."

I reached for the doorknob, but Yael's arm shot in front of me before I could grab it. The second his flesh touched the metal, it sizzled. "You should be careful," he said as he pulled away from the molten metal, hissing while I contemplated the double meaning of his words.

Myra stepped up and conjured a ball of water in front of her, then doused the metal handle with it. Steam rose off of it for a moment, and Myra pulled it open once she deemed it cool enough. "She *should* be careful," she said as she cast a wary glance at Yael before she stepped inside. "And remember to never trust a fae."

CHAPTER 25
ROWE

I finished the double from hell and bolted from *The Riff-Raff* as quickly as I could. Myra and Yael had barely spoken to me since our conversation in the alley, which was unnerving given their normal behavior. I felt their heavy stares on my back as I walked through the kitchen and dining areas. I caught their sideways glances and tense expressions as I rushed around, trying not to let my thoughts run wild. But Myra's question haunted me all through my shift, and by the time my double was over, all I wanted to do was bail.

I wanted to ask Volker about what had happened the night before.

I wanted to ask him why the queen had wanted my mother's necklace.

As I rolled down the sidewalk on my board, sticking to the light as much as possible in that part of downtown, I considered all the reasons someone like the queen might have wanted the necklace. Myra had said the stones were connected, but why? If it wasn't to suppress my abilities then . . . .

Ice slid down my back as a theory niggled in the back of my mind. What if the gabbro somehow stole my power? It would make sense of why I couldn't feel my magic and why the queen would want it, but my mother's ordinary witch status undermined that idea. She wasn't strong or powerful like she should have been if my theory was correct.

But it would definitely make the necklace worth killing for.

And it would also have given the queen the power necessary to overthrow the Moonlight Wraith. But why would she have waited so long to do it? Why not take him out as soon as she'd obtained it? And why leave me with Fire and Fluorite? I realized that she couldn't have kidnapped me without potential repercussions, but she would have been the leader of Air and Amethyst—a powerful, crafty bitch capable of getting away with murder—with a House full of fae at her disposal. Would it really have been so difficult to abduct me without fallout?

That didn't seem likely.

My mind wandered further as I rode through the cold, clear night. The nearly full moon watched over me as I made my way through the quiet streets of No Man's Land, wondering if Volker was out there somewhere, skulking in the shadows, watching me. Or if he'd returned to the queen's place to obtain the necklace. If the rumors of a disturbance at the embassy were true, security would surely be tighter, and the element of surprise was potentially lost. Whatever had happened, it was gossip-worthy, which didn't bode well. Something had gone wrong on his recon mission.

I needed to have a sober conversation with him ASAP. With any luck, he'd be waiting for me at my apartment.

The thought of him leaning over my bed flashed in my mind, and I quickened my pace.

As I neared the edge of the nightlife district, the streetlights grew fewer, as did those walking the streets. A gust of wind blew past, and I tucked my chin into the collar of my leather jacket as my auburn hair danced around me in the gale. Barely able to see, I tried to navigate the curb to the upcoming intersection, but my front wheels caught in a sewer grate, and I went flying into the road. A gnarly crack sounded from my board just before I slammed into the unforgiving pavement. But it was my board that took the biggest hit. I crawled over to find the deck ripped from the front wheels.

There'd be no riding it home. And there would likely be no fixing it, either.

"Well shit," I mumbled as I tucked it under my arm. Frustrated, I continued the long walk home. "Another problem I didn't need."

I hurried through the increasing darkness, my footsteps echoing for what seemed like forever off the large brick buildings hemming me in; the driving beat to my commute home. My phone vibrated in my back pocket, and I fished it out to see Andreas' name on the screen. I sighed, not sure I was up for that phone call. I hadn't spoken with him since our bench encounter the night before, and I'd conveniently ignored his texts while I was at work. But there'd be no avoiding him indefinitely.

The thought of him showing up at my place when Volker was there popped into my head, and I quickly answered the call. "Hey," I said, glancing over my shoulder at the sound of a can rattling down the way.

"Hey yourself." I could practically hear the smile in his voice. "What's up?"

"Just walking home from work."

"Walking?"

"Yeah, I just broke my board. The crowning glory to my evening."

"That good, huh? Was Myra on a rampage?"

I choked on a laugh; if only he knew. "No more than usual. Ravi was extra testy, though, so that was fun."

He laughed lightly. "I forgot you were working all day today. I was starting to think you were trying to avoid me—"

"Of course not." *But maybe a little . . .* "I woke up late and had to race to the restaurant. We were slammed all day, so I didn't get two seconds to myself."

"Rough morning?"

"The roughest."

"Well, you did hit the bottle pretty hard last night. I thought you were going to shank me if I tried to take it from you before you left in such a hurry."

"Talking about your dead mother does seem to make chugging a bottle of whiskey sound like a good idea," I replied. "And I might have stabbed you if you'd tried, so I'm glad you didn't."

The scuff of boots on pavement echoed down the street, and I spun around to see what was behind me. Apparently, my already frayed nerves had left me a little jumpy.

"About our conversation," he said, pulling my attention back with his serious tone, "do you remember everything we talked about? Or were you more wasted than I realized at the time?"

"Nope. I remember." *Unfortunately . . .*

"Do we need to discuss that any further?"

"One hundred percent no." Silence met my reply, and that sickening feeling in my gut started to churn for the eight millionth time that night. "Why?"

"I'm worried about you, that's why."

"Because you think I'm losing my mind?"

More silence. "Because I'm worried that maybe you did something after you left," he explained, hedging his words. "Something crazy."

"I walked home without my shoes on—does that count?"

"I'm being serious, Rowe."

"So am I! Pretty sure I still have a piece of glass in my pinky toe."

"*Rowe*!"

"*What*?"

"Did you do anything I should know about last night?"

Like try to kiss a fae assassin in my bedroom?

"I went home, Andreas. That's it. I passed out with my precious bottle still in my hand and woke up late for work." More silence. "What's this all about, anyway? What is it you think I did?"

Faint footfalls drifted up the street, and my heart raced as adrenaline surged through my veins. Another glance over my shoulder told me I was still alone, but somehow, it just didn't feel that way. My head swiveled from side to side, a weak attempt to find where the sounds were coming from, but all that I found were empty streets and alleys and flickering lights.

"Rowe . . . " Andreas' hesitation only ratcheted my anxiety higher as I hurried to get home. "There are rumors about something going down at the Air and Amethyst embassy estate, and I just need to know you didn't have anything to do with it."

"Why does everyone think I did something?" I replied, my voice a little too high-pitched to sound normal.

"Everyone?" he repeated. "Who's everyone?"

Shit.

"Myra and Yael were giving me shit about it, but I told them I didn't have anything to do with it."

His silence put me on edge.

"Something allegedly happened at the embassy last night, and after our conversation . . . " He let his words trail off, allowing me the chance to put the pieces together for myself.

I didn't love the picture they made.

"You what? Think I rolled up to her well-guarded home with no power to call on and strolled in like I owned the place so I could try to kill her?" His lack of reply was not comforting for many reasons. "Are you on glue?"

"I just—"

"Just think I left your house after consuming half a bottle of Jack Daniels and decided that was a great time to try to get revenge?"

"I think you're confused about all this necklace and power stuff, and they've opened up a wound that never really healed—and you're not exactly thinking clearly at the moment."

"Not thinking clearly is one thing. Going after the queen of Air and Amethyst is some next-level crazy, Andreas."

I heard him take a calming breath, and I tried to do the same, though for different reasons. He was way too close for comfort.

"You're not yourself lately, Rowe—"

"I could say the same about you," I countered, trying to turn the attention to him. "You've been totally weird lately."

Glass smashed in the background, and I barely stifled a scream as I jumped around to see where it came from. Once again, no one was there.

"What was that noise?" he asked, ignoring my comment entirely.

"A broken bottle, maybe? I think someone is fucking with me, but I don't see anyone."

"Where are you?" he asked, concern in his tone. "I'll come get you."

"I'm just about to reach Sinclair Avenue from Monroe Street, but it's nothing. I'm just on edge."

"I'm coming anyway," he said. Seconds later, I heard the sound of his car door slamming and the engine roaring to life through the phone. A small sense of relief washed over me. "Don't hang up until you see me."

"And abandon our conversation? I wouldn't dream of it."

"What were we just talking about?" he asked as the thrum of his car filled the background.

"You being a weirdo lately, too."

"Right. That."

I forced a laugh, trying to lighten the mood, but with every step I took, those taunting footsteps continued. The cadence was erratic and disjointed, like a broken rhythm section, and it was clear that it wasn't just one person making them. They seemed to come from everywhere.

Behind me. Above me. All around me.

The only constant was that they grew louder with every passing second. *Run,* my gut begged, but I'd learned long ago that predators loved to chase their prey. Playing that role often made things worse.

"Andreas," I said softly, my voice shaking, "something's wrong . . . "

"What's happening?"

"I'm being followed. I can't see anyone, but I can hear them—"

"Just keep going," he said, his voice calm as he gave the order. "Don't stop for anything."

My heart hammered against my chest and my pulse thundered in my ears until I couldn't withstand the urge to run any longer. With phone in hand, I tossed my board away and bolted down the road, my legs pumping hard as my boots hit the pavement.

"What's happening?" Andreas yelled into the phone.

I opened my mouth to answer, but eerie laughter echoed through the night, cutting me off. "Hurry, Andreas!" I screamed as I pushed myself as hard as I could run, my lungs burning as I fought for breath. But it didn't matter.

I was essentially human.

Those that hunted me were not.

As I neared the edge of Fire and Fluorite's territory—Andreas shouting at me as I fled—a hand shot out from an alleyway and hauled me backward. My phone fell to the ground, its light the last I saw before I disappeared into the darkness. Andreas would never find me in time, and I knew it.

As the promise of death slammed into me, the shadows of the alley swallowed my screams.

CHAPTER 26
ROWE

Pain sliced through my head as my body slammed against a brick building, then fell to the ground. Unable to brace myself, my skull bounced off the pavement, ears ringing and vision swimming. I tried to force myself up onto my hands and was met with a hard kick to the ribs for my efforts. I collapsed back down, gasping for breath and trying to keep myself from throwing up. Something was broken—I knew that much based on my vomit reflex—but that was the least of my worries. Whoever had attacked me didn't seem too keen on stopping at that.

"What next?" a male asked, his voice muddled by the ringing in my ears. His question was met with laughter that sounded fuzzy and muted, like I was listening from under water.

Another not-so-great sign.

While they debated how to break me further, I tried to drag myself out of the alley. It was pitiful and desperate, but I knew Andreas was coming for me. I just needed to get away—get somewhere that he could find me easily. Every second he wasted searching was a second I didn't have, and I knew it, even in my concussed state.

"Oh no, you don't," a voice called before grabbing me by the ankles and dragging me backward. Sharp, stinging pain radiated from my leg, and I looked down to see blood blooming through a slice in my jeans. I let my gaze drift upward to see who my assailants were, but they were shrouded in darkness, a random cloud offering no moonlight for me to see them. "We've got plans for you."

"I'm not . . . really . . . a planner," I grunted out in response, hoping to buy myself time however I could. If making them laugh at me fit the bill, then so be it.

It was better than dying.

"Too bad," another said before he stomped me in the lower back. The fact that it didn't immediately break told me one of two things: either these assholes were human, or they were holding back. The latter seemed more realistic, but it begged the question: why? "Orders are orders," he continued, hauling my head up by my hair. "You know how it is."

I managed to slip my arm in front of me right before he slammed my face into the ground. My forehead bounced off my arm, leaving my vision full of stars. "Orders . . . from who? And why?" I asked, hating how weak I sounded in the face of what I knew was coming. "Why me? What did I do?"

Laughter was the only response I got.

And that was when I felt it, felt my will to live—to fight—slowly slipping away. Because this was nothing more than an errand for them; a directive they'd turned into a game just for shits and giggles. They knew there was nothing I could do to stop them. My fate was literally in their hands.

What a crowning end to the life I'd led to die in a dirty alley for no other reason than that someone had ordered it.

Maybe it was a mercy of sorts. Maybe it would save me from a lifetime of being used.

I lifted my head to look down the alley to where Andreas would eventually stand, searching for me. He'd find my body. He'd take me home and do right by me. As the pounding in my head grew, I rested my cheek on my arm and closed my eyes. Visions of Volker assaulted my mind. Delusions of him avenging me, of his wrath befalling all who'd hurt me. But without me, he'd never get his vengeance.

A strange sadness washed over me as my vision began to fade. "I'm sorry," I whispered as darkness came for me.

Then bright light suddenly assailed me through my closed lids, and I wondered if Andreas' car had turned down the alleyway. I tried to open my eyes to see, but the light was just too punishing. Shouting erupted, footsteps pounded against the pavement, and all the while, that blinding light remained. I shielded my eyes and tried to roll over in an attempt to see what was going on, but my body was too weak and battered for the task.

All I wanted to do was close my eyes and sleep forever.

But as I felt the deep abyss of death open its arms to welcome me, something dragged me up to the surface again with just one touch. Something warm and gentle grazed my cheek, and I tried to force my eyes open to see.

"Now is not the time for death," a voice whispered in my ear before another, more jarring call eclipsed it.

"Rowe!" Andreas' shout reached me from somewhere in the distance. "Rowe, where are you?"

The hand on my cheek slipped around my neck and down my back, the pain in each abating slightly along with it. "I will see you soon," the voice said softly before the warmth of that hand disappeared altogether.

Then the alley went dark.

A heartbeat later, I heard the skidding of sneakers against concrete as Andreas arrived. "Sweet gods, Rowe," he gasped, running to my side. He crashed down beside me and gently pushed my hair from my face. My eyes fluttered open to find him staring back, concern etching his brow. "You're okay now. I've got you."

"I know."

"Don't talk," he said softly. "Just rest while I take you home. You need a healer, but first, we have to get you out of here." He gently worked his hands beneath my battered body and scooped me off the ground. With hurried but steady steps, he rushed down the alley. "It'll be okay, Rowe . . . you'll be okay . . . "

The cloud above passed and moonlight shone down on me.

"The light," I said, as my eyes drifted shut yet again.

"Light?" he asked. "What light?"

His worried words were the last thing I remembered before sleep overtook me and dreams of a moonlight angel filled my mind.

"What happened to her?" Shade's worried voice pulled me from my coma-like state, and I tried to lift my head to see him, but my body didn't respond.

"I don't know—she was basically unconscious when I found her, and that hasn't changed," Andreas explained, his tone matching his father's. "I was talking to her on the phone while she walked home from work. Everything was fine until she said something about being followed. I got in my truck to pick her up—" His voice cut off, and I tried to open my eyes. "Then I heard her scream, and the line went dead."

I forced my lids open slowly to see Andreas and Shade hovering near the living room couch, Shade's hand on his son's shoulder to comfort him. I let out a painful sound as I tried to shift my body to see them better, and their collective attention snapped to me.

"Rowe," Andreas said, rushing over. He crouched down next to me and took my hand gently in his, careful not to jostle me in the process. "You're okay. You're at our house."

"Everything hurts," I said as I tried to sit up and instantly regretted the decision. The throbbing in my head had returned with a vengeance, but now it was accompanied by pounding in my back and leg—ribs, too, because why not, right?

He helped prop me up with a pillow and leaned me back against it. "But you're not dying, so that's something." His warm brown eyes searched my face for any shred of reaction to his joke and narrowed when he didn't get one. But my face felt like it might explode at any moment, so smiling was right out for the time being. "What happened, Rowe? Do you remember anything?"

I pressed my hand to my forehead where the bulk of the pain resided and took a deep breath. "Not much . . . "

"I know this is hard and that you're hurting right now," Shade added as he slowly approached, "but I need you to tell us what you can."

"I heard someone following me—"

"I know. We were on the phone," Andreas said. "Do you remember what happened after that?"

I closed my eyes and tried to think about how the chaos of the night had played out while a bass drum pounded in my cranium. "Someone grabbed me—pulled me into the alley, I think."

Andreas nodded. "That's where I found you."

"It was dark . . . someone hit me in the head. I remember slamming down on the ground . . . then it gets fuzzy, but I'm guessing they beat me up pretty good, given how I feel."

"How many were there?" Shade asked, his voice gentler than it had been in weeks.

"I . . . I don't know."

"Did you see them? Maybe recognize someone?"

"It all happened so fast and it was so dark—I didn't ever see their faces." My frustration spilled into my voice and Andreas squeezed my hand—one of the few parts of my body that didn't hurt—to comfort me.

"That's okay. Maybe you recognized something else? A voice? Maybe a House pendant?"

"All I remember is ringing in my ears and pain in my body, and a blinding light . . . "

Andreas cast a concerned look to his father. "Well, I'm glad you didn't go into the light, crazy girl. And I'm sorry I didn't get to you sooner."

"It's not your fault."

"We are going to find who did this," Shade said as he loomed near my feet. "I promise. But for now, we need to keep this quiet. The instability of Fire and Fluorite is a problem right now, and word getting out that someone is out there trying to pick off our weakest members will do nothing to help the situation."

Andreas shot to his feet. "You want to keep this quiet?"

"Just until we can find out who did it and deal with them accordingly," his father said, palms out to ward off his son's growing rage.

"We need to hunt them down and make an example of what happens to someone who comes after the House of Fire and Fluorite."

"And we will, but—"

"It's okay, Andreas," I said, trying once again to push myself up. "Your dad is right. He needs to do what's best for the House right now."

"Rowe," Shade said, sympathetic eyes meeting mine, "please lie back and rest. I've sent for a healer—"

"No," I argued, pain lancing through my side as I shifted toward the edge of the couch. "That will only alert someone to what's going on. The fewer people that know, the better."

Before he could respond, a buzzing sounded in the room. I looked over to see my cell phone sitting on the table, a little worse for the wear but still intact. Andreas picked it up and checked the screen. His expression soured. "It's Myra."

I exhaled hard. "She'll keep calling if I don't answer," I replied. His resigned expression said he knew I was right. He offered the phone and I answered the call, quickly putting the phone to my ear.

"Are you okay?" she shouted by way of greeting. "I heard something happened on the edge of No Man's Land tonight—the part you go through to get home."

"I'm fine-ish—"

"So it was you?"

"Yep."

She cursed creatively under her breath. "Where are you now? Do I need to come get you?"

"Andreas found me and brought me to his place," I said.

"Are you hurt?"

"I said I was fine—"

"Concussion for sure. Heavily bruised. Sliced-open leg," Andreas said over me. "Probably a fracture or two, but we don't know because she's being a stubborn ass."

More muttered cursing. "Rowe, I'm so sorry."

"You didn't beat me up, so there's no need for you to apologize—"

"Maybe not, but—" She cut herself off, realizing the others could clearly overhear our conversation. "We shouldn't have let you go home alone."

"I absolve you of your guilt. Yael, too, if he's even capable of any."

"He is," she said softly. "He went pale when someone came in talking about an attack in that part of No Man's Land. He's the one that pieced together the location and time and realized it could have been you."

"If he feels bad, tell him he can be the one to break it to Ravi that I won't be in until I feel less shitty."

"Deal," she said, laughing lightly. It died off, leaving an awkward silence in its wake. "Rowe . . . are you going to be okay? For real?"

"She is," Andreas said, leaning in closer. "I'll make sure of it."

His reply was initially met with silence. "Maybe I was wrong about the puppy dog," she said, sounding irritated at that realization.

"Don't worry," I said. "I won't tell anyone."

"Good." Indistinguishable voices sounded in the background on her end, and I heard her muffle the phone to reply. "Hey, I have to go. Call me later so I know you're all right?"

"Careful, Myra. That sounds a lot like checking in on me, which would imply that you care. We can't have that ruining your cold-hearted bitch reputation, now can we?"

"Tell the puppy dog to keep his mouth shut, and we should be good."

At that, I actually laughed, then clutched my burning ribs. "Deal."

"I'll talk to you soon, then. And be careful, Rowe . . . I mean it." The line went dead, and I tossed the phone down by my legs. I noticed the bandage around my calf and the missing part of my pant leg that must have been cut off in the process. Guess I'd forgotten about that injury.

I looked up to find Shade and Andreas staring at me and forced a smile. "Myra grows on you over time."

"Like Adora and Danni?" Andreas replied. "I'll have to take your word for it." He shifted slightly as he looked at me. "Why does Myra think she shouldn't have let you go home alone tonight?"

I shot him a look that begged him to put the pieces together so we didn't have to spell it out in front of his father, who didn't need my drama to deal with on top of the House bullshit he was buried in.

"Myra's a bit paranoid about everything," I said, hoping the generic response would work.

"Seems like she was right to be tonight," Shade replied, eyes narrowing. "Do you remember anything else about the attack?"

I shook my head. "Nothing. But maybe I will after some sleep."

"I'll take you to my room," Andreas said, hooking his arm behind my back. "You can stay there tonight."

Once again, visions of Volker assaulted my mind. If something really had gone down at the queen's, then I needed to see him—to make sure everything really was okay. And to find out what the fuck had happened.

I sure as hell couldn't do that in Andreas' bedroom.

"I'm fine, really. Just a little banged up. Let's not play 'baby the human' tonight, okay? My ego has been battered enough already. I just want to go home."

"Rowe, there's no way," he argued, his arm going stiff behind me. "You need to stay."

"I appreciate your concern, but I'd feel better in my own bed where I can sleep off this nightmare evening."

"You can't be alone," Andreas argued. "Someone needs to keep an eye on you."

"I'll be fine. I'm pretty sure I still have a couple of Mom's old healing potions lying around somewhere that might help. Or there's that edible I've been saving for a rainy day . . . "

His expression soured. "I'm not sure this is the time for recreational drug use."

I forced a sly smile. "Isn't it always time for that?"

"Andreas is right, Rowe. You really shouldn't be alone," Shade said from behind his son. The second I opened my mouth to argue, he put up his palm to deflect my impending rant. "But as long as you have one of your mother's potions to help you, I'll allow it—for tonight." He shifted his gaze to his son. "Take her home and make sure she has something to help take the edge off her damage since she's as stubborn as her mother and won't see a healer."

"Thank you," I said softly as I eased myself upright and swung my legs off the couch. The second my toes hit the floor and I attempted to put weight on them, my knees buckled and I lurched forward—right into Andreas' arms.

"I'm carrying you out," he said as he shifted me in his arms.

"No, you're not."

"Rowe, you don't have to prove anything to us. We know you're tough."

"I'm not trying to prove it to you," I argued, cutting him off, tears welling in my eyes. "I need to prove it to myself."

Sympathy flashed in his expression, but he still didn't look happy about the situation. The fact that he didn't launch into an argument was a win. I disentangled myself delicately from his arms and tried to take a step onto my wounded leg. Andreas looped his arm around my waist to help me, and together, we headed for the door.

"Make sure she's settled before you return," Shade reminded him as he followed us into the grand foyer. "She will be safe there for now, but there will be no leaving our territory until we know more about this. We can't be complacent."

"I will."

Andreas and I shuffled to the doorway at an embarrassing pace, but he never said a thing. The pain in my leg and the bandage tying it off made for an awkward gait, not that I was trying to take off at a sprint. Pretty sure my head would have exploded immediately.

Not one for goodbyes, I opened the door and hopped outside without another word. The chill of the air permeated deeper than expected, and I shivered. I was exhausted and broken, and all I wanted to do was curl up and sleep for a week.

Andreas helped me to his truck in silence, then opened the passenger door. I stared at the elevated seat and took a deep breath. "Have you ever considered a compact hybrid? It's better for the environment and friends who got their asses beat."

He choked on a laugh, then scooped me up in his arms before I could argue. "It's not that high." He placed me in the seat gently. "Besides, the back is so handy for piling bodies . . . " Before I could even comment, he climbed over top of me with the seatbelt in tow. I winced when it pressed against my ribs. Andreas flinched and pulled away. "I'm sorry, but I have to put this on. I can't risk you getting hurt on the way home."

"It'll just add to the story."

He flashed me a playful grin. "I'd rather not, if it's all the same to you." He closed the door and ran around to the driver's side. The hinges creaked as he hopped in next to me. The engine revved to life, and we were on our way. "Is there anything else you want to tell me?" he asked, hesitation in his tone as he spoke. "Maybe something you didn't want to say in front of Dad?"

His meaning slammed into my addled mind. "No, nothing like that."

He let out a tiny sigh of relief as he wove through the neighborhood, headed toward the meeting hall. As he drove, I tried to grab hold of the fragmented memories floating around in my mind. The snippets of voices and muffled words. Through the jumbled mess, the memory of a bright light and a male voice floated to the forefront until I could almost grab it—almost hear him. "Now is not the time for death," I whispered as the words solidified in my mind.

"What?" Andreas asked, panic in his voice as he turned onto the main road. "What is it? Do you remember something."

"Sort of . . . "

He dared a glance at me as he sped down the street. "What is it?" I stared out the window as the weight of the memory pressed down on me. "Say something, Rowe—please. You're scaring me—"

"It's nothing helpful," I said. "Just thinking about that light again." Silence. "Did you see anything when you found me? Any sign of the guys that did it?"

His grip on the wheel tightened. "I was too focused on your body lying there, unmoving, to even notice. I was blinded by the need to help you." He exhaled hard and his shoulders slumped forward. "I'm sorry, Rowe. I should have paid better attention, but I . . . " His jaw flexed as he fought against the emotion rising within him.

I slowly reached over and rested my hand on his arm. "It's okay, Andreas. You found me. You saved me. I'm here because of you."

His arm tightened under my hand, and I looked over to see him staring back. "Are you sure there's nothing else?" he asked. "Nothing else that can help me find who did this?"

I let out a breath. "No. Not right now."

"It just doesn't make any sense . . . why would someone try to kill you?"

"I don't know. Maybe your dad is right. Maybe someone is trying to send him a message—rattle him somehow."

"They're going to really wish they hadn't," he muttered under his breath, his temper simmering just below the surface.

"You need to let your father sort this out. And if he wants to keep it under the radar as much as possible until he knows more, then let him do that."

"He should be mounting a search party to hunt those bastards down and kill them," he replied, venom in his tone. "That's how you show people the House is still strong. How you tell others not to fuck with what's yours."

"But you and I both know that it's not that simple right now."

"The hell it isn't."

I shifted in my seat, and a wave of nausea nearly did me in. Clutching my head and the door handle, I tried to steady myself while Andreas side-eyed me, concern furrowing his brow.

"Your loyalty is one of your best qualities, Andreas, but right now, I think Shade is right about this, and you need to let it go."

He inhaled hard and let it out in one long breath. "Fine. But so help me, if I find out who did this, I will flay them alive."

"I'd expect nothing less." I forced a smile in return, but the tension it created in my head had me cutting that shit out real quick. "Ow . . . concussions really fucking hurt. Zero stars. Do not recommend."

"You need a healer."

"I need to not get jumped in alleys."

At that, he growled as he rolled up to the tiny alley beside the meeting house that led to my apartment in the back and parked the truck. The two of us sat alone in the stillness and quiet for a moment. Then he turned and looked at me, amber flecks in his eyes glowing as his wolf peeked through. "I really want you to stay with us," he said, his voice low and rumbling. "With *me* . . . "

"I know," I said, squeezing his arm, "but I need this—and I need you to respect why."

The beast within backed away, leaving the man before me. "We wouldn't be here if I didn't."

I quirked a brow at him. "Oh really? I didn't realize abduction was on the table otherwise. Is that one of your skill sets I wasn't aware of?"

He stared at me in silence for a beat longer than was comfortable. Combined with the weight of his stare, I found myself squirming in my seat. "I have many skill sets you don't know about."

The awkwardness increased and the tension skyrocketed. I

quickly opened the door. "I should get to bed." I struggled with the seatbelt, which was apparently hell-bent on holding me hostage, before it finally relented, and I carefully turned in my seat, ready to escape the pressure cooker the truck had become.

I tried to step down and missed the foot rail, which sent me lurching forward. But Andreas was somehow there, arms out to catch me. "I am definitely carrying you this time," he said as he looped his arm under my legs and hefted me up.

"I can walk."

"Not without hurting yourself more, so if it's all the same to you, I'll make sure you get inside before you manage to add to your injuries." He had me halfway to the back door by the time I opened my mouth to argue, so I didn't bother. Instead, I rested my head against his shoulder, enjoying the comfort I felt as I closed my eyes.

"No sleeping yet," he said softly. "And unless you want me to search your pockets, you're going to have to give me your keys."

My eyes shot open and my body went rigid at the thought of him rummaging around in my tight pants. If he noticed, he had the good manners not to laugh.

I pulled them out and handed them over, the vision of him feeling me up in search of them still steamrolling over all other conscious thought. But the second they jangled in the door, realization stabbed me like a knife through the heart, because the odds were pretty fucking high that there was a fae assassin who loved to lurk in my apartment waiting inside. And if Andreas saw him, that wouldn't end well for anybody.

The deadbolt turned over, and panic flooded my system for the second time that night. "I'll be fine," I said loudly as I tried—painfully—to wriggle out of his hold. "You can put me down and head home."

He looked at me like I'd taken leave of every one of my senses. "Not a chance." His grip on me tightened enough to keep me in place, but not enough to cause further damage. "I've been directed to make sure you've taken something and are set up for the night, and that's what I intend to do. And if you argue with me, I'll sit next to your bed all night long and watch you sleep . . . or climb in with you . . . "

I swallowed hard. "That won't be necessary."

He laughed as he pushed the door open, the sound of it warming, but not enough to eclipse the icy dread floating in my veins. His hand reached for the light switch, but I swatted it away. "No lights!" I practically screamed. Because if the Moonlight Wraith was indeed waiting for me in my room, I needed him to do that fun little disappearing trick before Andreas saw him. I had no clue if he could scent him, and I closed my eyes and said a quick prayer that he couldn't. Then I took a deep breath and tried not to act like a complete crazy person. "They hurt my head."

"Good thing I can see well in the dark, then, because I'm pretty sure your room is a disaster."

"As always."

Andreas navigated the dark room as he fulfilled his father's order. I was able to find one of my mother's healing potions in the medicine cabinet, and I downed the bitter liquid with a water chaser to cut the vile, herbal taste. I had no idea how effective it would be after so many years, but it was what I had to work with—and better than nothing.

"Here," Andreas said, holding up a tee and shorts in the bathroom doorway. "Let's get you into these."

"I'm good," I said, pushing past him, headed for the bed.

"You're covered in dirt and blood, Rowe—"

"I'll wash everything tomorrow. I just want to sleep now."

Without further argument, he followed me and helped get me settled in bed. He laid my phone on the nightstand next to a glass of water and my fluorite ring. "I took it off just in case you had broken fingers. I didn't want them to swell up around it."

"Thanks . . . "

"And I texted Dad to let him know you're all set," he said as he hovered next to my bed. "Are you sure you don't want me to stay?"

"I'll be fine," I said with a smile. "And I'll call if I need anything."

"You'd better." Instead of leaving, he gingerly sat down next to me on the bed—no easy feat for a guy his size—then took my hand in his. "I'm glad I got to you in time tonight . . . "

"Me too."

"I don't know what I'd do if something ever happened to you."

"You'd have to have someone else clean your house—"

"I'm serious, Rowe."

"So am I." I gave him a tiny, less painful smile, but it didn't put a dent in his somber façade. I gave his hand a tiny squeeze. "Thank you for always being there for me—you and your father both. I owe you so much."

He lingered on the edge of my bed for a moment before releasing my hand. He slowly stood, then laid a throw blanket on top of me. "I'll check on you tomorrow." He turned away and walked out the back door, shutting it softly behind him.

My exhausted mind played over the way he'd looked at me, but it was too weak to really unpack it all. My eyes drifted closed again, and all I wanted to do was sleep until the realities of my life faded away. But as the deep pull of slumber threatened to drag me down and never let go, a voice echoed softly in my ear, yanking me back up again.

"You and I need to talk." My eyes shot open to find glowing silver eyes illuminating my room, with the Moonlight Wraith at the center of it. "*Now*."

CHAPTER 27
ROWE

His stare dimmed, which was a blessing all its own, and as my eyes adjusted to the darkness yet again, Volker walked over and hovered at the edge of my bed.

"I see you survived the night." His eyes focused on my various bruises and cuts. "*Barely.*" Though his brow was creased with worry, anger seemed to seep into his tone.

"I was attacked on my way home from the restaurant tonight," I replied, letting a little of my own anger cut into my voice. "Andreas found me and took me to his house. I woke up there a little bit ago, filled them in on the few details I remember, then told them I wanted to go home, because I was pretty sure you'd be here waiting to tell me about whatever the hell happened last night with the queen."

He reached over and turned on the lamp by my bed. The faint light illuminated his tense expression as he looked me over. "You're still wounded," he said, disdain in his tone.

"Shade wanted to send for a healer, but I wouldn't let him."

His eyes skimmed over my face, which undoubtedly was covered in various shades of bruising that had started to numb a bit, thanks to my mother's potion. Then his gaze drifted lower, as though he could see the injuries that lay beneath my blanket. "Then you should let me."

I pushed myself up onto my elbows and attempted to pull my body back so I could lean against the headboard. It hurt a little, and my limbs felt exhausted, but I tried nonetheless—all while Volker watched me like a hawk. My arm buckled under my weight, and his hand shot out reflexively.

"No," I said, pulling back as he reached for me, hurting my ribs with the twisting motion. I sucked in a breath through my teeth and tried to calm my breathing so I didn't make it any worse. "I can do it."

His hand slowly withdrew, but he remained poised near the bed, leaning toward me. "My offer was not an indictment of your ability," he replied as his arm fell to his side. "And I cannot help but find it ironic that you won't accept help from the one who saved you, but you'll allow the shifter to play white knight and carry you in like a child."

My eyes went wide and I stared at him, trying to make sense of his words. Then the image of a blinding silhouette flashed in my mind, along with the disembodied voice that had accompanied it. "That was you," I said, realizing that, to someone who hadn't just had the shit knocked out of them, that point should have been obvious. The fae assassin stood stoically next to my bed. "I . . . I couldn't remember everything before I started to black out. Bits and pieces are missing, but I remember the light—and a soothing sensation through my body—"

"Had it not been for your beloved shifter, I could have finished healing you before I turned my attention to those that harmed you," he said, his tone dripping with disdain. "His arrival was unfortunate for myriad reasons."

"If you saved me, then—" I cut myself off as realization dawned. "Volker . . . did you out yourself tonight?" I asked, the words barely a whisper. "Were you glamoured when you intervened?"

He shook his head. "I cannot do that and call my blade simultaneously. It was a choice between hiding my form or protecting you. I chose the latter, seeing that I did not plan for those in the alley to live."

All-encompassing fear took over, sending a shiver down my spine. I might have inadvertently exposed his secret to Yael and Myra, but hearing rumors of his presence was one thing; seeing the Moonlight Wraith in all his murderous glory was something else entirely. Something that would surely spread like wildfire once my attackers returned to whatever gutter they'd climbed out of. "Volker—"

"I will deal with those that have seen me," he said, "but I thought it best not to expose myself to your *friend*, given the consequences."

Because Volker would have had to kill Andreas to keep his return quiet. My stomach squirmed at the thought. "Thank you—for saving me. And for sparing Andreas."

"I did not do it for him." The slight glow in his eyes as he said those words impaled me through the heart. My breath caught in my throat, and I wondered if I was hallucinating, or if the hardened fae ruler really had just admitted to doing something solely for my benefit. "Now, perhaps you might allow me to finish healing your wounds."

I quickly shook my head, rattling my injured brain in the process. I clamped my hands on my skull and prayed that the spinning would stop. Apparently, Mom's potion wasn't working as well as I'd hoped. "I can't—"

"You're being ridiculous—"

"Andreas knows I took a potion to help me heal, but he and his father both know it would only take the edge off, at best, because of its age. If I'm suddenly fine in the morning when Andreas comes to check on me, it'll be suspicious as hell. Shade might like me, but if he thinks something fishy is going on, he won't hesitate to get answers—and he can be incredibly persuasive in an interrogation if he so chooses. I wouldn't last five minutes before I caved and told him anything he wanted to know. And I don't think you want that."

"No," he replied, the word so sharp it snapped from his mouth like a whip splitting the silence, "I don't."

The way light flared in his eyes as he said those words set me on edge, and I quickly looked away. "Great, then we agree."

"I don't like this," he continued.

"Then I guess it's a good thing it's not your problem to manage, isn't it?" I replied as I held my proverbial ground against the fae.

The muscles in his jaw flexed as he bit back his reply. Those glowing eyes drifted to the bruised, bare skin of my torso peeking out from my shirt. "It is very much my problem."

"It wouldn't be if you didn't need my power," I countered, too tired and beaten down to hide the hurt I felt at those words. And as much as I wanted him to refute them, he simply stood there, stoic as ever, and stared with the icy chill of a fae ruler. He slowly reached his hand toward my face, but I caught it before it could touch me. "I'm fine—"

"Your face says otherwise."

"I don't really have the strength to do this with you right now," I said, exhaustion plain in my tone. "You said we needed to talk about something?"

His eyes narrowed and he pulled up a chair to sit next to the bed. "And we will, but first you need to tell me everything that happened tonight."

I groaned at the thought of rehashing the night's events again, but I knew there was a zero percent chance of him letting it go, so I did. He listened intently, his impassive features giving nothing away.

Until a detail I hadn't remembered until that moment came crashing to the forefront of my mind. Something that changed everything. "Orders," I whispered, disbelief choking off the word.

Volker went rigid. "What did you say?"

"They said they had orders—that they were just doing what they were told."

Anger simmered in his glare. "I can think of only two reasons why someone would bother to attack a presumed-human affiliated with Fire and Fluorite." I flinched at his unwittingly harsh words. Even though I knew they were true, it hurt to have them spoken so casually—especially by him. His eyes narrowed as he watched my reaction, and realization dawned in their depths. "What I mean is—"

"I know what you mean," I said, interrupting an explanation that would have only served to make both my headache and the situation worse. "I'm nothing to them. Nobody is going to start a war over me, unless, of course, I'm just the beginning of a move on the House—or someone else knows about my powers."

"Precisely. But if they knew what you were, they wouldn't have attacked you. They'd have abducted you." Something about the way he spoke wasn't reassuring at all.

"That's super comforting," I muttered to myself. "Can't we just pretend it was powered-up assholes being assholes and forget about it?" I asked, my frustration slowly boiling over.

He stared at me, moonlight shining in his eyes. "Had it not appeared to be an assassination, then maybe," he countered, "but it did, so no."

I let out a sigh and rested my head back against the headboard. "None of this makes sense," I said, staring up at the ceiling. "I need a shower. Maybe that'll help, since it's apparent I won't be getting any sleep at the moment."

I gently lowered my legs over the edge of the bed and stood up slowly as Volker scrutinized my every move. With some difficulty I managed to walk to the bathroom and close the door behind me before I turned the shower on, praying the hot water would work. As I wavered on my feet, I heard the door click open, and I turned to find him staring at me unapologetically. "I don't need your help," I said as I stuck my fingers into the water stream to see if it was safe to enter yet.

"I think I'll be the one to decide that."

"Volker—"

"If it would make the little queen feel better, I'll avert my eyes while she undresses."

"It would."

As promised, he turned around to stare at the only picture in the room, a cheap print I'd found on my way home from work one day. With his focus elsewhere, I turned my back to him and carefully reached down to my hem. I tried to pull the tight t-shirt up over my head, but my ribs burned with every little twist and torque, and it wasn't long before I knew that the simple act of stripping wasn't going to be simple at all.

"Would you like to change your mind?" Volker asked, his low voice in my ear.

No.

"I don't think I can do this on my own," I said as tears welled in my eyes. Tears of frustration. Tears of pain.

His cool fingertips grazed my sides as he gripped my shirt, gently pulling it from my grasp. "Then I guess it's fortuitous that you don't have to." With great care and elegance, he maneuvered me out of my t-shirt. His finger slipped under the band of my bra and slid to the clasp. "Shall I assist with this as well?"

Goosebumps broke out across my skin at his touch. "Please . . . " The hooks released with ease, and I clutched the front against my chest.

I looked down at my ruined, skin-tight pants and groaned. There was no good (or modest) way to go about taking those off.

"It will be all right, little queen," he said softly as he reached around me to unfasten my jeans. "I promised I'd avert my eyes—and I cannot lie, remember?"

I stifled a laugh that threatened to become a sob as he slowly pushed my jeans over my hips, taking my underwear along for the ride. With my back to him, I had no idea if he'd kept his word or not, but I closed my eyes as though that would somehow make me invisible. Because it was one thing to fantasize about the fae assassin pulling my pants down—under very different circumstances—but it was quite another thing to be living the experience.

My body was a mess of adrenaline and hormones and warring emotions that I didn't have the energy for.

I felt the cool air on my thighs as he worked his way to my ankles with tactical precision until he gently lifted one foot at a time to free me of the rest of my clothes. "This bandage needs to come off, too," he said, fingers tracing around my calf to my shin where Shade had attempted to patch up my wound.

I opened my eyes in a panic and looked over my shoulder to find Volker crouched down, his face only inches from my left hip, his eyes closed, just as he'd promised. His fingers continued to drag along the tape on my shin as he awaited my answer. Grabbing a towel off the hook next to me, I dropped my bra and wrapped the fluffy white fabric around me. "You can open your eyes now."

His gaze slowly worked its way up my body until it met mine. Without looking, he easily removed the tape and gauze from my shin, then rose to face me, with only the silence building between us to fill the narrow gap separating our bodies.

He drew the shower curtain back and took my hand. "So you don't fall trying to get in," he explained. "I wouldn't want to offend your sensibilities by having to scoop your naked body out of the shower." A mischievous smile tugged at his lips, and I took the bait.

"I'm gonna need you to close your eyes again."

His smile widened. "Of course."

He did as I asked and turned his head for good measure before I dropped my towel and climbed into the shower. The warmth felt amazing, and I drew the curtain closed so I could brace my hands on the wall and let the water wash away the remnants of the evening. But when I looked down at the state of my body and the red swirling at my feet, I knew that wasn't possible. The tears that had threatened to escape only moments earlier trailed down my face along with the water as I released the emotions I'd suppressed. I'd nearly died that night—had essentially given up—and if it hadn't been for Volker, I might have.

But he'd come for me. Saved me. And even though I knew I shouldn't romanticize that fact, I couldn't seem to help myself.

I exhaled hard, trying to clear my muddled mind. I knew the

warm water wouldn't last forever—nor would the weak effects of my mother's potion—so I cleaned up as much as I could, then shut the water off and poked my hand out to grab the towel hanging on the hook nearby. The one I'd used to cover myself, then dropped on the floor.

I cursed under my breath.

"Are you in need of this?" Volker asked before the towel in question poked past the curtain.

"Thanks," I replied, still hidden behind the flimsy, semi-transparent barrier. With effort, I dried off as much of my body as I could, then wrapped the towel around me again and opened the curtain.

"I found this," Volker said, holding up a clean white tee.

"Thanks."

I reached to take it from him, but he pulled it away. "Turn around so I don't have to do this with my eyes closed." Not wanting to argue, I did as he asked, then rewrapped the towel around my waist. With skill I didn't possess, he managed to get the cropped tee over me without incident, leaving me only in need of bottoms.

When I turned back around, Volker's eyes quickly dropped to where the tee clung to my damp chest. I forced myself not to glance down and see just how see-through it had become.

"Now these," he said, drawing my attention to the black underwear dangling from his index finger.

My skin flushed red with embarrassment, but I was in deep. No point in stopping. "Yep."

Volker bent down and waited for me to carefully slip my feet through the holes. His pewter gaze slid up my legs along with the thin black fabric until both his hands and my underwear disappeared beneath the towel. His fingertips grazed my thighs, and I sucked in a painful breath at the contact as they continued to climb higher.

"I can do the rest," I said, reaching down to take over the job. Without argument, he released them and slowly stood. I yanked them up just in time for the towel to fall to the floor. Volker's eyes slid up my bare legs and beyond until they finally fixed on mine.

"Pants," I said out of nowhere. "I need pants."

"*Need* seems a strong word choice."

I swallowed hard, then carefully stepped past him to find whatever Andreas had pulled out for me earlier. I'd never been more aware of how naked I felt than I was at that moment, and I was willing to put on just about anything to escape being half-naked in Volker's presence.

"I've been wondering something," he said as I scrambled to locate anything to put on.

"Yeah? What's that?"

"How you convinced your precious wolf to bring you here and then leave," he said as he watched me intently.

I buried my head in my laundry basket, desperate to find pants. Any pants. *Where in the hell are those shorts Andreas found . . . ?*

"I told him I needed to prove to myself that I'd be okay alone."

"But you're not alone," Volker said in my ear, startling me. I yelped and whirled around to find him staring down at me, amused delight sparkling in his dark eyes—until he saw me wince and grab my ribs.

Then concern quickly took its place.

"True, but he doesn't know that," I countered, trying to control my breathing. "Unless you want me to tell him that the presumed-dead Moonlight Wraith is lurking behind me while I try to get dressed."

"I don't imagine that information would go over well—for many reasons," he said, taking a small step backward.

"I'm not interested in having this discussion again," I said with a sigh.

His eyes raked over my bare legs again, and I immediately picked up the pace.

"Finding pants is what I'm interested in right now," I said, turning to rifle through the basket one more time. But before I could, I felt his breath on my neck as he spoke, rustling the tiny baby hairs at my nape that had begun to dry.

"So I see . . . "

My heart sped at his words, and the aching in my ribs ramped up along with my breathing. Pain lanced my side, and I abandoned my fruitless search for pants and headed back to the bathroom. Whatever benefits my mother's healing potion had were definitely wearing off, and I wanted to wrap my ribs before the task became more painful than it was worth.

I grabbed a stretch bandage out of the vanity drawer and carefully hoisted my shirt up, tucking it under my arm to keep it in place. I'd made it maybe five seconds before I remembered why I hated those stupid wraps. The rolled-up section squeezed out of my hand and shot out of the bathroom, trailing across the floor. It stopped when it bumped into Volker's boot, and he bent down slowly to retrieve it. "Ugh, these things are impossible . . . "

"Then maybe you should let me help you, since you won't allow me to heal you." He rolled the wrap back up with nimble fingers and walked toward me, not stopping until his body was right next to mine, his hands grazing my ribcage. The second his skin met mine, my pain was eclipsed by something far more urgent, something warm and welcome coursing through my body.

I watched as he deftly wrapped my naked torso with gentleness I didn't fully understand. He tied it off with ease, but remained where he stood only inches from me. The tension filling that narrow space was unbearable.

"How did you find me tonight?" I asked, my voice soft and low. "How did you show up just in time?"

I forced myself to meet his gaze as he stared down at me, his expression unreadable. "Because I am never far away from what's important to me."

Important. Right. Because I was his ticket to vengeance, and that wouldn't go anywhere if I were dead. Somehow, barely dressed with him staring at me, I'd nearly forgotten that fact. Perhaps that was one of his powers, too. "Well, thanks again for saving me," I whispered.

He canted his head in a curious manner and his dark grey eyes began to glow. That eerie gaze slowly slid down my body until it fixed on my bandaged ribs. Then his hands fell upon them again. "I know you asked me not to, but I think you'll find this better than your bandage," he said as a different kind of warmth flowed through my body, emanating from him into me. With every passing second, I could feel my bones healing, knitting together in an obvious way, but I felt no pain. No ill effects at all. Mouth hanging open, I looked up at him to find him smiling—like *really smiling*—back at me. "Even if I didn't get your consent to fix them first."

"But Shade—"

"I have only healed what's inside," he explained. "I've left the bulk of your bruises and cuts for show, though you may want to leave this bandage in place, as well as one on your leg, to help sell the illusion."

"Okay . . . thank you. I feel like I owe you one now . . . "

His fingertips tightened around my newly healed ribs, and I sucked in a breath, but not from pain. "Never admit your indebtedness to a fae, little queen—we take that sort of thing quite seriously."

My mouth went dry at his words. "How seriously?"

Mischief blazed in his eyes. "I'm not sure you really want to know."

The way he was looking at me, I wasn't sure I did, either, but somebody needed to tell that to the warm sensation building between my legs at the thought. "I should probably find some pants and go to bed . . . "

Neither of us moved.

"You probably should." His eyes dropped to my skimpy underwear, and his fingers dug in a bit more. "You wouldn't want your little friend to show up tomorrow and find you like this."

"I wouldn't?"

His eyes flared. "*I* wouldn't."

I swallowed hard and shifted slightly, but his grip didn't relent. "My pants are in there," I said, pointing toward the basket in the other room.

"So they are . . . "

I couldn't take the intensity of the moment any longer, and I reached down to pull his hands away. This time, they moved, and I quickly darted to the laundry basket and dumped the whole thing out on the floor. I grabbed a pair of grey sweatpants and quickly bent over to pull them on.

"You'll probably want this, too," he said from the bathroom doorway. I stole a glance back at him to find him rummaging through his coat pockets for something, eyes fixed on me as I wriggled into my sweats, boobs jiggling in my wet, white top. He withdrew his hand and tossed something on the bed. "I found it in the alley where you were attacked," he explained as I walked over to the bed to see what it was. "I went back there to look for clues. It must have fallen off at some point, which is understandable, given the circumstances."

I stopped short of the bed, icy horror washing over me as I looked down to see a pale green crystal pendant lying on my comforter. A fluorite pendant.

My gaze snapped to the ring lying on my nightstand while every ounce of blood drained from my face. I stared at the crystal as dread and realization tightened my throat.

Volker, keen as always, took notice of my reaction. "Little queen . . . what's wrong?" he asked. But I couldn't answer. All I could do was walk over to the nightstand and pluck my ring from the surface, then slip it on my finger.

Volker's eyes went wide as he took in the ring, then narrowed to slits as the truth careened into him.

The pendant he'd found wasn't mine.

And that could only mean one thing.

CHAPTER 28
VOLKER

Anger roiled inside me.

When I'd learned that Rowe's attack hadn't been a random event, I immediately suspected Nyssa. I'd stolen the very thing she'd used to help overthrow me, and it would make sense for her to eliminate its power source so I couldn't use it against her. But to outsource the task to members of Fire and Fluorite made no sense at all.

And the pain of betrayal staring back at me in Rowe's eyes was more than I could bear.

Someone from her own House had done this to her—her allies. Her people. Those her mother had once turned to had turned on her, and the weight of that realization was certain to pull her down into a dark abyss. She had worked so hard to carve out a bit of happiness for herself there, and that had been all but set ablaze at the sight of that pendant.

I'd been a fool not to have considered the fact that it might not have been hers, but seeing her lying there broken and battered had undone something inside of me—that dark, feral beast within—and there had been no logic to be found. Even after I'd ensured she'd survive, all I could think about had been her whereabouts and her physical state. Andreas might have taken her away, but he could not do for her what I could.

So I'd waited for her return, the pendant in my pocket.

Now all I wanted to do was take back the moment I'd revealed it.

"I'm sorry, little queen," I said cautiously, daring a step closer to where she stood in silent disbelief. "I had no idea."

"My own House," she said as though she hadn't heard me, her mind clearly in a daze. Her faint voice hung in the air between us as we both stood unmoving. "It was my own House . . . my *family* . . . "

"They will pay for what they've done," I replied, that darkness rising within me once again as the despair in her expression grew. Her knees buckled, and I caught her as she crumpled. I lowered her to the floor and crouched next to her, staring into her bleary eyes as she processed this betrayal.

"My family," she repeated. "But *why*? Why would my own family do this to me? Am I that awful?"

The desperation in her voice nearly did me in. "Little queen—"

"Is my humanness *so* offensive that they wanted me dead?" she continued. "They didn't just try to kill me, Volker. They beat me—played with me like it was a *game*." A spark of something ignited deep within her emerald eyes, and it grew until the flames of anger burned, temporarily eclipsing her sadness. "Like my life doesn't fucking matter because I'm human."

"But you aren't," I countered, pushing her hair from her face. "You are so much more than that."

Her eyes narrowed to slits. "Well, that doesn't seem to really fucking matter, does it?"

"Only because they don't know."

"Like that would change anything." She got to her feet, determination and anger fueling her. "If they did, they'd just find a way to do exactly what you're doing—to use me." I flinched at her accusation.

But the truth was the only weapon she could wield in that moment, and I let her because she was angry. Because she was hurting. And I'd have given anything to take that away. "What good is the power if it can't really help me, anyway? What good is being a member of this House if it can't even protect me from itself?" Her questions remained unanswered as I stared at her in silence, my hands balling into fists. "My mother may have been a fool for bringing me to this place, but I was an even bigger one to think that being a member really meant anything." She choked on a morbid laugh that sounded more like a restrained sob. "The truth is, I'm dispensable . . . but at least I really understand that now."

I took a slow, measured step toward her. "Not to me, you're not—"

She cut me off with a dismissive wave. "Right, right, right. Because I'm the wellspring and you need me—I know."

"Little queen—"

"You know what I want in exchange for my power?" she asked, cutting me off. I stiffened at the question. "A world that doesn't care that I'm human. Can you give me that?" I said nothing in response, and she let out a mirthless laugh. "Yeah . . . I didn't think so."

"You have friends elsewhere," I said as I continued to inch closer. "The girl from the alley the night I met you . . . she is not from this House."

"No," she replied, disdain in her tone, "but let's be honest; even if Danni is with the king of Blood and Beryl, do you really think it'd be any different for me there, even with her protection? I mean, I have Shade and Andreas here, and that didn't seem to matter much tonight."

"If Elias is bonded to your friend, he might be more invested in your safety—"

"More than the man who was basically a father to me?" she countered, a frown tugging at her lips. "Do me a favor, Volker: don't try to placate me. It's not a good look. Brutal truth suits you better. And you and I both know what that truth is. There's no place for me in this House, or this world, for that matter," she said, sadness choking off her words. "And there never will be." Her tear-rimmed eyes looked to me, and fury flared deep inside. "Maybe that's why wellsprings go crazy. Maybe it's not the power—maybe it's the paranoia and isolation."

Something wild and feral rumbled in my chest. "That will never happen to you."

"It doesn't matter," she said as she walked to the edge of her bed and climbed in. Scooping the blanket up around her, she hid herself away. Her anger had abated, leaving behind little more than a shell of the being I'd first met in that alley.

And the beast inside me raged.

"I want to be alone now," she said. I could not ignore the sudden flat, dead tone of her voice. "Just go away—please."

"And if someone comes for you while I'm gone?"

She looked over at me, towering over her bed like the enemy, and answered with an icy calm that sent a chill down my spine. "Then I guess you'll have to avenge those who betrayed you without my help." The resignation in her voice was terrifying in a way I didn't fully understand, and the beast strained against his leash until I feared it would snap. "And if I'm still here tomorrow when you return, I guess you'll still have a chance to get what you came for."

"I don't like this—"

"And I don't care anymore," she said as she rolled away from me. "Just go."

"Little queen—*Rowe*—listen to me—"

"Know when to cut your losses, Volker," she said as she burrowed deep into the covers, the final bit of fight leaving her entirely. "Even I've figured that out . . . "

I stared at her back until I knew I could no longer withhold my growing rage. The darkness crept up my spine, spreading with every passing second until I could think of nothing but the dejection in her voice and the need for revenge. Without a word of goodbye, I disappeared into the ether, my mind singularly focused on vengeance for the one whose spirit they'd broken.

For Rowe.

For *my* little queen.

Let the hunt begin . . .

CHAPTER 29
VOLKER

It took only an hour to find them.

Their faces were etched into my memory, and I now knew their House of origin; it was only a matter of time before I tracked them down. And they made it easier still by sequestering themselves together at a home only blocks away from the little queen's.

As silent as the dead, I crept through the shadows, edging along the side of the brick façade toward the voices in the backyard. Hearty laughter rang out, and the distinctive clink of bottles followed. There was no remorse for their actions. No worry. No fear of retribution.

But retribution was coming.

My rage burned brighter still.

"Do you think she's even conscious yet?" a male asked as I crouched down at the edge of the house to survey my prey. They sat in chairs around a fire, feet kicked up as they lounged around like they hadn't just tried to kill one of their own.

"Probably, but it doesn't matter. She'll never know it was us that did it."

"The way she tried to crawl away," another said with a laugh. "Fucking pitiful—"

"What did you expect? She's human."

The way he said that word—like her life was of no consequence because of her humanity—made my blood boil.

"So what happens now?" a fourth male asked, leaning forward on his knees, the light of the flames flickering in his eyes.

"Now we wait," the original speaker said as he rose from his seat. No longer obscured by the others, I recognized him as their leader—the one who'd been closest to Rowe when she'd lain on the ground, wounded and helpless. I could feel my blade begging to be called forth—to cut him down and bathe in his blood.

But it was clear that he was the one with answers.

I'd let him live long enough to share them.

"What are we going to do about the guy that showed up?" one asked.

"I don't know who the fuck that was," the leader replied, "but I plan to find out."

"Then allow me to introduce myself," I said as I shot forth from the shadows, blade blazing in my hand. It sliced through the nearest shifter with ease, cleaving him in half. The leader and another were already on their feet, but the third was too stunned to respond quickly enough. He turned just in time to see my blade pierce his chest. With a sharp twist, I withdrew it, his heart skewered on the tip.

Momentum and speed carried me directly toward the one who'd mocked Rowe's pain—so I would give him his own. He'd already begun to shift, but the process was slower than I was, and it proved to be his downfall. He leapt at me in a state of half-change, but all that did was give me the perfect angle to slice through his flesh. I ducked as I raised my weapon and drew it across his belly as he arced over me. Blood rained down like the heavens themselves had opened up and purged the red liquid in torrents.

That left only the one in charge still standing; his anger and loyalty had kept him from fleeing, just as I'd known it would. He growled at me from across the fire pit, eyes glowing with a golden hue as his claws extended—his beast preparing to come out and play.

His eyes went wide as he took me in, blade gleaming in the night, then narrowed to slits. "I know you, he growled. "You're supposed to be dead."

"As you soon will be."

We circled the roaring fire, each sizing the other up with every passing step. He was the largest by far and undoubtedly the strongest, but that would not save him, and judging by the resignation in his eyes, he knew it.

"Why are you here?" he asked, the strength of his voice wavering slightly as his foot brushed against the lower half of his fallen comrade. He glanced down at him reflexively, and I sprang over the fire, blade drawn back to strike.

"You broke something very important to me," I replied, smiling like the devil.

"What the fuck are you talking about?" His ignorance only fueled my rage.

"A girl in an alley . . . does that help jog your memory?"

His expression bled from confusion to sly amusement. "Oh . . . that bitch. We definitely broke her—"

"I'm not here for you to tell me what I already know," I said, inching closer to the shifter. "I want to know who ordered the attack."

The firelight danced in his dark eyes as he smirked. "I don't know anything about that," he said, though his smug tone said otherwise. "But I *do* know she cried like a baby when I carved her leg open with the tip of my claw, and when I bounced her head off the pavement. I've never heard anything that pathetic in my life."

"You will momentarily," I said, heat creeping up my spine at the thought of what he'd done to her—and at his utter lack of remorse.

"Do what you want, but I'll never fucking tell you anything."

At that, I smiled. "That's what they all say—at first."

I lunged for him, my blade slicing his thigh clean to the bone, but not through it. No, this needed to last a while, needed to cause him pain like he'd caused Rowe. He needed to feel every slice, every blow. And even then, it wouldn't be enough.

He roared in anger as he turned, sweeping his clawed hand out in a wild arc. With a flick of my wrist, I sent that hand flying across the yard to land on one of his friends' corpses. The spurting blood sizzled in the fire, and he clutched his arm to his chest to staunch the flow until his shifter genes kicked in to heal the wound.

"I'll take you piece by piece if I must, but this would be easier if you'd just tell me what I want to know," I said as I stepped gracefully over his fallen comrade. "You won't live, of course, but your compliance would earn you a speedy demise—a mercy, to be certain."

He looked at me, eyes wide and wild like a caged animal, then smiled. "She must be a sweet piece if you're this angry about it." I spun and smashed the hilt of my blade into his mouth. He spit blood and teeth across the yard, then smiled again. "I should have had some when I had her face down in the alley. I bet that really would have made her scream—"

I plunged my blade into his belly and hoisted him above my head. His limp body slumped against my sword, his breath coming in shallow gasps as his fading power attempted to heal him. Dark eyes with hints of gold stared down at me as I looked up at my soon-to-be victim and watched as the reality of his death flashed in his eyes.

"You should never have laid a hand on my little queen," I said, my calm tone belying the storm raging inside. And with a jerk of my arm, the moonlight blade carved through him, drinking its fill of his bounty. His lifeless body fell to the ground at my feet and I turned to leave, anger still coursing through me. Anger that had driven my rash behavior.

But as I walked away, I realized that it didn't really matter. Nobody would ever hurt her again.

I'd make certain of that.

CHAPTER 30
ROWE

The light scuff of boots on hardwood woke me.

Memories of what had happened in the alley flashed in my mind seconds after the noise registered, and I threw the blankets back as I shot up in bed. Shadows in the far corner moved slowly until a foot edged its way into the sliver of light shining through the kitchen window. My breath lodged in my throat as fear captured me and held me tight, preventing me from moving. From fleeing. From doing anything other than sitting paralyzed, awaiting my fate.

A pant leg, wet with something nearly as dark as the fabric, soon followed, then the hem of a midnight blue coat—covered in blood.

A different kind of fear took hold of me, and I was on my unsteady feet in seconds, watching as Volker slipped fully into view. His coat fanned open to expose his white-stained-red shirt. Splotches of blood dotted their way up his neck and speckled his face, the contrast of deep burgundy against his pale skin as stark as it was alarming when combined with his slow pace.

Worry freed my feet, and I darted to him. "You're hurt," I said as I tore open his shirt to uncover the source of all that blood, as though I could do a damn thing if he were bleeding to death.

Volker remained steady and silent as I tugged and ripped at his clothes. My frantic efforts to find his injuries revealed nothing, and I pulled away, wild-eyed and breathing hard as I stared at him. His arm rose slowly and his fingertips grazed my temple, trailing lightly over my forehead to the other side in an arc, sweeping my wild hair from my face. "The blood isn't mine," he said as he lowered his arm, his body otherwise painfully still.

I looked up into those cold grey eyes and found a hint of warmth brewing, brightening their dark hue ever so slightly. "Whose is it, Volker?" I asked in a whisper. "Whose blood?"

His piercing stare narrowed. "It belonged to those who hurt you."

Silence. "Are they . . . "

"Dead?" he said, completing the thought I couldn't bring myself to say aloud. "Yes. All of them."

"You killed them." A statement, not a question.

"Yes." He stood before me as though he were awaiting a verdict about to be handed down. As if my judgment would somehow direct his next move. But it never came.

Instead, I asked the question that was running through my mind on repeat. "Because they could have ruined your plan?"

"*No.*" The fingertips still touching my side flexed for a split second. "So they could never hurt you again."

I leaned in closer. "Because you don't want to endanger your magical ticket to vengeance?" I asked, the words barely escaping.

The moonlight streaming in through my window highlighted the harsh planes of his face as his jaw muscles clenched. His fingers flexed again. "Because I never want to see the light in your eyes fade like that again," he said, his voice low and thick and husky. "See the spark deep within you die . . . "

"My spark didn't die." I reached down, took his other hand, and placed it gently on the bare skin peeking out of my v-neck—right over my heart. "It's still in here, alive and well. Just like me." My heart thundered wildly against my ribs like it was trying to free itself. To be closer to his touch.

But the icy fae seemed unfazed by its antics. "I see that."

"Is that why you came? To tell me the news?" I asked, pressing his hand tighter against my bare skin. "And to check on me?"

More silence. "Yes."

I leaned in closer. "Are those the only reasons?"

Hesitation. "No."

"Do you think I'm still in danger?"

"*Yes*," he all but growled in response, and his body tensed as I lifted my chin to better meet his gaze.

"You're afraid for me." He didn't refute my claim, and a strange sense of boldness washing over me. "Because you care about me."

That alien stare raked over my face like a starving man searching for food, and I nearly came undone. Without alcohol fueling me this time, I pushed up onto my tiptoes until my nose nearly brushed his. When he didn't pull away, my free hand wrapped around the back of his neck and pulled him closer to me. "I know I lectured you about consent the other day, but . . . " Without another word, I pressed my mouth to his and kissed him slowly—gently. The soft feel of his lips against mine was everything I'd imagined it would be, and thoughts of them on other parts of my body soon flooded my mind.

But that was not what this kiss was for. It was a thank-you of sorts. An acknowledgment of what he'd done for me.

I quickly pulled away, my lips parted. He watched me like a hawk about to strike as the inches between us increased and the heat rushing through me flushed my cheeks.

"*Little queen*," he said, that gruff edge returning to his perfect voice as his eyes drifted to my lips. "Do that again."

Every nerve in my body came to life at the raw need in his tone. My fingers trailed along his neck to the hair at his nape, toying with the sensitive area as my lips brushed the sharp line of his jaw. "You didn't ask nicely," I whispered.

His fingertips dug into my hips as his restraint began to wane, and I sucked in a breath. "Do that again . . . *please.*"

I could feel his intense stare on me as I slowly kissed my way along his cheekbone to the edge of his mouth, strategically avoiding his lips just to tease him—to enjoy the tiny bit of control I had over him in that moment. But it didn't last long. His hand captured the back of my head, fingers twining in my hair, and guided my mouth to his.

My lips pressed to his again, but this time was different. What had been a slow and controlled thank-you before quickly evolved to something deep and desperate and filled with the promise of what might come next. His tongue grazed the inside of my mouth and I moaned at the feel of it, which only seemed to drive him further. The second that sound escaped me, he fisted his hand in my hair and pulled me away, his eyes sparkling with delight like they always did when he knew he had the upper hand.

I took a deep breath to steady my nerves and my hormones, but it did nothing at all. The deadly, glorious fae before me, covered in the blood of our enemies, was way more than I could handle. It was like every fantasy I never knew I had was standing there before me, and my hormones were melting down by the second.

Apparently, he could sense as much and thought it would be fun to slowly torture me.

"That noise . . . " he said as he looked down at me with hungry eyes. "I've heard it once before—in this very room, in fact—just the other night while you were sleeping." He released my hair and let his finger trail down my neck, leaving a tingling trail in its wake. "Tell me something, little queen: what were you dreaming about?"

My mouth went dry at the thought of divulging the details of my midnight fantasy. "I . . . it was . . . "

"Something so scandalous that you can't bring yourself to tell me?" he said, taunting me wickedly as his finger grazed my collarbone, then traced the V of my shirt down to the point at the bottom. "There is no shame in sharing your subconscious desires, little queen." His heavy gaze dropped to where his finger tugged at my shirt's collar, dragging it down low enough to expose the swell of my breasts. "We all have them."

The way he said 'all' sent a shiver right through me.

"You were here," I said softly. "In my apartment."

His eyes shot back up to stare into mine. "Why was I here?"

I closed my eyes and pictured the fragments of the dream I could remember, but as with all dreams, the details had grown fuzzy. What had happened between us, however, had not. I remembered that so vividly that I could feel the rush of blood in my cheeks at the thought. "I don't remember."

His finger released my collar and his hand slipped down over my shirt between my breasts to my bare stomach. "What was I doing?"

"You seemed irritated at me about something," I said as he slowly walked around me, his hand trailing around my torso as he moved. Heat welled between my legs as his hand spiraled lower and lower.

"What happened?" he asked, stopping directly behind me, his lips at my ear.

"You stood like that," I said, swallowing down my nerves and anticipation. "Behind me."

"How very interesting." His voice was a low rumble in my ear, and the vibration echoed through my body in the most delicious way. "I wonder why I'd do such a thing." His tone was teasing, but it was so sexy that I didn't care. I leaned back against him, just as I had in my dream, and let my mind focus on what happened next.

"Your hand pressed flat against my belly and you pulled me tight against you," I whispered.

"And then what?" he asked, his fingers pressing into the soft flesh of my stomach as they had in my dream. "Did I punish you for whatever you'd done?"

"Yes . . . "

"How?"

I swallowed hard. "You . . . you teased me . . . with your fingers."

His hand drifted lower, his fingertips barely breaching the waistline of my sweatpants "And did you like it?" he asked as he nipped my ear. The sharp pain made me jump, but the warmth that followed melted that moment's tension. His hand against my stomach pressed me against the strength of his body, and I could feel the length of him against the small of my back.

"I don't know," I breathed.

Every muscle in his body went taut. "You don't know?"

"I woke up before we could . . . " My words trailed off as the memory of his finger inside of me drowned out all conscious thought. I bit my lip and arched my hips against his hold.

"I see." His voice grew serious for a moment, as though he were angry that I had no more to tell. His fingers traced back and forth below my waistband, as though he somehow knew that very act had almost undone me in that dream. "Then what exactly elicited that sound from you?"

"You played with me like you are now, drawing close, then pulling away just enough—"

"Enough to arouse but not to satisfy?" he asked, his fingers plunging lower and lower with every pass. I struggled against him to angle myself closer, the throbbing between my legs more than I could stand any longer. All I wanted was to feel him slip inside me and come completely unraveled. "That does sound like punishment . . . "

"It's torture," I said, the strain and want in my tone so thick I barely recognized my own voice.

"Oh, I promise you, little queen. It isn't."

His finger went still just millimeters from its destination, and all rational thought abandoned me. All I could think about was getting his hand lower at any cost. I'd have sold my soul to the devil himself right then if it would have gotten Volker inside of me.

And I swore the fae bastard knew it.

"You still haven't told me about the sound," he rumbled in my ear as his finger began its teasing dance again, "which is such a shame. I'd love to hear it again . . . "

I opened my mouth to say something—anything—but the

moment I did, his finger dipped inside me, and everything in my body went rigid. A storm of pleasure raged between my legs, and a ragged cry escaped me.

He held me captive, fingers working against my sensitive skin as I quaked and moaned and tried to control my breathing. "There it is," he whispered as his teeth grazed my earlobe. "Would you like to see how your dream should have ended, little queen?"

His words barely registered, but I managed to answer. "*Yes.*"

"Good. Because what you saw that night was just the prologue."

His fingers pulled free, leaving me panting and desperate for them to return. Without warning, he spun me around and picked me up, his hands cupping my ass as he carried me over to the kitchen counter, kissing me along the way. He set me down gently, then grabbed the waistband of my pants. "Are you particularly attached to these?" he breathed against my mouth.

"No—"

The sound of ripping fabric echoed through the room as he tore them apart to get to me. My hips jolted forward into his hard body with the force, and he grabbed my face, kissing me hard as I sat there on the cold counter in my underwear, not giving a single shit about that. All I wanted was him.

I pushed his wool coat off his shoulders, and he slipped his arms out without skipping a beat. His thumb was on my core, sliding back and forth over the thin black fabric still covering me like he was trying to tease me to death. "Volker . . . please . . . "

"Are you ready for what comes next?" he asked, his wicked voice full of taunting.

"*Yes!*"

He pulled away and smirked at me before he bent down next to the cabinet, his face level with where my hips balanced precariously on the counter's edge, and lightly brushed his nose across my core. My legs closed around him reflexively, but he held them back, then slid his hand up my thigh to snag the edge of my underwear. "And what about these, little queen?"

"Rip them," I replied, frustration driving my response.

In a flash, they were gone, leaving me bare before him. But his eyes weren't on the prize he'd just uncovered. Instead, they were fixed on mine. "Should I promise to keep them closed again?" he teased, amusement twinkling in his eyes.

"No—"

"Then neither can you. You're going to keep them on me the whole time, or I'll stop."

His tongue flicked over my soft flesh and I gasped, which was all the encouragement he needed. Seconds later, his face was buried between my legs, his tongue making lazy circles around my clit. I gripped the countertop and held on for dear life as his pace increased, and my mind went blank except for the myriad visions I'd had of him and me together. But my eyes never left his. I watched him watching me and bit my lip, doing all I could to hold on—to not let it come to an end too quickly.

But that seemed to be out of my control, and the delicious release I craved began to swell. It grew and grew until I knew I couldn't hold on any longer, and it seemed Volker knew it, too. Seconds before what promised to be the orgasm of a lifetime hit, he pulled away and scooped me off the counter, headed for the bed. He laid me down and hovered over me as I writhed against the sheets.

"I need you to understand something, little queen," he said, a dark note of urgency in his voice as he tugged my shirt over my head. His eyes raked over my bare skin for a moment, making me squirm. "I might have taken your pain away earlier, but that does not mean I will be gentle. If you wish to turn back, now is the time."

"I don't want to," I said as burning need tore through my body.

A rumbling approval sounded before he ripped his ruined shirt off, and my gaze went wide as he unfastened his pants. I watched with rapt attention as they slid down his legs, underwear in tow, revealing the rest of his glorious body. I swallowed hard at the sight and rubbed my thighs together as the ache for him increased. He stood beside the bed like a Greek statue, his pale skin resembling the marble they were cut from. Beautiful death, I'd thought when I'd first seen him, and that moniker rang through my mind as he climbed on top of me with the stealth of an assassin.

"I have half a mind to drag this out until you can stand it no longer," he said as he spread my legs with his knees, "because I can be extremely patient when it comes to things I want, as you know. But . . . " He planted his hands on either side of my head, caging me in, and whatever cognition had returned went right out the window. Those grey eyes bore into mine, and in that moment, nothing else in the world existed; just the press of his cool skin against mine, the heat throbbing between my thighs, and the promise of so much more that I couldn't fully understand in that moment but wanted all the same. " . . . the other half wants to plunge inside you like a wild beast and only stop once you've made that sound again."

He inhaled deeply and threw his head back as if he were drinking in that memory. When his gaze fell upon mine again, silver glowed in its depths. His hand tangled in my hair and his grip tightened.

I sucked in a breath of my own.

"Many times, to be precise," he all but growled as he lowered his face to mine.

"So many times," I replied as my eyes rolled back in my head at the thought.

"No . . . keep them open." I did as he asked and found him staring down at me, a hint of concern etched in the corners of his eyes. "I need to see the light in them when I touch you." I locked my gaze on his and held it as his grip on my hair loosened and he drew the back of his hand along my cheek. "You are unlike anything I've ever met."

He pressed his hips closer and the tip of him rubbed against me. With excruciating slowness, he rocked his hips back and forth, sliding along my delicate skin until he barely slipped inside. I gasped as he pushed further and further until the full length of him was buried deep inside of me. A tiny moan escaped me as he withdrew at the same pace.

"I meant what I said, *Rowe*: there is no turning back."

Rowe . . . I loved the sound of my name on his lips. I reached up and cupped his face in my hands. "And I meant what I said: I don't want to."

The smirk I loved to hate, or hated to love, returned. "Good."

Then he slammed himself inside me, and I gasped as pain met pleasure in a way it never had before. His pace was anything but gentle, and I wrapped my legs tightly around his waist just to hold on. A low, guttural sound escaped him as my thighs clamped down.

Gone was the cold, calculating fae assassin I knew, leaving a wild, untamed creature in his place. A being of fire and impulse and passion, pumping hard between my legs as I dug my nails into his flesh and cried his name. His lips tangled with mine, teeth nipping and tongue claiming as our bodies moved as one. Fingertips dug into my hips to leverage me as that delicious sensation grew in my core again.

"Volker," I gasped as he nipped my breast.

"Not yet," he rumbled in response, his body growing tighter with every roll of his hips against mine. "Not until I say . . . "

I threw my head back, desperate for breath and for release, but he captured my face in his hand and pulled it back to his. "I need to see that light, my little queen," he said again as he held my chin captive, what little restraint he still possessed unraveling by the second. I did as he demanded and stared into his eyes as my climax threatened to release. His pewter gaze glowed silver as he leaned in closer and growled one word. "*Now.*"

With that simple command, any shred of control I'd mustered dissipated. My orgasm ripped through me as I cried out, but Volker's hold was unrelenting, and I watched as his body finally gave in, too. A primal sound escaped him and echoed through my apartment as he thrust one final time.

The tension wracking him slowly abated, and his grip on my hips slackened, but his eyes never left mine. And as our heartbeats slowed and our breaths steadied, he pressed his forehead to mine, then gently kissed my lips. "It's still there," he said softly, relief tainting his tone. "It's still there . . . "

"Maybe even a little brighter now, I imagine."

He pulled away to look at me through his tousled hair, and I reached up to brush it from his face. His eyes darkened as I slowly extended my hand until my fingertips met the stray pieces. I continued on, pushing his icy-white hair from his face. I raked my hand through the side until it wrapped around the back of his head, toying with the short strands.

The way he watched me as I did it warmed me deep inside.

"You should get some rest," he said, gently pulling my hand away so he could roll to his side. "Before I change my mind and decide to flip you over and take you from behind . . . "

"I need to get up." I moved to climb out of the bed, but his arm slung around my waist and pulled me in tight to his body.

"Trying to escape already, my little queen? I thought you understood the rules."

He nipped my neck, and I let out a nervous laugh. "I understand the rules just fine, but that doesn't change the fact that I need a shower—as do you."

"I'm not yet done with you," he said, running the tip of his nose along my ear.

"Then maybe you should join me . . . " I attempted to hoist his arm off me, but it was clear it wouldn't be going anywhere until he wanted it to.

"Stay," he murmured in my ear.

"Fine—but at least let me turn up the heat first. You're not exactly the warmest cuddle buddy." I shifted to climb out of bed again, and this time he allowed it. Naked as could be, I darted across the dark room and squinted at the thermostat until I could make out the numbers, then turned the dial up to a reasonable temperature. With the Moonlight Wraith watching my every step, I hurried back to the bed and launched myself under the blanket.

"I will have to make sure I have extra blankets in my room once I retake the House of Air and Amethyst," he said as I snuggled in deep under the comforter.

As his words registered, I flipped around in one smooth motion to face him. "What do you mean?"

"Were you planning to stay here?" he asked, darkness filtering into his expression. "Amongst those who'd betray you?'

In truth, I hadn't thought about it. The gut punch of learning who'd attacked me had been swept away by sleep and by all that had just transpired between Volker and me. The lack of pain had allowed my brain to block out the reality that my situation was less than desirable, at best. I closed my eyes, wishing I could block it out again.

"I don't know . . . "

"*Rowe—*"

"I know that doesn't make sense, but this is all I've ever known. All I can remember," I said. "It feels wrong."

"That was before your House fell apart and some of your 'family' turned on you." It was impossible to ignore the note of disdain when he said that word.

"But Shade—he needs my help. And Andreas . . . " I let my argument trail off, knowing that I'd likely just made things worse. Volker stared at me with that eerie, calm expression I could never read. "I just . . . I need a little time to figure out what to tell them."

"Nothing, until the queen has been defeated."

"Obviously," I said, shoving him playfully. Surprisingly, he took the bait, and a hint of a smile graced his face. I couldn't help but smile back. "I haven't put up with all of this just to have that plan go to shit."

The smile widened to a grin. "I didn't realize my presence was such a hardship."

"I mean, you are a bit of a pain in the ass at times—"

"I see—"

"—and you have some definite diva behaviors—"

"*Diva* behaviors?"

"—but you're surprisingly sweet when you want to be, and kind—"

"Facts that I will need you to keep to yourself, for my reputation's sake."

"Of course. I'd hate to undermine all that terror you've cultivated for decades—"

"*Centuries*, my little queen. *Centuries*."

I shot up on my elbow to stare down at him. "Wait. How old *are* you?"

"Old enough to rarely give in to impulse," he said, scooping me underneath him as he rolled on top of me, "except where a particular little royal is involved."

He kissed his way down my neck and I squirmed beneath him, laughing at his antics. "I do tend to bring out the worst in some people."

He went deadly still, then slowly pulled away to look at me. "No. You do quite the opposite. You are a light in the darkness I never knew existed. A beacon I cannot deny, though I've tried."

"Are you sure that's not just my power calling to you somehow?" I whispered, his sudden change in intensity overwhelming me.

"No, it's not," he replied with an assuredness I didn't understand. "It's something else entirely." He traced my jaw with his finger, and my body shivered. "It seems like you need to be warmed up again." His hand trailed down my neck, along my side, and over the curve of my hip until it drifted across my upper thigh. The blankets haphazardly draped across my body went flying across the room, and Volker smiled at me devilishly as he slowly worked his way down the length of my body until he lingered just above my core. "Perhaps you don't need sleep after all . . . "

Before I could argue, his tongue grazed my delicate skin, and I cried out for the third (or fourth . . . or fifth) time that night.

The Moonlight Wraith was sure to be the death of me—just not in the way I'd always imagined.

CHAPTER 31
ROWE

I awoke the next morning a bit achy (in the best possible way) with a rogue assassin at my back, his arm draped over me protectively. A spot of dried blood still speckled the pale flesh of his chest, a grim reminder of what he'd done the night before, and a wave of panic washed over me when I realized what that meant. The deaths of those responsible for my attack would soon be discovered, and even more chaos would erupt among the House. If Shade was looking for a common cause to unite us, he had it.

The hunt for the killer would be on soon.

That thought drove me out of bed, startling Volker in the process. He sat up and surveyed the room, moonlight blade in his hand, until his gaze fell upon my naked body. The blade disappeared, and a smug smile graced his face. "Have the ramifications of your actions finally hit you?" he asked as he nestled back against the headboard with his arms folded behind his head, casual as could be.

The weight of his hungry stare penetrated my rush of fear, and I scrambled to find something to cover myself with. His heavy wool coat was closest, so I snatched it up and threw it on, doing my best to ignore the dark stains adorning it. The fabric hung awkwardly from my much smaller frame like a parent's clothing on a child. It took effort to fish my hands out of the long sleeves, but once I did, I pulled the coat closed around me so I could continue my panic attack fully covered.

"No, the ramifications of yours just did." His eyebrow quirked at my response. "You murdered members of Fire and Fluorite, Volker. That won't go unnoticed—"

"That's not a concern."

"It feels like a big one. Huge, in fact. Unless you disposed of all the bodies . . . " I considered that notion for a moment, a million macabre ways to do just that assaulting my mind.

"I did not," he replied, stopping my morbid train of thought cold. "They are where I left them, but once found, the trail I left will lead exactly where I wished."

His smile could only mean one thing. "You set the queen up." He nodded. "But why? Why bother, if your whole goal is to kill her?"

"Because," he said, shifting his position. The blanket jostled in the process and slipped further down his body, until visions of what lay just beyond its edge flashed in my mind. "Your House is in need of stability and, potentially, an ally. If it comes out that the queen attacked Fire and Fluorite's members, and I kill the queen, I can spin that to suit my purposes with your new Alpha Supreme—the one you see as a father."

"You think Shade will owe you one?"

He shrugged ambivalently. "It cannot hurt to use the deaths of those that harmed you to work in my favor." His eyes darkened as he leaned forward, arms dropping to his sides. "But that is not why I did it." The ferocity in his stare was a weapon all its own, and something deep inside me stirred the longer it held. "I already explained my motives."

"You did," I said weakly, swallowing down the anticipation rising within me, because as much as I liked the idea of lying in bed with Volker all day, that wasn't an option for myriad reasons. "And I appreciate them."

At that, he smiled. "You showed me that appreciation last night—multiple times, in fact."

Blood flushed my cheeks, and I tried not to squirm under his gaze. "What can I say? I'm all about gratitude."

"You most certainly are. Perhaps you should come back over here and remind me."

"Nope," I said, scurrying away from the edge of the bed as he reached for me. "I have to pee, and Andreas is sure to show up here soon to make sure I'm still alive. Besides, you have a necklace to steal so you can kill the queen." Before he could even try to sidetrack me with any more of his sexy promises, I bolted for the bathroom and locked the door.

One look in the mirror had me questioning Volker's eyesight. He'd looked at me like nothing would have pleased him more than to pin me down and ravage me again for breakfast, but I was beyond a mess. On top of the bruises he'd allowed to remain on my face when he'd healed me, my mascara lay smudged beneath my eyes, and my hair was a wild tangle of red waves. My lips were swollen and bruised, and split along the top edge where he'd nipped me. I looked like I'd lost a fight, which was ironic for obvious reasons, but that apparently hadn't fazed him.

I couldn't help but smile at the thought.

I quickly finished up in the bathroom, then pulled his coat tight around me as I cracked the door open. I'd half expected him to be standing by the door, naked as could be, prepared to throw me over his shoulder and carry me back to bed. Instead, he was next to the bed fastening his pants, dark eyes watching my every move as I crossed the room.

"Rowe, there's something I need to—"

"I'm sure there are lots of things you need," I said, laughing as I cut him off, "but what we really need to do is come up with a plan for how we're going to get the necklace back." The lapels of his coat fell open, and I quickly shoved my hands into the pockets to hold it closed.

A pained expression tainted his face just as my fingers brushed against something craggy and cool. The second my skin made contact, a strange sense of familiarity washed over me, and I staggered back a step as I fished it from the depths of his pocket.

Dangling from my closed hand was a chain that mirrored my own, and I opened my palm to find a gabbro stone looking back at me. A cold wave of dread slammed into me, and I stumbled backward again as I rubbed the stone between my fingers. "I know this stone," I said softly as unwanted memories rushed through my mind. Memories of sitting in my mother's lap playing with the necklace around her neck. The one with the gabbro that matched mine.

"It's not what you—"

"It's my mother's," I said, the pieces of the puzzle falling into place like a line of dominoes. "This feeling . . . I felt it in the streets the other day, which means . . . " I cut myself short, allowing the reality of the situation to fully set in. "That was the queen I ran into. She was wearing this when I saw her."

Volker flinched almost imperceptibly, but his silence spoke volumes.

It hit like a bullet to the chest.

"Please let me explain—"

"How did you get it, Volker?"

"I stole it."

The rumors of a disturbance at the embassy suddenly made much more sense. "The last I knew, you were only going there the other night to surveil her routine."

He shrugged with the unapologetic ambivalence of a king. "The opportunity presented itself, so I took it."

His words were like a blow to the gut. "And you didn't think I'd want to know? That I had a right to know?"

He bristled at my challenge. "Yes, you did, which is why I rushed back to tell you, but you were drunk with your wolf, which made it rather difficult. And then last night—" His expression softened at the reference to my attack, but it was too late. I was too mad to give a shit about his sympathy.

"Oh, I see. I was too injured for you to mention that you'd gotten the thing we needed to sort out my power and get your revenge, is that it?"

"It was not the right time—"

"Because I was half dead, or because there's no such thing as a right time?"

"*Rowe*—"

"You should have snatched me from that party and dragged me home so you could figure out how to break the spell and make my power yours . . . but you didn't." The jagged edges of the stone bit into my palm as I clenched my fist. "Why didn't you, Volker? Why didn't you do everything you could that night to undo the spell binding my power?"

Something like pain flashed in his eyes before they hardened like the killer he truly was. "Because it isn't necessary."

Icy fingers seized my heart and held it hostage. "Why not?" I asked, the words barely a whisper. "Why don't you need to break the spell?"

"Because your necklace doesn't bind your power."

Memories of my last conversation with Yael and Myra slammed into me. "That's it," I muttered to myself. "You didn't keep it from me because it wasn't the right time; you didn't tell me because you don't need to break the spell. Because my mother's necklace doesn't stifle my magic at all."

"No, it doesn't." His stoic expression was more than I could take.

"Tell me what it does."

"It does what I've suspected it did since I saw it hanging from the queen's neck a few days ago. It siphons it."

Those fingers clenched my heart harder still.

It all finally made sense. My mother's murder. Volker's overthrowing. The powers I'd never felt. In truth, I'd been a fool not to see it sooner. The queen would have no use for a talisman that bound my powers.

But she sure as hell had use for one that drained them from me.

"It takes them," I said softly. "It channels them into the one that wears it . . . "

Volker's brow furrowed. "So it seems."

I glanced at the innocuous stone, thinking about the lies my mother had told me, then looked back at him. "How do you know for sure?" I asked, my voice low and thick with emotion and ready to break like the rest of me. Like my heart. "Tell me how you know, Volker. I want to hear you say it . . . "

"Because I've worn it ever since—felt the rush of your magic heighten my own." He dared a step closer, and I retreated a pace in return. "I used it last night to avenge you. I had planned to tell you about it when I came here—"

"But instead you thought you'd just fuck me another way?" I asked, my sadness fusing with my pain and anger. "Is that it? You thought you'd just bang the clueless bitch for fun because you were riding your killing high?"

"*No*—"

"Bullshit, Volker!" I yelled, throwing his bloody shirt at him for good measure. "You had ample opportunity to whip out this stone and tell me the truth, but instead, you chose to fuck me stupid—which I guess worked really well, overall. If I hadn't slipped your jacket on, I never would have realized what you'd done. You could have run out of here with your little magic-sucking stone and killed the queen. Then you could have disappeared to rule Air and Amethyst with it, and I'd have been none the wiser."

"The fact that I didn't should tell you something—"

"It tells me nothing I didn't already know, but it makes me wonder what else you might be keeping from me," I said, my anger growing. "What secrets you're hiding away. Like maybe you know who ordered the hit on me? Or maybe you know who my father is?" The way he flinched at the mention of my father made my hair stand on end. "Holy shit . . . you do, don't you? You know who he is—"

"I knew him," he corrected. "Past tense."

The room closed in around me. "He was the last wellspring," I whispered, my knees buckling as I took a step back. He lunged to catch my arm, but I sidestepped him, slapping his hand away. "You bastard . . . you killed him—"

"He killed himself," he argued, taking a step closer. "Be mad at me for not telling you, but do not blame me for his death."

"Why should I believe you? You're a liar!" I shouted at him. "You betrayed me!"

"I did *not* betray you," he yelled back in frustration. "I didn't tell you because it seemed cruel after giving you the details of his demise. At the time, I didn't care about my methods, but now—" He cut himself off, taking a breath to steady his anger. "Now I do. So be mad at me if you must, but I didn't betray you. I wouldn't."

I struggled against my anger until the fight finally left me, tears instead of rage now filling my eyes. "It sure feels like you did."

Fear flashed in his eyes as the spark in mine undoubtedly faded yet again. "I care about you, Rowe. More than anything I ever have in my life," he said, daring another step toward me.

My arms fell to my sides as I stood there, staring at his desperate expression as my heart shattered to pieces. "More than your precious revenge?"

His jaw tensed as he inhaled sharply. "*Yes . . .* "

I choked on a sob. "I thought you said you couldn't lie." He flinched, though this time he did nothing to hide it. Or maybe that particular blow landed harder than expected. "But I guess it doesn't really matter anymore, does it? You did what you did, and you got what you wanted." I grabbed his hand and turned it palm up, then dropped my mother's necklace into it. "I hope it was worth it."

"*Rowe—*"

"Just go kill the queen," I said as I turned away, "and stay the fuck out of my life."

"I can't do that."

I looked back over my shoulder. "Can't what? Kill the queen?"

He shook his head. "Can't stay out of your life."

My gaze dropped to the necklace in his hand, and his words made sense. "Of course you can't . . . I guess we'll always be tied together now, won't we?"

His angry expression was response enough.

It would have to be.

"Rowe?" Andreas called from outside the door right before he tried the knob. The deadbolt caught, but the way he shook the door, it wouldn't hold for long. "Rowe, open the door—"

"Looks like it's time for you to go get that revenge," I whispered as I turned toward the back door. But I didn't make it far before Andreas kicked it in and stormed the room, eyes wide and wild. The second they landed on me, wrapped in the Moonlight Wraith's coat, they glowed amber.

A quick glance over my shoulder confirmed that Volker was gone.

Forever.

CHAPTER 32
ROWE

"What the fuck is going on, Rowe?"

Andreas hurried toward me, but he slowed when I went rigid at his approach. I clutched the coat tighter and hung my head, embarrassment, anger, and shame swirling through me, along with a few other emotions I didn't have the time or bandwidth to unpack right then. I wanted to scream. I wanted to cry. I wanted to punch the shit out of something, then curl up in a ball and fade into the ether. But I knew that couldn't happen.

So I did the next best thing.

"I did something," I said weakly, hating the sound of it.

The tightness in his shoulders released, and he took a slow, careful step closer, his arm reaching toward me. "Whose coat is this?" he asked, the rough edge of his wolf plain in his tone.

"I should have told you before," I said, ignoring his question. "I should have trusted you to trust me, but I didn't, and now everything is a fucking mess, and it's all my fault."

"I need you to tell me now." His hands gently cupped my neck and he lowered his head to level his gaze with mine. "Get dressed, then come sit with me. I need to know everything."

I sniffled hard, doing all I could to fight back the tears, and did as he'd asked. Turning my back to him, I pulled some jeans from the pile of laundry I'd dumped on the floor and threw them on. I tossed Volker's coat to the floor, then yanked a black tank top over my head. When I turned around, I found Andreas staring at the coat like it was the enemy.

"Start at the beginning," he said, gesturing for me to sit on the bed. It squeaked under the weight of us on its edge, the shrill sound breaking the silence and growing tension in the room. But it was a temporary reprieve at best, because I knew there was no way to avoid telling him what I had to.

So I did.

I told him every detail I could recall. Volker's ambush in the alley. His demands. The truth about my power and the necklaces that channeled it. And the queen he was off to kill with the aid of my magic.

My cheeks burned scarlet with shame, and I couldn't bring myself to meet Andreas' gaze, but he slowly lifted my chin to face him, his eyes staring back at me kindly, even after everything I'd just admitted. After everything I'd done. With a tiny sense of relief coursing through me, I took a deep breath to prepare the other truth bomb I had to drop.

About the fluorite pendant Volker had found in the alley and the House members he'd killed.

As I spoke those words, I watched Andreas' soft expression harden to a murderous mask. "He's a liar, Rowe. Tell me you don't believe any of that."

But I had, and I did. Because maybe Andreas was blind to how some of our House felt about me, but I certainly wasn't. Throw in its fractured state, and I could totally see that someone might use me to send a message to Shade—or to undermine his authority. If he couldn't keep his most vulnerable members safe, he wasn't fit to lead.

And that wouldn't end well for him. Or for Andreas.

"I don't think so, Andreas—not about that."

"Why? Because the Wraith has proven himself so trustworthy? So honest?"

"He used me, but he never lied to me—not outright, anyway."

"That sounds a lot like splitting hairs, Rowe."

"He can't lie."

He pinned incredulous eyes on me. "Why would you think that?"

"Because he told me he can't."

"And if that's a lie?" Hearing the words out loud that I'd thought in my mind a million times sobered me, and I felt my resolve slipping away. "Rowe," he said, cupping my cheek, "we're talking about the Moonlight Wraith. Do you have any idea how dangerous he is? How he got to be the king of Air and Amethyst? Because I can assure you, it wasn't by noble means. He's a stone-cold killer." The second those words left his mouth, his eyes narrowed, as if something had just dawned on him and he was working through the details before he spoke again. "You're lucky to be alive. You should have told me."

"I thought I could handle it," I said weakly. "I know it sounds stupid when I say it out loud, but he threatened everyone I cared about—including you—so it was a risk I had to take."

"And then he employed his manipulations," Andreas continued, sympathy in his voice. "Let me guess; he made you feel special. Important. Sold you a bunch of pretty lies, and you believed them."

"No . . . it wasn't like that."

Or was it?

"Then tell me how it was, Rowe, because I'm struggling to understand how you could be so easily swayed by a notorious killer—one overthrown by his own kind. Were they wrong about him, too? Are you the only one who understands him? Because there's no greater red flag than that."

"He—" I cut myself off, realizing that Andreas' view of how things had gone down was not only possible, but probable.

"He what, Rowe?" he asked softly, pushing a stray strand of hair over my shoulder. "Manipulated you? Is using you to get his revenge, while creating even more havoc in our House?"

"He doesn't care about Fire and Fluorite."

"Doesn't he?" he countered, raking his hand through his hair. "There's nothing a fae like him loves more than power, Rowe. What better way to amass it than to not only regain his hold on Air and Amethyst, but to then use that to overtake Fire and Fluorite? No one could stand against him then."

"No . . . "

He held my gaze for a moment, pity in his eyes. "*No*? For fuck's sake, Rowe, what does he have over you? Why do you still want to see some good in him when there isn't any?" He cut his anger short and stared at me for a moment, realization dawning in his deep brown eyes. "Oh shit, Rowe . . . please tell me you haven't actually fallen for him." My lack of response said enough for Andreas' composure to wholly unravel. "For fuck's sake, he's a killer!"

"I know that!" I yelled at him. "I know he's a killer—but so is your father! So are you!"

"That's hardly the same thing, and you know it."

"I grew up in a culture steeped in violence, Andreas," I countered. "Violence that took my mother from me. And now her killer is going to get the justice she deserves. So maybe I fucked up and maybe I got played, but I can wallow in that shame with a smile on my tear-stained face, knowing that the bitch who murdered my mother is dead. And if you can't understand that, then you're not who I thought you were."

The sting of my words showed in his face for a moment before he wiped it clean, his second-in-command countenance falling into place. "We need to get you out of here," he said, taking my arm. "Grab whatever you need, because you can't come back here again—"

"Seriously?"

"We can't risk it."

"He can find me no matter where I am, but he doesn't need to now—he got what he wanted." The double meaning cut deep, and I tried not to show the hurt I felt as I spoke the words. Judging by the tension in Andreas' face, I failed.

"Just grab the basics. I can send someone for the rest later." He ushered me to my closet and grabbed a duffel off the shelf, then tossed it to me.

"Where are we going?"

"My place, for now," was his only answer.

I started stuffing clothes into the bag mindlessly until it barely zipped shut. Andreas emerged from the bathroom with my toiletry bag tucked under his arm. He took the heavy duffel from me and threw it over his shoulder with ease.

"What about your dad?" I asked as he led me to the back door.

"He had to go out of town this morning. We'll tell him when he returns."

With nothing really left to say, we climbed into his truck and drove in silence until we reached his family home. Parked in the garage, he killed the engine, and the two of us sat there, unmoving.

"You're mad," I finally said, dreading his response but needing one all the same. I forced myself to turn and look at him, arms folded tight across my stomach. "I'm sorry, Andreas . . . "

He reached over and cupped my face in his hand, his thumb stroking away the rogue tear trailing down my cheek. "I know you are. It's not your fault." He leaned forward to close the distance between us and pressed his lips to my forehead. "I love you, Rowe . . . and I need you to trust me right now. Can you do that?"

"I've always trusted you."

He pulled away enough for me to see his smile light up his face, dimple and all. "Good, because it might be you and me against the world for a while. Can you handle that?"

I smiled in return at the friend who'd had my back for as long as I could remember. "I can handle that."

He released my face and climbed out of the truck. Following his lead, I hopped out and met him by the tailgate, duffel in tow. He took my free hand in his and led the way into the house. A strange sense of peace settled in, eclipsing the lingering sadness and betrayal. Volker might have broken my heart, but Andreas would help pick up the pieces.

With a deep breath, I straightened my shoulders and notched my chin higher as we walked through the kitchen and down the hall past Shade's office. I looked at the closed door, shame flooding me again at the thought of having to tell him what I'd done. I was still focused on it as Andreas took a sudden turn into the living room just before we reached the staircase. I slammed into his back, then staggered back a step to steady myself.

"Yo . . . maybe you should warn a girl the next time you—"

My words cut short as I looked past him at the woman standing in the living room, smiling wickedly at me, her long black gown flaring out around her.

"Hello, Rowe," the queen of Air and Amethyst said. "It's so nice to finally meet you."

CHAPTER 33
ROWE

Time stopped.

The world narrowed, my singular focus on the queen before me, smiling like the murderous serpent she was. My mother's killer stared back with delight from the far side of the room, sunlight spilling in through the massive wall of windows behind her. And with every passing second that seemed to move in eternally slow motion, I realized why she'd come.

Volker had stolen the necklace—the one fueled by my power—which had left her vulnerable to his attack. Without it, he'd said, she would fail.

But my death would level the playing field.

She took a step toward us, and I edged closer to Andreas, who'd stood there in silence since we'd entered the room. Not a good sign. He wasn't a loose cannon, but he was powerful, and not one to back down from a fight. The fact that he hadn't said or done anything at all told me things were way worse than I could even comprehend. He was being careful—*calculated*—two things I'd never associated with him before. My heart lodged higher in my throat at the thought.

I'd sent Volker away to get his revenge. How ironic that, in doing so, I might have signed both of our death warrants. Necklace or not, one didn't become the queen of a House without great power. I was about to find out how much.

"You seem surprised to see me," she said, amusement brightening her dark eyes. "I wonder why that is."

"Because you're alone, in the wrong territory," I replied, hoping that pointing out that fact might make her rethink whatever diabolical plan—that surely ended in my death—she had.

"Am I?" she asked as she took another soundless step forward. It was as if she absorbed the reverberation entirely, which made me wonder exactly what her power was. Neither Volker nor Yael had ever bothered to mention it, and I'd never thought to ask. I hadn't needed to, with Volker in the picture.

Yet another fucking oversight on my part. One likely to lead to my death.

My hand wrapped around Andreas' arm, and he went rigid. I wondered if she had frozen him with a spell of some sort. I really wanted to kick myself for not knowing her abilities.

"Tell me something, Rowe." She clasped her hands behind her back to make herself look less threatening, but it had the opposite effect. Sweat trickled down my back, and panic gripped my lungs in a vise. I was a mouse trapped in a cage, waiting for the cat to strike.

"What?"

"I heard a rumor that you've been helping the Moonlight Wraith . . . why would you choose to do such a thing?"

"I'm not sure I really had a choice in the matter . . . "

"But there is always a choice," she argued, her midnight skirt flowing around her as she took another step closer, "and it seems as though you chose to conspire with him—to use your power to help him." She pinned her sharp stare on me, and I clamped down harder on Andreas' bicep as fear gripped me tighter. The cut of his muscles bit into my palm, helping to clear my head.

If he couldn't get us out of this, I would have to.

Somehow.

"Volker isn't really the type to offer options," I replied, "but I imagine you already know that."

Her gaze snapped to Andreas' hardened face, then back to me. "No, he isn't, is he? Perhaps you are just a victim of circumstance—much like myself."

"You're no *victim*," I said, choking on the word. "You're a murderer. You killed my mother—chopped her fucking head off—just so you could have my power!" I was shouting at this point and gave zero fucks about it. My unresolved emotions about my mother's death came bubbling up in a fury and erupted all over the room. If I was going to die there, then I would do so confronting the truth of her murder—and the one who had caused it.

"Is that what you think?" she asked, her mocking tone enough to unravel what little control I had left. "Or is that what you've been told?"

"That's what I know," I snapped back, taking a step forward. "I saw the body."

"So her corpse told you this?" she asked, leaning forward in conspiratorial fashion. "I'll admit, I don't know if it could or not. I cannot converse with the dead . . . "

I lunged toward her, wanting to rip her flowing brown hair from her head, but Andreas caught my arm and drew me back to him. Shocked that he'd moved at all, I looked back at him and found concern etched deep in his brow. "Don't," he said, his grip firm but not punishing.

"Ah, he speaks," the queen taunted, her voice rising with feigned delight. "I wondered when you might join in, Andreas."

"Why are you here, Nyssa?"

"She's come to kill me," I answered for her. No need to mince words. "Volker has my mother's necklace now, and she knows he plans to use it to kill her—and he will, won't he? He'll have the power he needs to cut you down like you did him, so you want to eliminate his advantage. That's about the size of it, right?"

Her smile widened, and every hair on my body stood on end. It bordered on maniacal, the amusement in her eyes too wild and wicked to be housed in a fully sane person. I'd hit the nail on the head, and in some twisted way, it pleased her. "That would certainly even the odds," she crooned as she stepped closer, "but it would be such a shame to destroy something so full of power, don't you think?"

When I didn't respond, she looked to Andreas for one.

Instead, she got the resounding crash of the front door being knocked off its hinges echoing down the hall. Startled, I looked over my shoulder to find Shade storming into the room, eyes glowing yellow and teeth bared in a human snarl. But he wouldn't remain that way for long if the queen didn't back down.

"Shade!" I called as he entered the room.

His gaze quickly cut to me. "Are you two all right?" he asked as he moved through the room.

"Better now," I answered.

"Good. Now somebody start explaining to me why the queen of Air and Amethyst has invaded our territory and my home."

"I was looking for the wellspring," she replied, as though that were obvious.

Shade didn't even flinch at her words. "You're not welcome here, Nyssa," he all but growled, "so I will give you five seconds to leave and never come back."

She quirked an eyebrow at him in challenge. "And if I don't?"

He stepped up shoulder-to-shoulder with his son. "Then I will consider it an act of aggression against this pack and this House, and I will respond in kind."

"Your assessment of the situation is in error," she said, picking a fallen hair from her impeccable gown.

"I think it's just fine."

"I'm not leaving without Rowe—"

"And Rowe is a member of my pack and my House, and therefore under my protection," he countered. "She goes nowhere unless I allow it."

"Is that so?"

"That's so."

The corner of her mouth curled in a lazy smirk. "How very interesting indeed."

"This is my fault," I said, turning guilt-filled eyes to Shade. "I should have told you the truth from the beginning, but I knew he'd come after you if I did—"

"Who?" he asked, daring a glance at me before again fixing his gaze on the threat in the room.

"The Moonlight Wraith."

"He's dead, Rowe."

"It turns out he's not," the queen answered for me, "but I'll correct that once I leave here."

"Then leave." The authority in Shade's tone filled the room, but the queen remained unfazed. Her absolute audacity would have been awe-inspiring under other circumstances.

"Not until I get what I came for."

Shade took a step forward. "Five," he said, starting his countdown. "Four . . . " His claws shot out from the ends of his fingers in warning.

"You weren't supposed to get involved in this," she said as she shifted her stance and raised her hands in front of her.

"Three . . . " He edged in front of Andreas and me.

"You still have time to walk away—"

"So do you. *Two . . .* " he said, his voice booming over the queen's. "Andreas, get ready."

The queen glanced beyond him to where we stood, then smiled.

Andreas moved to join his father, and I held my breath as I waited for Shade to say "one." The queen stood unfazed and smiled at him as though he couldn't possibly hurt her. Her blasé manner made my hackles rise just as that bizarre slow-motion feeling set in again.

I knew something was wrong.

And as Shade uttered his final word, I watched in horror as an arm looped around his neck and ripped his head free of his body.

Blood sprayed through the room, raining red down upon us all, as his limp body hit the floor.

Right at his son's feet.

"You weren't supposed to come back," Andreas said, his voice flat and calm and unlike anything I'd ever heard from him before. And as he turned his blood-stained face to me, I saw the devil in it. "I think we need to talk."

CHAPTER 34
ROWE

"I wondered how you planned to handle that," the queen said as she sashayed over to us, gliding through the pooling blood as though it weren't even there. Andreas watched her as I stood there, mouth agape, unable to process what I'd just seen. I didn't scream—didn't run—didn't do anything at all. Tears streamed down my face as I tried to reconcile the fact that the man who'd all but raised me was dead—at the hands of his son.

"I thought I had handled it," Andreas replied. "Sending him out of town didn't work, apparently."

"So it seems."

I stumbled back a step. "You killed him," I stammered, hands shaking as I held them up in defense, as though that would do anything at all. "What . . . how . . . *why?*"

Andreas looked at the body on the floor. "I thought that was obvious. He got in the way."

My bottom lip trembled in fear. Things were far worse than I ever could have imagined. "What has she done to you?" I asked, terrified of the answer.

At that, he laughed. "Nothing at all."

The icy sickle of death dragged down my spine. "What is wrong with you, Andreas? He was your father!"

He shrugged ambivalently. "I'm loyal to power." Cruel eyes drifted over to the queen, then back to me. "Why do you think I chose you, Rowe? Why I did everything I have for you?" My stomach roiled as he spoke. "My father knew what you were—what you could be—and he squandered that power, just like your pathetic mother." He took a step toward me, and I retreated. "Do you know what she said to me when I confronted her about it?" he continued. My body went still. "She said she was *helping* you—*protecting* you. Can you believe that? All that power she took and then squandered? She could have ruled this House if she'd wanted to, but instead, she channeled it into potions and trinkets. So now, I'll rule instead."

Anger simmered in my veins as that reality helped cut through the haze.

He reached over to grab my necklace, but I batted his hand away. "You're not going to rule anything once Volker finds me. He has my mother's necklace," I said, a dark satisfaction growing inside. "His powers are his again—and he's going to kill you both."

"He has *part* of your mother's necklace," Andreas corrected, leaning in close to me. The psychotic delight in his deep brown eyes shook my newfound resolve. "The part I traded to the queen. The part spelled to receive your magic—once it travels through *me*."

Shock coursed through me.

It hadn't even occurred to me to question the size of my mother's necklace; I'd been so angry when I'd found it in Volker's pocket, and so young when I'd last seen her wearing it. I mean, everything looks big to you when you're a kid, right? I'd thought it was just time and me growing up that might have dwarfed it slightly. Until that moment, everything that had happened hadn't fully made sense. But the pieces were slowly starting to fall into place, and the picture they showed was a twisted one.

"It was you," I whispered, disbelief holding my vocal cords hostage. "*You* killed her . . . "

"Once I realized there was no other way to remove her necklace, I knew it was the only way," he said, as though he were merely stating a fact and not admitting to the cold-blooded killing of my mother. "I suspected there was magic involved in keeping it in place, since you lost your fluorite ring incessantly when you were younger, but never the gabbro. When you were older, I tried taking it off to see, and I could feel the magic coursing through it. I knew your mother's would be the same."

"So you cut her head off?" I asked, nausea rolling through me once again at the thought.

"I slit her throat first," he said, as though the alternative would have been barbaric. "After she died, the necklace still wouldn't let go, so I did what I needed to do. Once it was off her body, the magic holding the chain together disappeared."

The world closed in around me. My knees buckled and I collapsed to the floor, gasping for breath. Panic choked me, and a small part of me hoped it would end me right then and there. Death would be a welcome alternative to the twisted reality I was living.

"Where is it?" I asked. "Where is my mother's gabbro?"

He canted his head. "Somewhere safe. Somewhere you'll never find it." A smirk tugged at the corner of his mouth. "It's embarrassing to think how close you've been to it before and never noticed."

"But it has to be on you to work," I said, thinking of how the stone in Volker's pocket had seemed to come to life when I'd touched it. How I hadn't sensed it was there until I'd brushed up against it. "But I can't feel it . . . " I closed my eyes to escape his taunting and tried to pull up a memory of Andreas with anything I'd ever seen on him that could have been the gabbro glamoured or magicked somehow. But every time, I came up short. "You're lying," I finally said. "I could feel the gabbro when she wore it." I jerked my head toward the regal bitch looming nearby. "If you had it, I'd know."

"Except you wouldn't—not if I'd planned for that possibility," he countered, looking far too pleased with himself for my liking. "The great thing about magic, Rowe, is that it can do just about anything, provided you know who to turn to and what to ask—and have enough time to bring it all together. And I had all the time in the world." His gaze cut around the room. "Nobody would have respected a seventeen-year-old Alpha Supreme, so I knew I had to bide my time—learn the politics of running a House. Wait for the perfect opportunity to make my move; one that wouldn't arouse suspicion." His wicked smile made me want to vomit. "I guess I should thank your girl Danni for handing me one on a platter. The chaos she caused was exactly what I needed."

"You're a monster," I said as my anger grew. "There's no way you'll get away with it, either. Not once I tell everyone what you did."

"You won't get the chance."

The queen moved closer, and the two of them stared down at me. Not a shred of emotion could be found between them. "What shall we do with her?" the queen asked.

"You'll need to look like you've taken her captive," Andreas explained. "I will conceal myself somewhere until the right moment." His gaze turned to his dead father. "His body will help sell the lie."

"She'll need to be silenced," the queen pointed out, "or she will ruin everything."

"She'll be quiet," he said, his narrowed gaze drifting slowly back to me, "or I'll hunt down her precious friends and kill them. I'll start with Adora, because I've been dying to strangle that bitch for a long time now. Then I'll take out those rejects at *The Riff-Raff*—the mermaid, in particular. I'd love nothing more than to carve out those judgmental blue eyes of hers with my claws. I'll finish with Dannika . . . that should cause quite a stir, I think. Killing the king of Blood and Beryl's mate . . . "

"You'd start a war," I said, the words escaping on a whisper.

"I believe I would." His smile was anything but friendly as he thought of the chaos that would result.

To think I'd been worried about Volker having control of my power; what havoc he could wreak on Portland, and on the world in general. There was no way Andreas could be allowed to have that kind of power.

And with that realization came a strange sense of calm. I knew what I needed to do.

The two of them discussed how and where to bind me like complete fucking sociopaths while I sat slumped on the floor. My stillness seemed to lull them into a false sense of security where I was concerned, and I waited until they were arrogant enough to turn their backs on me. There wasn't a square inch of that home that I hadn't scrubbed or dusted. Wasn't a cabinet or drawer I hadn't organized. I knew it like it was my own.

Which was why I knew about the serrated dagger in the side table only three feet behind me.

"That wasn't the agreement, Andreas," the queen said, her tone taking a notable turn.

"Well, things have changed, thanks to you not ensuring the Wraith's death," he snapped at her.

Their voices continued to rise as their disagreement escalated, a nasty side effect of one too many masterminds in the room, and I used their distraction to inch backward, silently sliding across the hardwood floor. My movements were painstakingly slow, but I was almost there. If the two of them could keep disagreeing for a bit longer, I'd be good.

"Do not play me for a lovestruck child, Andreas. I will not sacrifice myself to secure your prize." The queen's words cut through my focus. "We are in this together, because you cannot possibly fight off the other Houses without my aid, wellspring or otherwise. You'd do well to remember that."

"And you'd do well to remember the terms of our agreement," he replied, jaw flexing with restrained anger. "You are currently without your gabbro. Your power isn't enough to test me alone, Nyssa." His eyes raked over her as my hand drifted toward the drawer in the dark wood side table. "And though I've enjoyed our time together, you are not irreplaceable."

She looked up at him through her lashes. "Perhaps not, but do not assume the one who replaces me will be as amenable to our alliance."

I closed my eyes and said a little prayer as I reached to slide the drawer open. It was the quieter of the two tables, but far from silent. But all I needed was enough time to secure the blade. Then I'd control the situation.

Andreas cupped her cheek and stroked it once as his head lowered to her ear. My heart caught in my throat as I watched, wondering if he'd rip her head from her body as he had his father's. But instead, he leaned in close and whispered something I couldn't hear. Her body went rigid, and I knew I was out of time.

With the two of them distracted, I threw the drawer open and snatched the dagger. Springing to my feet, I scrambled backward as the two of them lunged for me. But they stopped short the second they realized what I intended to do.

"Don't," I said, inching toward the doorway.

Andreas' upper lip curled as an animal snarl escaped him. "I cannot let you leave, Rowe. That would ruin everything."

"I don't plan on leaving," I said, stopping in the center of the large entryway. "That wouldn't stop you—and you'd never stop hunting me."

His dark brown eyes flared gold. "No, I wouldn't."

"This ends now." Though my voice wavered, my hand did not.

Maybe madness really was a consequence of my gift, because as I held the blade to my own throat, the sharp tip digging into my flesh enough to make me bleed, I felt no fear. Sadness, yes. Regret, for sure. But not fear.

For the first time in my life, I knew that what I was about to do could save the lives of hundreds—maybe thousands, or even more. Maybe that was really why wellsprings' lives ended in suicide. Maybe it wasn't madness at all.

And maybe with my death, the wellspring line would end forever.

With great power comes great responsibility. My mother always used to say that. And though I wouldn't get to avenge her death, I knew she'd have been proud that I'd heeded that lesson.

"I can't let you have my power anymore," I said as I pressed the blade deeper. The queen's eyes were wild with rage. Andreas dared a step closer, and I smiled. "Volker is going to skin you alive when he finds you . . . I wish I could be here to see it."

The muscles in Andreas' shoulders bunched as he prepared to launch himself at me—a tell he'd had since our younger years—but he'd never make it in time. With a deep breath, I slashed the razor-sharp blade across my throat. It carved easily through flesh and muscle until it came free on the other side.

The queen's screams filled the air as I collapsed, blood spurting wildly from my neck. I quickly placed the tip of the blade under my ribs, aiming up to pierce my heart before unconsciousness could take me, but someone ripped it from my grasp.

"Now is not the time for death, little queen," a voice rasped in my ear. "At least not yours."

CHAPTER 35
VOLKER

I had never known fear before that day.

But standing in the hall of the Alpha Supreme's home, watching her slide a blade through her own throat, remedied that for me in an instant. Nothing mattered in that moment but saving her—even if she still hated me. I'd have gladly suffered the pain I'd felt when she'd dismissed me a thousand times over rather than see her dead.

But those that had forced her hand would know no mercy.

I flashed to her aid, catching her before she could fall. The wolf and the queen were already rushing over to staunch the bleeding, but both stopped short when I appeared. I pried the blade from Rowe's hand and cupped her neck. With my magic stabilized, courtesy of her mother's gabbro, the bleeding stopped immediately. Tissue knit and mended until all that was left was unmarred alabaster skin covering an unblemished throat.

"It seems I made it here just in time," I whispered in her ear as I hauled her to her feet. Eyes full of relief and sorrow met mine, the regret she felt buried in their depths. "I know, my little queen . . . I don't blame you. I should have told you right away." My gaze cut to the wolf and Nyssa, standing in the middle of the room, anger blazing in the former's glare while concern tainted the latter's. The queen no longer held an advantage over me, and she knew it.

The wolf, however, didn't share that realization.

"He has part of my mother's stone," Rowe rasped, rubbing her throat as she leaned into my side. "It was him all along—he's the one who killed her." The slight shake in her voice when she spoke sent fire roaring through my veins. The anguish he'd caused her would be paid for in blood—and slowly.

"That would explain why the power from this one is weaker than expected."

"And why you cannot win," Andreas added, the confidence of foregone victory tainting his tone.

I looked from him to the queen, then back again. "You make many assumptions with that statement, wolf. The wellspring's power does not make you invulnerable, nor unbeatable. You can most certainly die."

"Maybe," he said, clasping his hands behind his back in a casual display of superiority, "but you are outnumbered and overpowered. You will not leave here alive. And Rowe will be mine."

My moonlight blade appeared of its own volition. "Rowe will *never* be yours," I countered. "She will be with whomever she chooses." My blade raised, I tucked her into my side with my free arm and hugged her tightly. "And for now, that appears to be me."

"And once I've ripped your head off, it will be me."

"I'd rather die," she said, her voice strong and loud this time, brimming with anger. "Or did slicing my own throat not make that clear?"

"That won't be necessary," I said, squeezing her gently before I let her go. "Andreas seems to be working under the preconceived notion that your power in addition to his is enough to defeat me. But that assumes that his power rivaled mine before he had the stone." I smiled wickedly at the wolf poised to attack. "And I am most certain that it did not. So you may be powerful now, little wolf, but even combined with Nyssa, your victory is not guaranteed." I raised my blade in challenge, then turned to the queen. "You'd be wise to leave now if you wish to die another day."

"You cannot blame me for what I did," she said, her voice devolving to a near snarl. "You would have done the same."

"Perhaps," I said, inching forward, silvery-blue light cutting a path before me, "but I didn't. You, however, did. That was your mistake to answer for, not mine."

Andreas turned his eyes to Rowe, and it was as if his entire persona changed. He slipped easily back into the character he'd played for years—the one he'd used to keep her close. To manipulate her.

"If you come with me willingly, I'll spare him," he said softly. "All you have to do is leave with me."

I felt her shift behind me, and the darkness within me stirred. She would sacrifice herself to keep me safe—would live her life as a hostage to ensure mine.

"No," I said, throwing my arm out to block her. "He lies, but you already know this. He has no honor." My eyes drifted to the decapitated body at my feet. "He killed your mother, presumably his father, and—" My words cut short when something I had yet to realize assaulted my mind, the pieces of his plan falling into their places. "—I'm willing to bet that he manufactured your attack," I said, daring a glance back at her. "It was Andreas who sent those shifters after you in the alley." Her eyes went wide with disbelief at first, but as the shock wore off, her expression changed. "Isn't that true, Andreas?"

His laughter filled the room as he clapped slowly. "So clever, Moonlight Wraith. It's unfortunate that I can't keep you as a pet, too. You would come in so handy." When I said nothing in response, any sign of his amusement fell away. "I knew I was losing her . . . I needed something to drive her closer to me. Something I could later use against you."

"You underestimated us both."

His expression soured. "A mistake I won't make again." His eyes glowed yellow and his claws shot forth. The queen swirled her hands before her, summoning her winds, prepared to use her air magic against us.

I smiled at the sight. "You just did."

With a mighty shove, I knocked Rowe through the living room entrance, then disappeared from sight. I rematerialized behind Andreas just as a gale-force gust slammed into me. The queen's anticipation of my next move combined with her cries of warning were enough to drive Andreas from where he stood only seconds before my blade would have cleaved him in half. I dared a glance at where Rowe stood, knife in hand, tracking Andreas as he hurried toward her.

Fast as lightning, I shot into the air and drew my sword back to skewer him, but Rowe's gaze gave me away. Andreas spun around and shredded my shirt with his steel-like claws. Blood welled on my chest as I landed and rolled across the hardwood floor. I wasted no time in striking again, launching myself at the wolf. My blade sang as it cut through the air in a blur of blue light. Andreas ducked and wove with uncanny speed, but as I'd told him, he was not invulnerable, and one tiny mistake illustrated as much. The moonlight blade sliced across his abdomen, slashing through skin as though it were air.

He looked down at the wound and smiled.

I pressed forward, prepared to capitalize on the moment, but a sharp, cold pain made me falter. I looked down to find a spear of swirling wind piercing my side. With no time to extract it, I feinted a blow at Andreas, then kicked out his leg instead. It buckled, and I quickly drove my knee into his face. The force knocked him backward, and he flipped over the back of the sofa.

"Volker!" Rowe screamed, and I turned just in time to find Nyssa upon me, another spear of wind drawn back to pierce my heart. Before she could throw it, I drove my sword up through her ribcage and into her heart. Her eyes went wide as she felt her life draining into my blade.

"You should never have crossed me," I whispered as I yanked my sword free. Her limp body fell to the floor, but I relished the view for only a fraction of a second. I looked back just as Rowe cried my name again.

A force struck me hard from behind, but I didn't fall forward; and when I glanced down, I saw why. A clawed hand jutted through my chest, covered in blood and bone. Weak but determined, I lifted my blade to cut it off, but Andreas caught my arm and easily snapped it backward, the hollow sound of bones breaking filling the room, soon followed by the sound of Rowe's screams.

"I guess you weren't as strong as you thought," he growled in my ear. "And now she will be mine forever."

With a ruthless tug, his hand ripped back through my chest the way it had come, leaving a hole too large to heal quickly. Blood poured from the wound, and I dropped to my knees next to Nyssa.

I'd won that battle, but I'd lost the war.

I forced myself to turn and face Rowe, who stood wide-eyed in the doorway, shock taking over. "I guess it's my turn to say I'm sorry, my little queen." I collapsed to the floor, my life fading with every passing second, but I held her gaze until I felt the darkness closing in around me and gave her one last order. "*Run . . .*"

CHAPTER 36
ROWE

I watched in horror, my heart in my throat, as Andreas leaned over Volker's slumped form, arm raised to seal the Wraith's fate with one final blow. The queen was dead. Shade was dead. And if I did nothing, Volker would soon follow.

Andreas would win.

The dagger in my hand burned as I threw myself at Andreas and caught his arm before he could finish Volker off. I drove the blade deep into his flesh—or at least I tried to. The metal met something so hard it shattered, and Andreas let loose a howl before he threw me off. I landed in a puddle of Volker's blood, right next to the moonlight blade still clutched in his hand and shining faintly.

It gave me hope that he was still alive—that not all was lost just yet.

I slowly moved to shelter it with my body to conceal it from Andreas.

"You stupid bitch," he snapped, pulling up his sleeve to inspect his arm. His hand rubbed over the scar he'd had for as long as I could remember, and something niggled at the back of my mind. "You could have ruined *everything*."

"By stabbing your arm?" I asked, knowing damn well that wasn't how. But playing dumb would force him to explain. Men like him needed you to understand the magnificence of their plans. Their egos demanded it.

His angry eyes cut to me, and I tried not to shy away. "Has the fact that you've never seen the gabbro on me still not crossed your mind?"

Beneath me, my hand closed around the moonlight blade's hilt and crushed it in my grip. The bleeding from Volker's wound had slowed, but the hole was still gaping and ominous. His eyes fluttered half-open, and I silently begged him not to move.

To hold on a little longer.

"I couldn't risk it being seen," Andreas continued, "and I couldn't find anyone with a spell to lock it on as your mother had. So . . . " He shrugged ambivalently. "I carved a hole in my arm and buried it there. The magic of the stone wouldn't allow it to heal normally, so the scar remained."

"And you just explained that away with ease, didn't you?" I asked. "Just one little lie, and nobody questioned it."

At that, he smiled. "Not even my father."

I dared a glance down to see Volker's eyes fall shut and the blade's glow dim.

I knew time was running out.

I didn't know if I could kill Andreas while he possessed the stone, but removing it from him could seal Volker's fate. If the piece of my mother's stone he possessed was keeping him alive by way of the power channeled from Andreas', then the second that connection was broken, his power would wane again, and he'd die.

Unless I could give it to him in time.

"Do it," a faint voice whispered so quietly I wondered if I'd truly heard it. But I looked down at those steel-grey eyes for what I feared could be the last time and realized what he was saying.

He wanted me to try—regardless of the cost.

"Still not dead yet?" Andreas said, leaning over Volker and me. "Well, I can take care of that for you."

Andreas raised that clawed hand again, and adrenaline shot through me. As it sliced down through the air, I sprang to my feet, sword in hand, and swung at his arm, aiming for his shoulder. If I could cut it off, then I could get the stone.

But my timing was off, and the moonlight blade sped towards his upper arm where his scar and the gabbro were. The sword sliced through his flesh until it crashed into something far harder. A blinding flash of eerie blue light, followed by an explosion of power strong enough to knock me backward, filled the room. I crashed to the ground, panic lodged in my throat as I looked to where Andreas' arm hung half-severed from his body, blood spraying in arcs from the wound.

And there, in the pool of blood below, lay the shattered stone.

"No," I gasped as the moonlight blade dimmed in my hands.

Andreas seethed with anger, clutching his spurting wound. "I'm going to *kill you* for that," he snarled as he stormed toward me.

The sword flared to life as I scrambled to my feet, and I raised it high. I felt the power it held—the magic thrumming through it—as though it were my own.

Andreas reached for me and I ducked; then, taking a play from Volker's arsenal, I drove the blade up through Andreas' ribs, just as Volker had the queen's. Andreas' eyes filled with disbelief as I thrust it in hilt-deep. "That's for my mother," I said as his weight sagged against the sword and me. Before he collapsed, I gave the blade a brutal twist. "That's for your father." I yanked the sword free, and Andreas fell at my feet, unmoving. "And that's for Volker."

Tears welled in my eyes as I turned to see if I had indeed sealed the fae assassin's fate—and found him lurking right behind me, smiling wickedly. "You were doing such a wonderful job on your own," he explained, spreading his arms wide. "I didn't want to interrupt."

Without responding, I dove at him and locked my arms around his waist. "You're alive . . . "

He rested his head atop mine and hugged me back. "Thanks to your power—and my ability to heal, it seems."

"But the stone," I said, sniffling hard. "I destroyed it . . . "

"And you thought I'd die if you severed the magic?" he finished for me. I nodded against his chest, and he pried me off him just enough to see my face. He carefully wiped away the rogue tears with the back of his hand. "I'll admit, I assumed as much myself, but when I saw you pick up the moonlight blade, I wondered . . . "

"Wondered what?"

He smiled again, but this time, it was genuine. "An interesting fact about that sword is that only I can wield it. It answers to me alone, which is why you employing it was so telling."

"I don't understand," I said, shaking my head. "This doesn't make sense."

"Seeing you hold the blade told me that our connection ran deeper than the fragment of your mother's stone." His smile widened. "It meant that the blood exchange we made was more successful than we thought. It didn't fail, per se—the magic of the gabbro simply blocked it. The harder we tried to overcome it, the more pain it caused you. But it never failed." His words slowly trickled into my brain until the truth soaked in. "I would have loved to tell you that at the time, but I was a bit busy trying not to bleed to death."

"Wait . . . are you saying that—"

"You are now connected to my magic?" He glanced down at the blade in my hand. "Yes, I am." His hand closed around mine, and he gently slipped the weapon from my grip. "For now, perhaps it's best that I hold on to this."

I giggled, then pressed up onto my toes to reach his face. "Worried it might start to like me more than you?"

His lips pressed to mine in a gentle kiss. "You do have a way of charming everyone around you."

I opened my mouth to answer when something scuffed the floor behind me. I turned to look but only got a glimpse of Andreas' hunched-over body. He let out a howl as he lunged for me, but Volker swung me behind him as the blade flared in his hand. It cut through the air in an effortless arc toward Andreas's head, slicing through his neck with ease, and Andreas wavered on his feet for a moment before his head dropped to the floor seconds before his body did.

Volker hovered over him, eyes flaring silver. "I told you she will never be yours." He looked over his shoulder at me, eyes dimming to show the emotion they held. "She's *my* little queen."

I let out a nervous laugh that quickly turned to a sob. Volker was immediately at my side, arms wrapped around me, holding me tightly to him.

"What do we do now?" I asked between ragged breaths. "What do *I* do?"

"We cannot stay here," he said, surveying the room, "and you cannot stay with Fire and Fluorite."

I wiped my face clean with the back of my sleeve and nodded a little too enthusiastically. "Okay . . . okay . . . "

"Little queen," he said, hands clamping my shoulders to steady me, "*Rowe* . . . I know you didn't have a true choice in this, but if you want it, you have a home with Air and Amethyst—even if you wish to rescind your bond to me."

And there it was, the final act that dispelled any notion that he wanted me only for my power. Even without it, he was offering me a refuge in his House. And at his side.

"Does that mean I get to be queen?" I asked, forcing a smile.

He did the same in return. "If you choose to be with me, then yes, but that's a dubious honor, to be sure." His smile faltered for a moment, and my heart fell right along with it. "But it would not change who and what I am, my little queen. I am the Moonlight Wraith, with all that implies."

I weighed his words for a moment. "Maybe who you are isn't as bad as you think," I replied, taking his hand in mine. "Maybe I like you because of it."

Though he tried, he could not hide the amusement on his face. "Then I'm afraid the madness has already set in, and there's no hope for you."

"Guess I might as well make the best of it," I said with a shrug. "I mean, there have to be some perks to being the Moonlight Wraith's girlfriend, right? Like maybe a king-size bed? Or a soaker tub? OH! A personal chef?"

While I listed off the most ridiculous demands I could think of, he took my hand and led me away from the carnage in Shade's home. From my past. There was nothing there for me anymore—nothing more for him, either.

Volker had gotten his revenge.

And so had I.

EPILOGUE
ROWE

Two weeks later, the pain of death and betrayal had subsided a little, but I doubted it would ever truly fade. It was so hard to reconcile my past with what had transpired—what Andreas had become—that I found my mind spinning in circles in the quiet moments, which were far more plentiful now that I was no longer with Fire and Fluorite.

Luckily, I had the chaos of Air and Amethyst to fill that void.

It hadn't taken long for Volker to reclaim his place as king, but that was not without its challenges.

"Explain to me again who Feyre and Lady Oleander Price are?" I asked, staring up at the crystal chandelier lofted high above his bed at the embassy.

"They were my most loyal aids," he said with a sigh, "and ambassadors for the House. Also ruthless killers, when necessary."

"And they've just been chillin' over at the House of Gold and Garnet since you were overthrown?"

"I don't think 'chillin'' would be the most appropriate word choice, but yes, they found refuge with Vesperus after Nyssa usurped me."

"So they ran?" I asked, sitting up to watch him get undressed. Standing there in nothing but his unfastened pants, moonlight streaming in through the massive windows at his back, he looked like a marble statue, all pale skin carved with shadows.

He took notice of me staring and quirked his brow in amusement. "They lived to fight another day," he replied, taking a step toward the bed. "Something you know much about."

"I guess—"

"If it is their loyalty you question, don't. Their fealty was pledged to me in blood long ago—and it is binding. Vesperus and I may not be friends, but we both do things according to the old ways, so I know he will honor the bond."

The weight of his words and their implications pressed down on me. "Pledged in *blood* . . . does that mean—"

"Your bond to me is not the same, my little queen. Your power is yours to do with as you wish, and as I've told you before, you can leave at any time." He stopped beside the bed and stared down at me. "But I'd be lying if I said I wanted that."

"And you can't lie, so . . . " A wicked smile stretched across his face, and my heart began to race. "Volker, would you want me to stay even if I didn't have power to offer?"

Slowly, he crawled onto the bed, stopping only once his formidable frame loomed above me. "I would have you any way I could get you," he replied, "wellspring or otherwise."

Butterflies fluttered in my belly as he bent down to kiss my neck. "That's good to hear."

His teeth grazed my jaw, and I nearly jumped out of my skin. "Do you require any further assurances or should I continue what I'm doing uninterrupted?"

"That," I said, sighing heavily as he climbed between my legs. "You should do that."

His naked torso pressed against me and I arched up into him, tipping my head back to further expose my neck. He rumbled his approval as his lips trailed down the delicate flesh along the plunging neckline of my shirt. The fabric stretched tight as he pulled it lower, exposing the tops of my breasts.

I side-eyed him and found those fathomless grey eyes staring back at me with delight.

Then his bedroom door flew open, and panic surged through me.

He shot off the bed with me right behind him, the familiar silver-blue aura of his moonlight blade glowing around us.

Yael hovered in the open doorway, looking paler than usual at the sight of his leader poised to kill, then retreated a step. "My apologies for the intrusion," he said, lowering his head, "but there is a call for you—from Vesperus."

Volker lowered his weapon, but Yael's eyes remained wide. "Tell him I will return his call at a more convenient time."

"Forgive me, but he says it's urgent."

Volker let out a breath and turned to me; then his eyes went as wide as Yael's. "It appears I have pressing matters here as well. Tell him I will call him back shortly—once I deal with this."

Adrenaline still pumping through my veins, I stared back at him, trying to figure out what I'd missed. Then I noted the angle of his gaze and followed it all the way to my hand—and the glowing dagger clasped in it. I yelped when I realized what it was, but I didn't dare let it go until Volker took it gently from my palm.

"Leave us," he told Yael.

He did so without a word.

"I . . . I don't . . . " I stammered. "I didn't . . . "

"Well, this is surprising," he said, turning the dagger over in his hand, "but not wholly unexpected, I suppose."

"Um . . . it sure is to me!"

He handed it back, and it quickly disappeared. "You were able to wield the moonlight blade against Andreas," he explained. "I knew then that our bond allowed you access to my magic on some level, as no other is able to do what you did. But that . . . "—he nodded toward my open palm where the dagger had just been—" . . . that, I did not think was possible." Amusement tugged at his expression. "You called it to protect me."

"Well," I said, flustered, confused, and oddly embarrassed, "I just got you . . . you can't blame me for not wanting to lose you already. And besides, you were usurped once . . . I'm just being cautious!"

"You're being *protective*," he said, disappearing in a flash, only to reappear at my back. His arm wrapped around my waist and pulled me closer to him. "And I think I like it—very much." His hips ground against me, illustrating exactly how much he enjoyed it.

"Care to expand on that?" I asked, reaching my hand between us to cup the length of him. He sucked in a breath through his teeth, and I knew his otherwise unshakable resolve was crumbling at record pace.

In response to my challenge, I found myself on my back once again, pinned to the bed by the Moonlight Wraith, his eyes glowing silver as he stared down at me. "I will expand on that for as long as you remain at my side, my little queen," he replied in a deep, husky tone that nearly undid me right then and there. "If you'll let me."

"I will—on one condition."

He pulled away enough to better assess me, his serious face in full force. "Name it."

I thought about my new position and power and the words he'd just spoken to me—more specifically, the name he'd used—then took a deep breath. "I want a cool nickname like yours."

For a moment, he just stared at me like I'd lost my damn mind.

Then he smiled. Then he laughed—like *really* laughed.

With one poorly timed outburst, I'd successfully derailed the moment.

"A nickname?" he asked between breaths as he calmed himself.

"I don't want to be 'little queen'," I explained, "except when we're alone, of course." I waggled my brows at him, and he shook his head as he tried to school his expression to one of understanding. He failed miserably. No matter how hard he tried, his amusement was plain.

"What shall I call you, then?"

"I don't know, something cool like the Midnight Shadow, or the Starlight Killer—"

"But your magic is not of the night, as mine is, even though you seem to share a bit of it," he said as he gently brushed a stray piece of hair from my face. "And you're not a true killer. Your 'nickname', as you call it, should be a true reflection of who and what you are, not just a random title."

"Okay . . . " I tried not to let my disappointment show. There was no cool way to use 'wellspring', and what else was there?

"Your name has always meant 'queen'. And now, given your position at my side, it is more befitting than ever."

I let out a sigh. "Fine. I guess it's 'little queen' forever, then—"

"No," he said, taking my chin in his hand and forcing me to meet his gaze, "not 'little' . . . " He stared at me in silence for a moment until a smirk slowly bloomed on his face. "*Rebel.* To honor your connection to your mother through the music you love. To honor the creature you became in her absence."

The Rebel Queen . . .

I mulled the title over and over in my mind until I loved the sound of it. It felt right. It felt like who I'd become. "It's perfect." I reached up and took his face in my hands, then pulled his mouth to mine. "Thank you."

"I'd rather you show me your gratitude," he said, letting the weight of his body down upon mine, "if that's all right with you, *Rebel Queen.*"

"Oh, it is . . . but what about your call with Vesperus?" I asked as he unfastened my pants.

He shot me a look that could have melted glass. "I know why Vesperus wishes to talk to me, but the disturbances in the night's magic are the least of my concerns right now." My jeans flew across the room, and Volker slid along the length of me until we were face to face. "I have much more pressing matters to attend to at the moment."

I threw my head back and laughed as he ripped my shirt free and began kissing his way across my body. He was good and riled up, which meant I was in for it, not that that was a bad thing. I'd never felt more desired in my life—and not just in the bedroom. Volker and I had become a team—a partnership—and together, I was convinced there was nothing we couldn't do. The future was ours to shape; our story to write.

We'd have a fairy tale ending if it killed me.

A happily ever after for the Moonlight Wraith and his Rebel Queen.

BEFORE YOU GO...

Leaving reviews is one of the best ways to support authors. Got a second?

Review Queen Me on Amazon

Review Queen Me on Goodreads

Can't get enough of Immortal Vices & Virtues? While it's recommended they be read in order, they are all standalone and can be read in any order you want.

Check out the entire series on Amazon.

Want a head's up for each new release without following the authors everywhere?
Text "IMMORTAL" (844) 506 -1510

MORE BY AMBER LYNN NATUSCH

The *CAGED* Series

CAGED

HAUNTED

FRAMED

SCARRED

FRACTURED

TARNISHED

STRAYED

CONCEALED

BETRAYED

The *UNBORN* Series

UNBORN

UNSEEN

UNSPOKEN

UNMADE

UNBOUND

The *BLUE-EYED BOMB* Series

LIVE WIRE

KILLSWITCH

DEAD ZONE

WARHEAD

The *FORCE OF NATURE* Series

FROM THE ASHES

INTO THE STORM

BEYOND THE SHADOWS

BENEATH THE DUST

THROUGH THE ETHER

The *WITCHES OF THE GILDED LILIES* Series

A CURSE OF NIGHTSHADE

The *SUPERNATURAL MISFITS ACADEMY* Series

ROGUE REFORMATORY: BUSTED

ROGUE REFORMATORY: BROKEN

ROGUE REFORMATORY: BREAKOUT

Contemporary Romance

UNDERTOW

About the Author

Amber Lynn Natusch is the author of the bestselling *Caged*, as well as the *Light and Shadow* series with Shannon Morton. She was born and raised in Winnipeg, and speaks sarcasm fluently because of her Canadian roots. She loves to dance and sing in her kitchen—much to the detriment of those near her—but spends most of her time running a practice with her husband, raising two small children, and attempting to write when she can lock herself in the bathroom for ten minutes of peace and quiet.

She has many hidden talents, most of which should not be mentioned but include putting her foot in her mouth, acting inappropriately when nervous, swearing like a sailor when provoked, and not listening when she should. She's obsessed with home renovation shows, should never be caffeinated, and loves snow. Amber has a deep-seated fear of clowns and deep water . . . especially clowns swimming in deep water.

For more including release dates, visit:

amberlynnnatusch.com

www.ingramcontent.com/pod-product-compliance
Lightning Source LLC
Chambersburg PA
CBHW021623030826
48979CB00036B/1923/J
* 9 7 8 1 9 5 9 0 1 0 0 1 2 *